ALL I STOLE FROM YOU

ALL I STOLE FROM YOU

AVA BELLOWS

A NOVEL

HARPER  PERENNIAL

Published by Harper Perennial, an imprint of HarperCollins Publishers Ltd

First edition

HarperCollins Publishers Ltd
Bay Adelaide Centre, East Tower
22 Adelaide Street West, 41st Floor
Toronto, Ontario, Canada
M5H 4E3

www.harpercollins.ca

Library and Archives Canada Cataloguing in Publication

Title: All I stole from you : a novel / Ava Bellows. Names: Bellows, Ava, author.
Identifiers: Canadiana (print) 20220178410 | Canadiana (ebook) 20220178429
ISBN 9781443466806 (softcover) | ISBN 9781443466813 (ebook)
Classification: LCC PS8603.E5545 A75 2022 | DDC C813/.6—dc23

Printed and bound in the United States of America

LSC/H 9 8 7 6 5 4 3 2 1

To the memory of Henry Carr, a boy whose big open heart changed the course of my life. He is (and forever will be) at the very center of me. Henry, if you're reading this wherever you are, just float. Talk back soon.

She is so naked and singular.
She is the sum of yourself and your dream.
Climb her like a monument, step after step.
She is solid.

As for me, I am a watercolor.
I wash off.
—Anne Sexton, "For My Lover, Returning to His Wife"

PROLOGUE

Ingrid,

You said you wanted to know everything. I'm not sure I'm ready to tell you everything. I'm not sure I'm ready to relive everything, but after all you've given me, your forgiveness, your wisdom, your kindness, Rob . . . I owe you this much. You told me to spare no detail, so I've done my best here, though it might not be enough for you. Or maybe it's too much. I don't know. All I know is that this is everything that happened, and I've written this letter in as much detail as I could muster.

—Maggie

PART I

Mistakes Were Made

1

Just for the record, I didn't go to the party with the intention of ruining a marriage. I want to make that clear. I didn't even want to go in the first place.

Henry, the latest DJ in a too-long line of DJs, had broken up with me in a "later, babe" text four days before, leaving me to revert to a uniform consisting strictly of sweatpants and sports bras. Shirts are not required when dealing with heartache, though of course there's also the whole Jackson thing. We'll get to that, though. Just not right now.

Rob and I met in August, three nights after I swore off men and a week after I resumed smoking. My ex said in the Program, you deal with things in the order in which they're killing you, and men seemed a more pressing poison. I always used to tell people that if doctors or grownups had tried to appeal to my sense of vanity and not my sense of mortality, I never would've started smoking, but they hadn't, so I had.

So, the party. Thrown by and for someone I wasn't close to.

The only reason I was there was that Dani, my roommate, told me she'd do all our dishes for a month if I went with her, and in my grief I'd been doing a lot of baking, so I could use a dishwasher.

It was Dani's boyfriend's thirty-fifth, and he did what any guy who liked Leonardo DiCaprio a little too much would: he rented a boat to take him and his hundred closest acquaintances along the coast for six hours.

Everything was fine and infidelityless until elevenish. I spent the first chunk of the party seeking out dinghies I could use for an escape and nodding at C-list auteurs as they explained the plots of my father's movies to me because apparently I "just didn't get them."

It wasn't until I grabbed another Craig-tini (your standard martini, but like every other drink on the menu, Craig-ified with a toothpick displaying a photo of Craig with Leo) and snuck out onto the deck to resume poisoning my lungs that things got complicated.

I was sitting on the bench, happy to be wearing the too-expensive coat I had stolen from my ex's ex as I lit up and looked out into the sky, when the door opened and someone stumbled out.

I didn't look up, hoping if I stayed small and quiet and smoking, whoever it was would go back inside to the Craig-tinis and not-teurs, but luck was not on my side, evidently.

"Can I bum one?"

If you could punch a voice, I would've punched his. No one has a right to sound as good as he did. Still does. I'd always been a sucker for an English accent, so I was fucked from the start.

I wordlessly handed him one, staring straight ahead.

What I should've done was left. Gone back inside to the Craig-tinis and the mindless nodding and the store-bought chips and top-shelf liquor, or else I should've just jumped into the ocean and started towards land.

Instead, I handed him the cigarette, and even though I didn't look at him, our fingers brushed, which was so much better and so, so much worse because the second we touched, a jolt of electricity or lust or a mix of the two shot up through my fingers and into my spine.

"Thanks," he said, picking up the lighter that lay between us, a kind of border, and lighting his cigarette.

This is when I made my second mistake. This is when I, thinking it safe, glanced at him.

Or it started as a glance, at least, and then quickly morphed into a gawk or a gape or a combination of the two.

Even seated, he was tall. Taller than me, at least, which was good enough. I'd mistaken height for attractiveness before, but that didn't happen this time. His hair was shaggy and unkempt and the kind of greasy that I liked. His lips were full and edible looking and his scruff caught the light of the flame, turning gold and orange and blue.

It was then that I made my third and thus far most fatal mistake. I met his eyes.

In my defense, I thought I'd be okay. I thought he'd be looking at the cigarette or the ocean or the Craig-pick in the old-fashioned in his hand, but no. He was looking at me. Or gaping. Or gawking. Some combination of the two, but the bottom line is that his eyes did it, so if you're looking for a bad guy, if you're looking for something to blame, blame his eyes.

Big and green and fenced in by eyelashes I'm sure the women inside would've paid hundreds of dollars for.

I should've looked away, I know that, okay. Of course I know that.

"Hi," he breathed out, still gape-gawking.

"Hi," I said, though I can't be sure I didn't whisper it or sing it in Italian.

I looked away, busying myself with downing the rest of the now-watery Craig-tini.

"You know there's a party going on in there, right?"

"Really? I had no idea," I said, trying not to look him directly in the eyes.

"Yeah. Just thought you should know. Doesn't seem your thing, though," he replied.

What I should've said was nothing. But the thing is, talking to him with his accent and his height and his gape-gawking made me forget about Henry and Jackson and everything else, so I spoke.

"What makes you say that?"

"No reason, really. Other than the fact that you looked like you were considering jumping into the water the second you and your friend got here. And the whole solo smoking thing," he said, nodding his chin to my smoke.

Now do you understand why I stayed? You don't have to. I'm not sure I would understand either, but when he said that, when he decided to tell me he had seen me, he had *noticed* me, I felt every nerve in my body light up, and I liked that feeling.

"So, you've been stalking me, then."

I would like to note that the fact that I played it *that* cool is *very* impressive to me to this day.

"Can you stalk someone if you're both in the same enclosed space?"

"I think so. It's ideal for lazy stalkers."

I glanced over in time to catch him scratching his chin as he let out a "hmmm," and I had to grab another smoke from the pack to ensure I didn't reach up and stroke his chin too.

He spoke again. "You're right, but I'm not a stalker, so you're in the clear."

"Oh good. I'm not in the mood to evade stalkers tonight," I said through my smile.

"I'd imagine not. I'm Rob, by the way."

He extended his hand (I'll get to it), and I extended mine. "Maggie."

He took my hand in his and shook it once, twice.

I'm surprised I didn't dissolve into the air or otherwise explode into a tiny, nicotine-fueled fireworks show.

Okay, the hand. But I'm only getting to it because once we'd stopped shaking, his didn't let go of mine. Or mine didn't let go of his. Or both.

I'll start by saying that I've always loved hands. Other people's, not my own. I have "peasant hands," apparently. My grandmother said that to me twenty minutes before she died. She also told me she was pretty sure my uncle was gay, but he'd come out of the closet years before, so I wound up fixating on the whole hands thing.

Back to Rob's hand, then. No more distractions, I swear. It was calloused and warm and made me think of loaves of bread straight out of the oven, which made my mouth water, a ridiculous thing to have your body do while shaking someone's hand. His fingers were long and slim except for where they ballooned at the knuckles. His hand was veiny in the way that I've always envied, but not as veiny as my grandmother's hands, whose skin was so thin and veins so bulging, I worried they'd burst and she'd bleed to death.

This was just his right hand. I hadn't yet seen his left one, okay?

I don't remember who let go first, so let's just say it was me. I like the way that sounds, and besides, I have clammy hands so I'm big on letting go.

"So, Maggie, why are you at a party you don't want to attend and can't escape?"

"My roommate dragged me. I was too tired to fight her."

"Long week?"

"Very. You?"

"My week?"

"No, why are you at the party? Your week too, though, I guess," I said, biting the inside of my cheek so as not to keep smiling.

"Oh. Right. I've known Craig for a while and he was in the parlor the other day and invited me, so here I am."

"The parlor?"

"Yeah, the tattoo parlor. I'm—"

"Tell me you're not a tattoo artist."

"I'm not a tattoo artist," he said, grinning.

"Okay, good. Good. Is that true?"

". . . No, it's not."

I groaned. He laughed. I groaned again because fuck him for having a laugh that sounded the way a lit fireplace felt.

"Really?"

"Really what?"

"Nothing. Never mind. Nothing. It's nothing."

"It's very obviously not nothing," he said, laughing.

"No, ignore me. You've tattooed Craig, then."

"I have, yeah."

A quick word on Craig: I didn't particularly like him; he had a penchant for over-pronouncing French words, finishing my yogurt, talking down to me about the "industry of film," and calling me "Mags," a nickname he hadn't earned, but I didn't *dislike* him either. He loved Dani, and he bought wine for our apartment when he came to stay with us and had a cute dog he'd sometimes bring over, and he'd hooked me up with several well-paying house-sitting jobs. All of this made the constant shirtlessness tolerable. And that one tattoo on his shoulder.

Craig had twenty-seven tattoos in total, all of them garbage (Roman numerals representing nothing just because he "liked the way it looked," a Ferris Bueller quote credited to Plato, a grape that will turn into a raisin as he ages), but the one on his shoulder was different.

It was a portrait of his sister, who'd died when she was nine and he was fifteen. Car accident.

I only knew this because one night when Dani was asleep, I walked Dottie, his dog, with him, and he told me. For some reason, people often tell me about the deaths of their loved ones.

My therapist once told me that I have a very "approachable" face.

When she said that, I said, "thank you," and then spent the rest of the week avoiding mirrors.

But Craig's sister-tattoo was special. It was gray and shadowy, made up of thin lines and shading, but it felt alive. Kind of like how people say when you're in a room with the *Mona Lisa*, you think that her eyes are following you. Craig's tattoo of his sister was my favorite thing about him, and I'd often find myself staring at her as he wandered shirtless throughout our apartment, eating my snacks and leaving a trail of crumbs in his wake.

Back to Rob.

"Which one?" I asked, regretting the question as soon as I'd asked it.

"Which tattoo?"

"Yeah."

I'm sure you know where this went. I'm going to tell you anyway, just so it's here, in print. Just so I can show you that this is all his fault, really.

"The one on his shoulder. It's a portrait of his sister and—"

This is where I started to laugh. He laughed too, but there's no way we were laughing at the same thing.

"What?"

"Nothing."

"Come on, out with it." He laughed as he said it. I already loved making him laugh.

"It's really nothing, it's just, of *course* you did that one." I groaned.

"It's that bad?"

"No! *No.* It's . . . I love it, actually. It's my favorite."

I had stopped laughing at that point, but I wasn't looking at him. Instead, I fiddled with the Craig-pick and tried to look cool and mysterious, two things that I have never in my life been accused of being.

"Thank you."

"You're welcome. It's . . . you're really good," I said, blushing. I'm not sure why, but I felt embarrassed saying it.

"For all you know, the rest of my work could be shit."

"Maybe, but I doubt it."

I wondered how many calories flirting burned.

"You're too kind."

He smiled at me then, so I lit another cigarette to keep from using my mouth to say something stupid. Or kiss him. Or say something stupid and *then* kiss him.

"So . . ." he continued, trailing off.

"So."

"So, what do you do?"

"I house-sit."

"Professionally?"

"Yep. I'm a world-renowned house sitter," I replied, sitting up straighter than I had been, taking on an air of self-importance that didn't feel real.

"I don't think I've ever met one of those before."

"You've never met a house sitter?"

"Not a world-renowned one, at least."

"There aren't many of us. We're very rare."

"I don't doubt it," he said, eyebrows raised.

This is the part where I could have told him that while I'm a professional, world-renowned house sitter, I wait for my managers to email me the scripts for auditions to play rape victims or murder victims or some other kinds of victims, but I was still trying to be cool and mysterious, and there is nothing cool about being a struggling actress and having to fight to be part of projects written by and for men about hot but wounded women.

It was then that Dani came out, stumbling on her bare feet as if they were stilettos, laughing at something she'd heard inside.

"Mags Mags Mags Maggie Margaret," she sang, plopping herself on my lap and running her hands through my perpetually tangled hair. I'm still unsure if I wanted to kiss her or hit her for killing whatever had been in the air just a second before.

"Hi, bud. You good?"

"So good. I am *so* good," Dani said, stretching each word out longer than necessary.

"What's up, Dan? Where are your shoes?"

"They're somewhere. I don't know; it's not important."

"What's important, then?"

"I have to tell you something," she shouted. "It's a secret!"

"I'm listening."

"Okay. Are you ready?"

It's in moments like these that I'm grateful for my years of nannying experience.

"Very ready."

"I found your soul mate."

The whole "soul mate" thing is a game Dani plays. Mostly when she's drunk, but occasionally when she's sober. Dani, amateur tarot reader and life coach, is a big believer in soul mates. Also in both crystals and manifesting, so ever since Jackson, my last real boyfriend, broke my heart, she's been manifesting my soul mate while filling every surface of our apartment with crystals that she cleanses in salt once a month.

"Have you, now?"

"Yup. He's tall and broody and cute and tall—"

I wanted to jump into the ocean right then and there.

"You said tall already," I muttered.

"Because he is! Tall. He's tall. Ish. Taller than Craig, at least. *And* English, which I know you *love,* AND you know that tattoo Craig has? His sister?"

". . . Yeah, Dan. I know it."

"*Grrrrrrreat,* 'cause he did it! How cool is that?"

I could *feel* Rob's laughter. I wanted death. Or murder.

"Very cool, Dani. Very cool," I uttered, looking at my shoes and her toes.

I could feel Rob's eyes on me as Dani continued to buzz and trill, but

I refused to look at him. Instead, I focused on Dani's copper-painted toenails and tried to tune her out, listening instead to the waves as they slapped against the boat. It didn't work all that well; Dani's loud when she wants to be, and she wanted to be.

"Wanna go find him with me? He's got an R name. Richard or Reggie or Rudy or—"

"Rob?" Rob interjected, grinning.

"YOU FOUND HIM WITHOUT ME?!"

I couldn't tell if she was happy or upset.

"It would seem so," said I, the death-or-murder-wisher.

Dani clambered off my lap, grabbing Rob's old-Craig-shioned as she stood.

"I'm gonna go, then! Soul mates!! I knew it!"

She turned to leave, but spun back, pointing at Rob and sloshing his old-Craig-shioned onto his jeans.

"You be nice to her, 'kay? She's sad and that makes me sad and I don't like to be sad at parties."

"Yes ma'am."

Dani studied his face for a moment longer before stumbling back into the party, leaving us to silence. It was decided. Death, not murder.

"So . . ."

"So," I said, looking out into the black water ahead of us.

"You're sad?"

I'd never been more relieved to talk about my emotional well-being. At that point, I would've disclosed my entire sexual history just to get away from the whole soul mate topic. It also helped that the Craig-tinis had just settled into my bloodstream, rendering everything a little blurry around the edges, making me forget about my desire to seem cool and unaffected by everything.

"Yeah," I said, "I am."

"Just general sadness or is it more specialized?"

This I wasn't expecting. In my experience, telling a cute guy about my emotional inner life was a surefire conversation ender. The emotionally inept ones got uncomfortable and either left or changed the subject before leaving, and the "complex" ones (actors) liked to think that they were the only ones fraught with emotions, so the conversation would quickly morph into a "trauma-off," which I'd forfeit.

"Do you want the cool answer or the real sadness spiel?"

This is when I looked again. Another mistake. I'd never before experienced being "drunk in" by someone. In fact, I hate that phrase. It made me picture a giant bringing a pint glass up to his mouth, drinking me up. An effluvia smoothie. But there wasn't a better phrase for what he was doing.

I liked it. A lot. And it scared me. A lot. My clammy hands got clammier, and I wanted badly to look away, but I'm competitive, and if this was a staring contest, I was going to win.

"The spiel, please."

I took a deep breath, still staring.

"I'm good. I'm here. I want to hear it all," he said, melting me.

Fucker.

"I've been dumped. By a DJ, which is . . . it's a lot of things, but it's not so great for the ego, especially after, after . . . never mind. And I haven't booked anything in months and my dad's in town shooting something and I can't bring myself to see him, 'cause then I'd have to *see him,* you know? And I'm at this point where I guess I've just resigned myself to a life of shitty parties and commitment-phobic DJs, except for the fact that I've decided to swear off men, which should be easier than it is, just because most men are just . . . *men,* and my sister's pregnant again, which is great, it's great, but it's also shitty, because how is it that we were raised by the same people and *I'm* the only one of us who managed to get fucked up enough that I'm being dumped by squatting DJs and dragged to parties on boats and picking the wrong people to love? And this is all just extra stuff, really, but I don't want to talk about my sadness anymore 'cause then I'll cry. I'm a crier."

It all just came spilling out. Well, not everything, exactly. I'd neglected to mention Jackson, but only because I knew that if I mentioned him, I would break down. That still happens, sometimes.

Silence wrapped itself around us like a blanket. I refused to look at Rob. I could feel him looking at me. Gawking. Gaping. Gazing. Whatever it was, it felt too warm, too kind, too understanding for me to be able to cope with right then, so I kept my eyes planted on the black waves ahead of us and wished that I'd said more and that I'd said less all at once.

"Maggie," he murmured, but I cut him off.

"That was a lot. I know. I'm sorry, I'm not normally like that. I can go back to pretending to be cool and casual and—"

I shut up then because he used his hand to brush away a tear from my cheek.

"It's okay. You're okay."

His hand was warm and I tried not to nuzzle into it, but all I could think about was that it had been so long since I'd felt that comfortable around someone who wasn't Dani.

"Yeah?"

His hand was still touching my face. I'd never before been turned on by anything so closely related to my tears.

"Yes," he said, and I looked at his fingers.

"I'm not so sure about that. I'm a bit of a mess. Clearly."

I tried to look down, but he tilted my chin so I was forced to resume our staring contest. Or not forced so much as encouraged. Despite the momentary silence, I could barely hear what was going on inside the party.

"You're not a mess," he replied.

"No?"

"No."

"Are you sure about that, because it feels like unloading a therapy session's worth of bullshit onto a perfect stranger is the sort of behavior of utter messes."

His hand didn't move from my chin. My eyes traveled from his eyes to his lips, which he licked.

I didn't realize that my sadness could be used to get guys to want to kiss me. If I'd known that sooner, I wouldn't have spent so much money on low-cut shirts.

"You're not a mess. You're wonderful."

It was then that I kissed him. And yes, I kissed him and not the other way around, so maybe I *am* the one to blame, but considering the hands and the staring and the "you're wonderful," I don't think that the kiss was entirely my fault. Plus, he kissed me back. If I wanted to save face, I'd say that it was a chaste kiss, but we both know that would be a lie, and I decided that I wouldn't lie to you. There have been enough lies, don't you think?

So no, it wasn't a chaste kiss, but it wasn't a rip-your-clothes-off, *The Notebook*–style kiss either. On the spectrum of peck to Gosling, it was somewhere in the middle. That's what I'll say. I don't want to say much more about it, because I want to keep some things for myself. I don't deserve much, but I deserve that. I'll say this one last thing about the kiss, though. It was great. I'm sorry.

2

No more apologies, back to the kiss. The kiss that had me forgetting where my lips ended and his started. The kiss that gave me the excuse to (finally) wind my fingers through his hair while his hands moved from my waist to my shoulders to the sides of my face. The kiss that ended when he pulled away. Obviously. But *he* pulled away.

"Fuck," he said, running his hand through his hair.

"Bad fuck or good fuck?"

"Maggie, I—"

"Oh. Bad fuck, then."

I stood up, but the boat lurched forward, knocking me towards Rob, who stood and grabbed my shoulders, steadying me with his hands. Plural. As in his right and left hand. As in when I looked down, I saw The Ring.

I'd like to say that I felt as though I'd had the wind knocked out of me, only because it sounds good. It's the sort of thing you should feel when you realize that the person whose lips you've just kissed and bitten and melted into is married, but it wouldn't be true. Instead, I felt numb. Totally, completely numb. Of course he was married. Of. Fucking. Course.

I took a step back, away from The Ring and the hand and the height and hair and scruff and eyes and lips and . . . fuck.

"Oh," I said.

He looked down at The Ring on his finger like he'd never noticed it before. Like it was a birthmark or freckle that I'd pointed out to him. *This old thing? Huh. Never noticed it.* Like that.

"Maggie—"

"*Fuck* makes a lot more sense now, I guess." I tried to laugh, but it sounded hollow.

"Yeah."

"I don't know what to say. I'm sorry. I'm drunk and I didn't think and—"

"Maggie." He reached towards me (with his left hand, the fucker), but I took another step back, half wishing I had stepped back enough to accidentally fall overboard, half wishing that instead I'd taken a step forward.

"It's okay," he said, and I could tell that he was going to continue, but I couldn't stop looking from his mouth to his ring, and it was making me dizzy, and sad and horny and then sad again, so I stopped him.

"It's not okay. It's not. I'm sorry. If I keep standing here, I'm gonna say that so many times it'll lose meaning, which I don't want because I am. Sorry. I'm sorry. I'm just gonna go back inside and leave you to the whole married thing."

At that point I was gesturing with my whole body, ultimately catapulting my Craig-pick to the ground. I'm not sure why I bothered picking it up, but I did. It was stuck and I struggled to get it, but that was okay. I needed to focus my attention on something other than the married guy in front of me.

Craig-pick in hand, I turned on my heels to return to the bar and the probably-not-married not-teurs. Out of the corner of my eye, I saw him reach for me, but either I was too fast, or he stopped himself.

Despite my escape, there was a problem. I'm sure you've worked it out by now. You're smart, after all. I'm gonna say it anyway, just in case.

When you're on a boat, it's very hard to avoid people. It's almost impossible, actually.

3

It was a little after midnight and we weren't set to dock until two, leaving me with ninety minutes to go before I could successfully get away, so I did what anyone trying to avoid someone at a party does: I went to the bathroom.

The bathroom was big, bigger than any party-boat bathroom should be, and cleaner than most public bathrooms, but it reeked of designer perfumes that absolutely did not mix well and the stalls were full of girls talking to each other about who they were planning to go home with, a subject I couldn't be around, so after a few minutes, I left. Another escape. Eighty-five minutes to go.

I took a lap around the party, grabbed another Craig-tini, and went to find Dani, hoping that would eat up about eighty minutes or so. Evidently, I was off by seventy-five. Dani was easy to find.

She was sitting on Craig's lap on one of the couches (Dani preferred laps over chairs), reading people's palms, a skill I didn't know she had and didn't want to be a guinea pig for, so I surveyed the party once more.

I watched as people danced to Lorde remixes, envying the way they all moved so freely. I was a shitty dancer. I was always a little too aware of the fact that I was being watched when I danced. It felt staged. Maybe they had that feeling too and just didn't care, or maybe they were just good dancers, or maybe they were all too drunk to think about anything other than bass and rhythm.

Joey, Craig's best friend, strutted towards me as I leaned against the wall. He always strutted. He must have back problems, the way he leads with his hips.

"Margaret," he said, smirking at me. He always smirked.

"Joseph."

"How are you on this lovely evening?"

"I'm just fine. How're you?"

"I'm spectacular," he crowed.

He was always either "spectacular" or "stellar." Those were his only two states of existence.

When Jackson broke up with me, Craig tried to set me up with Joey. Not because he thought we'd get along, really. It was just math. I was single. Joey was single. I was heartbroken. Joey was . . . sad. Perfect match!

We went on one date. He took me to see his ex's movie, some romantic drama about people with terminal illnesses falling in love, and spent the rest of the night telling me that she'd been "much hotter" when they were together. I didn't tell him I'd seen him cry when she kissed her costar on-screen. I just sat and nodded. Approachable face, I guess. Since then, we'd been friendly. He knew about Jackson, and I knew about Delilah, so we'd occasionally commiserate over brunch while Dani sat on Craig's lap, feeding him eggs Benedict.

I surveyed the crowd for a moment before asking, "Where's your date?"

Joey had boarded the boat with Liv, a hostess from Craig's favorite restaurant, the one with the eggs Benedict. She was tall, taller than Joey (not hard to be), and she had half of her head shaved. She was *very* cool, made all the more cool by the fact that she always sent our table free pancakes.

"Bathroom. She had a few too many mules. Or Craigs, I guess."

I laughed and he laughed too. Joey was funniest when he didn't mean to be.

"Are you guys having fun?"

"Yeah, I think so. She's pretty stellar," he said, blushing.

So *he* was spectacular, *she* was stellar.

Liv came bounding towards us, pupils huge and bra strap hanging off her shoulder.

She'd just applied more lipstick, so her lips were a deep purple, almost black, and her mascara was smudged. I was going to point it out to her, but I figured she'd probably done it on purpose. She was good at looking artfully disheveled. I envied that quality.

"Hiiiiiiiiiiii," she said, putting her hands on Joey's shoulders and whispering something in his ear. From up close, I could see a dusting of coke on her septum ring. Saving it for later, I guess.

Joey and Liv kept whispering to each other, so I slipped away.

On my second lap, I saw Rob deeply engrossed in a conversation with a not-teur, probably about being married, and I decided to sneak off back to the deck. I thought, once again, that I'd be safe. Which I was, actually. For about thirty minutes.

I spent the thirty minutes Instagram stalking Jackson's ex, Elsie, the rightful owner of my coat.

I let myself stalk Elsie on Instagram once a month, twice if I was feeling especially masochistic, but this time I stopped after coming across her engagement announcement photo.

I'd seen it before—it was three months old—but this time I stared at it. For a while. There she was, at her fiancé's parent's house in Montauk (I'd Instagram stalked her and Ray, her finance-bro fiancé, enough to know these things about their lives), kissing him passionately as she held her left hand up to the camera.

I stared at it and wondered who took the picture and how many times Elsie made them retake it. I thought about the rejected versions of this photo, sitting in her camera roll, never to be used or seen. The post had two hundred and forty-six likes. I wondered if she'd have gotten more with one of the rejects. I bet she did too.

This is when I decided to go full-on masochist and pulled up Jackson's Instagram. An account that was no longer active. Ghosts don't post on social media, after all. I scrolled through the same twenty-six photos I'd seen last night, and the night before, and almost every night since I got the call from his sponsor last year.

I'm not sure why they kept his Instagram up. I'm not sure who "they" is either. His parents, I suppose.

I knew I could have screenshotted the photos, keeping them in my camera roll where it would be easy and convenient, but there was something about having to search for him—as if he were just like anyone, just like he were alive—that I needed, so I searched for @careaboutmylife like I had every night since he'd died, going through the photos I'd already memorized.

I focused especially on the one of him that day at the beach in the hat. My hat. One of those big, floppy hats I'd bought on a whim, hoping that in purchasing it I would become a Hat Person, and then never wore outside. Jackson looked good in it, though. He was a Hat Person.

I loved that photo. I'd taken it. It was his one-year sober birthday and so we went to the beach and ate sheet cake with our hands and took naps in the sand and he told me he loved me and I got stuck in the car because fucking in Fiats without your feet falling asleep is nearly impossible to do. I loved that day. Four months before he dumped me, eight months before he died. I stared, forcing my eyes open until my vision got spotty and my eyes blurred.

That's when the door opened. I was putting my phone away. This time I looked up. I'll give you twenty dollars if you guess who it was. I'll even give you a hint: he's married. Or he was. At the time.

He looked at me, brow furrowed, with a humorless smile on his face and my purse in his hand. The left one.

"You left this," he said, simply.

"Right," I replied, trying to sound nonchalant, "thanks."

I felt him stare at me as the silence got thicker and more charged. I wasn't looking at him, though. Not his face, at least. I was staring at his ringed hand, the one gripping my purse. I was trying to figure out the easiest way to get it from him without having to touch him.

Maybe he could just throw it to me, I remember thinking. *That would be good of him. Considerate. If I touch him, I may kiss him again. I cannot kiss him again.*

He didn't throw it to me, though. He took a half step towards me, that same furrowed, pensive look on his face, and he extended his left hand to me, carefully, as if he was afraid that I'd bite it. I didn't.

I stood up, slowly, so as not to spook him, or so as not to spook myself, I'm not sure which, but I stood and walked towards him, head down, eyes planted firmly on the purse in front of me.

I lifted the purse from his grasp, careful not to touch him and even more careful to not appear careful.

"Thanks," I repeated from over my shoulder, ready to reenter the party. I almost did. I almost made it to the door, but it didn't work out that way. Not really.

"Fuck," I heard Rob say under his breath, more to himself than to me, before speaking louder. "Maggie, wait for a second, will you?"

I turned, gripping my purse like it was a lifeline.

"Before you escape again, would you let me say something?" he asked, eyebrows still furrowed. "Please?"

I opened my mouth, but I had nothing to say, and he'd already started talking again, so I closed it.

"I *was* kind of stalking you this time around. And you're right, the enclosed-space thing helps."

It was a joke, but I didn't laugh. I was staring at The Ring, which he must have noticed because he put his hand in his pocket as he continued.

"I don't quite know what to say, really. I haven't been in this situation before, but I want to apologize."

I opened my mouth again, this time with a few things to say, but he continued.

"I flirted with you and that's not something I do, but I saw you and we started talking and . . . and I don't know. I know I should have told you I was married or said something, but I didn't. I don't know why. I should have planned this all out a bit more, but the truth is I forgot myself when we started talking and then—"

"And then I kissed you," I said, not looking at him.

"And then you kissed me. But I wanted you to. I'd wanted to kiss you. From the second you accused me of stalking you, which I know I shouldn't say at all, I just don't want you to get off this boat thinking that you were in the wrong in any way. You weren't, I assure you. You didn't know."

So now we're in agreement that this is his fault, right?

"You're joking, right?"

"What?"

"Do you have to be so . . . charming about this?"

"I could pretend to be a dick if that'll help you," he joked.

"It won't work now."

He leaned back against the railing, and I knew I should go back to the party, but all I really wanted to do was walk up to him, take his ring off his finger, throw it in the ocean, and make him forget himself some more.

"So," I said, "you're married."

"Yes," he said, "I am."

"You know, you married folk should wear a sign or something. Just to make sure things like this don't happen."

"In fairness, I think that's what the rings are for."

I'm not sure if I laughed because it was funny or because I knew that if I didn't laugh, I'd cry, but the why doesn't matter. I laughed. Hard. A throw-my-head-back kind of laugh.

And he groaned. A throw-his-head-back kind of groan.

"What?" I said, genuinely confused. My laugh had been compared (by me) to the sound of a crow's foot being run over by a shopping cart, a witch's cackle, and an old dog's bark, but it had never elicited that reaction.

"You can't do that; that's not fair." He groaned again.

"Laugh? I can't laugh?"

"Not if you laugh like that, no."

"It's that bad?"

"No. Quite the opposite, actually."

"Oh," I whispered.

Oh.

"Yes. So if we're going to be friends, we've got to set up some ground rules. Starting with no more laughing like that."

"We're going to be friends? You and I?"

This is the part of the story that I like to call Playing with Fire.

"I think so. I'd like to be, anyway. If you'll have me."

If I had had just one more Craig-tini, I probably would have told him all of the ways that I would have liked to have had him, but I was sober enough to refrain from sharing that.

"That depends. How would you rank yourself as a friend?"

"So now I have to pitch myself?"

"Yep," I said, trying to pretend that I was enjoying the conversation more than I really was.

"Okay then. I'd give myself an eight."

"An eight? B territory?"

"I was trying to be modest," he exclaimed.

"Not a great pitching strategy."

"You're right, but I've not had much experience pitching myself. Or anything, really."

"Give me a general overview of the friendship. A logline."

"Our friendship in a sentence?"

"Yeah," I replied.

"Okay, then. Here goes . . . no more boat parties."

"That's it? That's all you've got?!"

"I was feeling pressured!"

"Fine, think on it."

"But in the meantime, friends?" he asked, smiling.

"We're really gonna be friends?"

"Is that really so strange?"

"I don't know, it's just . . . I mean, I did *just* kiss you. Like an hour ago. Maybe less."

"Yes, you did, but I don't think that should hinder our budding friendship."

He should have.

"No?" I asked, eyebrows raised.

"No."

"Why not?"

"Well, for starters, I'm married, as we've established—"

"We have," I said, humorlessly.

"Right. So now we've done the 'will they, won't they' thing and we did and we won't anymore."

"Okay, but—"

"Next, I'm a great friend, as we've also already established, and, judging by how you handled your shoeless friend, you are too, so it feels only right that we join forces . . ."

"Okay, that's fair—"

"And, lastly, most importantly, really, I love talking to you and I want to do that more. If you think my being married will make you feel odd, then I'll understand, but . . . I don't know, I just really enjoy talking with you. I don't see how my being married should complicate that," he finished, running his hand through his hair.

"That's your pitch," I said, dumbly.

"Yes."

". . . Okay."

"Yeah?"

"Yeah."

"Okay, great. Friends, then." He sounded pleased as he said it, and I smiled despite myself. Despite *you*.

"Friends."

Like I said: Playing. With. Fire.

It was then that the boat started to slow, and for the first time that night, I wished that the boat were miles away from the harbor, so I could have more time with my friend. My very cute, very married friend. But the boat was slowing, and it was time to go find Dani and her shoes. And besides, if I spent any more time with him, I would probably wind up kissing him again.

"Well, friend," I said, heading towards the door, "I guess it's time to go."

"You're free."

"I am. I'm free and you're married and we're friends."

"Excellent summary."

"Fuck off," I replied, smiling.

"Is that any way to talk to a friend?"

"It is for me, yeah."

"Noted."

"Well, I'll see you."

I made to leave, but he spoke, grabbing my wrist. "Maggie."

I turned. "What?"

"Friends typically have each other's numbers."

"Right. Of course."

So, I gave him my phone and he let go of my wrist to text himself from it, saving his number under "Rob." He placed it back in my hand gently, as if it were precious.

"Okay, so that's sorted, then."

I turned away again.

"Maggie."

"Yes, Rob."

"I don't know how you do things, but I normally hug my friends goodbye."

So, I turned back. And he wrapped his arms around me, and I wrapped mine around him and I can't prove it, there are no tapes to go back to and look at, but I'm almost positive he smelled my hair, which was much hotter than it sounds like it would be. I felt his scruff and his lips brush against my neck, and I had to bite my tongue to keep from moaning out loud as we pulled away from each other. Before I turned, he stopped me once more.

"Maggie," he said.

"Yeah?"

"Would you let me know when you get home? Just so I know you got back safe?"

I almost started laughing right then and there. It wasn't that he had said anything particularly funny, I just couldn't believe him.

"Yeah, I'll let you know."

And I turned, again, back to the door and into the party, where I found Dani and one of her shoes.

4

Dani had gone home with Craig that night, which I was both happy and sad about. Sad because I would have liked to commiserate with her on our porch as she told me all the gossip she'd heard while on people's laps, our standard post-party routine, and happy because if she had come home with me, she would have asked me about my maybe–soul mate Rob, and I would have had to tell her everything, and I was self-aware enough to know that I wasn't ready to hear myself talk about any of this out loud.

So, I piled into a Lyft and headed home, staring out the window and pretending that I was in an indie movie, a habit I indulged in after nights like this one or any time I was on public transit.

As I walked through my front door, kicking off my shoes and locking it behind me, I looked at my phone, pulling up Rob's contact, and texted him: **it's maggie, i'm home.**

I pressed Send with my eyes closed. Because, I reasoned, with my eyes closed, it was kind of like I hadn't done it at all. It was an accident, a slip of the thumb.

He called me a second later.

I stared at it for a bit as it rang, walking to my porch, bumping into my potted plants, as I debated declining the call. I answered as I sat down on my too-uncomfortable porch chair.

"Hello?" I said, voice scratchy. I'm not sure why. Maybe the cigarettes had finally given me Emma Stone's voice.

"Hi," he said. "You got home all right?"

"Yeah, it was uneventful."

"Not much traffic at two a.m., I suppose."

"Right."

It was quiet for a bit, and I moved the phone away from my ear and mouthed *get it together* to myself before bringing it back, trying to figure out how to stay on the phone with him.

"So I just wanted to let you know that I got home safe, so . . ."

"Okay good. Good, I'm glad. I just got in myself."

"Okay," I said, while lighting another cigarette. I'd told myself I could only smoke two a day, but that clearly had been thrown out the window.

"Are you smoking?" he asked, faux disapproval in his voice.

"Maybe," I said, exhaling.

"You know, smoking's bad for you."

"I don't recall you saying that when you asked me for one tonight."

I grinned despite myself. I knew that I was flirting, I *knew* that, and I didn't stop. I liked flirting with him. I was pretty sure I'd like doing just about everything with him, but the flirting ranked high on my list of things I had done with Rob thus far.

"Yeah, but I'm old. I'm allowed to trash my lungs. They're useless now," he said.

"You're not *that* old. What are you, thirty-four? Thirty-five?"

"Thirty-two, actually," he said, sounding smug.

So he's seven years older than me, I thought. Not the oldest guy I'd been with. I chose to see that as an accomplishment.

"See? Young enough for smoking to be bad still."

"Is it odd that hearing you say that makes me very happy?" he asked, and I grinned.

"Maybe a bit."

He laughed and I dug my nails into my palm, trying to make myself associate the sound of his laugh with pain. I didn't want to admit to myself just how far gone I was yet. I wouldn't let myself think about the fact that I was on the phone with someone who was married.

"Well, in any case, thank you for that."

"Not a problem."

We sat in silence, and I debated going inside, grabbing a sweater, and taking my bra off, but I worried that just by getting up, I would ruin the soft, easy quiet we had, and I didn't want to risk it. I wanted him to be with me, on the uncomfortable chairs on the porch, drinking a beer and listening to me complain about the party as I told stories he'd been there for.

He yawned then, and I could picture his face so clearly it was like he was right in front of me.

"You should go to sleep, it's late," I said, hating that I'd said it as soon as it was out of my mouth. I didn't want him to go to sleep. I wanted him to sit on the phone with me for hours. At least until I fell asleep. Sleep had been hard for me the past year, and I'd taken to crawling into bed with Dani or, when she was with Craig, turning on podcasts I had no interest in listening to just so it felt like I was around people.

"It's not that late."

"It's three a.m. That's late, Rob."

"You forget that I'm a tattoo artist, Maggie. We keep weird hours."

"Oh, yeah?"

"We're a nocturnal breed," he murmured.

I moved my chair around so that I could put my feet up on the porch railing. I hoped I was going to be on the phone for a while.

"What was that?"

"My chair. Trying to get comfy," I said, feeling self-conscious about the interruption.

"Where are you right now? You sound far away."

"Geographically or . . ."

"In the context of wherever you are right now. Are you house-sitting?"

I looked around at my surroundings. "No, I'm at my apartment. Not house-sitting for a little bit as of now. I'm on my porch. Or patio. I don't know what the difference is."

"A patio's normally detached and built into the ground. Porches are attached to your house. Or apartment."

"How do you know that?"

"Is that a weird thing to know?" he asked, sounding surprised.

"Maybe not, it just feels like a very specific thing to know about."

"We redid our house last year, so I now know too much about porches and decks and patios and backsplashes," he muttered.

For a second, just one second, I'd forgotten that he was a part of a "we"—then he said that. Maybe it was the hour or the drinks in my system or something I don't have a name for, but I hated that I'd forgotten and hated even more that he'd reminded me.

"So, which do you have, then?"

"Huh?"

"Deck, patio, or porch?"

"Oh. A deck," he said simply.

"Is that where you are?"

"No, I'm in bed."

I froze. In bed. The bed he shared with someone. Someone he was married to. While he was on the phone with me. I thought of my mom and then I thought of my father and then I got mad, not at anyone, just general anger. Or maybe I was sad. Both, really. I could feel myself going further and further down a path that had been trod by so many before me. A path that had ended my parents' marriage. A path I feared and hated and didn't want to get off. My voice sounded thick when I spoke.

"Is your wife there? Doesn't she mind you talking on the phone in bed at three a.m.?"

"No, Ingrid's out of town till the end of the month. Visiting family while she works on her writing."

"So, she's a writer?"

"A poet," he proclaimed.

I bit my tongue. A fucking poet? That's just perfect. Christ.

"Oh. Cool."

"Yeah, she's just released a new collection of poems, so now she's trying to prep a new one. Always churning something out," he said around a semistifled yawn.

"Sounds nice. How long's she been gone?"

"A little less than a month."

"Gotcha."

I didn't know what else to say, but I didn't want the call to end. And I didn't want to keep talking about this. He yawned again and I yawned too. I didn't know they were contagious through the phone.

"You should get some sleep, old man."

His voice was louder this time as he said, "You wound me! I thought you said I was young!"

"I did, but the constant yawning made me question myself."

"You were yawning too, you know. Why don't *you* get some sleep?"

"That's not gonna happen. I don't sleep much," I said, trying to sound casual.

"You don't?"

"No."

"And by 'much,' you mean . . ."

"About three or four hours a night. Five sometimes, if I take an Advil PM or something."

I looked around, trying to find something I could mention to change the subject. I didn't want to talk about sleep, 'cause then I'd have to talk about why I can't sleep and then I'd have to talk about Jackson.

"Maggie."

"Rob."

"That's not good for you," he cooed, almost the way a parent would to a child.

"Better or worse than smoking?"

"Worse. Equal. I don't know, but it's not good. You need sleep."

"I get sleep."

"You need more sleep."

He wasn't wrong. Dani said the same thing. My therapist too. Sometimes I'd come in for a session and she'd take one look at the circles under my eyes and tell me to get comfy on the couch and close my eyes and rest. On days like those, she'd wake me up after forty-five minutes with a cup of tea and a ginger candy, which I'd put in my mouth as I walked to the car, crying.

"I'll work on it," I said, my go-to response when anyone got on me about my sleeping.

"Do you want to talk about why you can't sleep?"

"Not tonight. Maybe another time."

"Okay. Want to hear why I can't sleep?"

"Yes, please," I said, as I moved from my porch to my bedroom, setting about taking my clothes off. I blushed when he spoke and dressed quickly, as if he could see me through the phone.

"Well, for starters, I made myself a cappuccino when I got in, so I'm riding a pretty strong caffeine high at the moment. I don't know about you, but I'm not much of a coffee drinker, so when I do, it's not pretty."

I was having a hard time believing that anything he did wasn't pretty, but I stayed quiet, closing my eyes as he continued. "And I'm working on a design for a client that's not coming together yet, which is frustrating the hell out of me and I can't stop thinking about it."

"What's the design?" I mumbled, eyes still closed. I pretended that the warmth of my phone was his breath.

"It's another portrait. It's for a friend of mine, actually. I don't know why I said 'client.' I think I was trying to sound more impressive than I am."

I snorted and he groaned.

"Maggie . . ."

"Does snorting fall under the no-laugh rule?"

"Absolutely."

"Copy that. Sorry. Carry on." I waved my hand through the air as I said it before realizing he couldn't see me or my many hand gestures.

"Where was I?"

"The tattoo for your friend."

"Right. It's a portrait of his wife."

"So, are you basing it on a photo or does she come and sit for you and you draw her there? I can't decide which one seems easier . . ."

"Nothing like that," Rob replied. "She passed away last year, so it's based on a photograph. One of the wedding photos, actually."

"Wow." Really? That's all I had to say?

"Yeah. It's not a light subject matter, I know."

"No. It's okay, I get it. I'm sorry."

"I guess it's not a conversation between the two of us if one of us doesn't apologize for something, but thank you," he said, and I could tell he meant it.

"I just . . ."

"I know. It's hard to know what to say to that. People and grief don't mix well."

"No, they don't," I said, trying not to sound bitter.

"So, to answer your question, it doesn't make drawing her easier. If anything, it's much more difficult. There's more pressure to get it right."

"I'd think that anytime you're designing something to go on some-one's skin for the rest of their life, there's a shit-ton of pressure."

He laughed and I closed my eyes again, sitting back against the pillows.

"Christ, you're right. How am I ever gonna tattoo someone without sweating through it now? What have you *done*?!"

"I'm sorry, I'm sorry! Forget it. I take it back." I grinned as I said it.

"You can't take it back, it's out there now."

"You'll work through it, I'm sure."

"Thanks for that. Have you got any tattoos? I'm not sure if I saw any . . ."

"Well, to be fair, I was pretty covered up. Hard to show off your tat-toos if you're in long sleeves and pants," I said, suddenly wishing I had worn a dress or a skirt or something that made my legs look good and showed him some more skin.

"You make a good point. So no neck or face tattoos, then. I know that for sure."

"Yeah, no neck or face tattoos for me."

"Other than that?"

I looked down at my wrist. "I've got three."

My fingers traced the lines of my tattoos as I spoke. They were no longer raised, and for the most part, I'd forgotten that they hadn't always been a part of my skin, but as I brushed against them, I imagined that Rob had done them. I imagined sitting in the chair, listening to the buzz and hum of the gun and looking down to see Rob, his brow furrowed in concentration as he focused solely on me. On my skin.

"And?"

"Yes?"

"Do I get to know what they are, or are you going to force me to guess?"

"I'm scared to know what you'd guess," I joked.

"I don't have much to go on, so I doubt they'd be good guesses. Come on, tell me. Friends should know these things about each other."

"You first."

"My tattoos?"

"Yeah. Your tattoos. What are they?"

"You're not gonna believe me," he said, and my mind conjured up images of inked mermaids and lyrics to songs I didn't know.

"What do you mean?"

"I don't have any."

"What?!"

"I know. It's bizarre."

"None?" I asked, my voice loud with shock.

"None."

The imagined mermaid and lyrics vanished from my mind and left me picturing him, his brown hair tousled, his green eyes wide, his skin bare. Warm. I dug my nails into my palms again and tried to shake the lust and the guilt and the shame that coursed through my body in waves that came hard and fast.

"I didn't know tattoo artists were allowed to not have tattoos."

"It's not encouraged, that's for sure."

"So why haven't you gotten one?"

"I don't know. I just never knew what I'd get," he replied, his voice soft again, his rough and honeyed accent back. "I spend my days giving people tattoos that mean something to them, you know? Really mean something. I just never had anything that meant enough to me to have it on me permanently, I suppose."

"Hmmmm . . ."

"What?"

"Nothing. It's just interesting. A tattooless tattoo artist."

"Rare, I know."

"So why be a tattoo artist, then? If you don't know what you'd get yourself."

"I didn't plan on it. I just knew I liked to draw, and I wanted to do something with that, but there's something about galleries that's always felt a bit inaccessible to me, you know? Exclusive, maybe. And one day in school, I found a book of old Romanian tattoos and I got obsessed. I remember finding one that said, 'I fuck well and I'm heavy on the beak,' which I loved, just for how utterly absurd it was. I wanted to know more about the guy who decided to brag about his sexual prowess on his skin, and then it just went from there. People with tattoos are kind of like walking galleries, and I wanted to be a part of that. I wanted to make art that I knew people would look at and appreciate and carry for the rest of their lives, so . . . tattoos."

I could feel the passion in his words as he spoke, talking about his favorite tattoos he'd seen, his favorites that he'd done, and I could feel myself drifting off a bit, on the precipice of sleep, when—

"Your turn," he proclaimed, smiling through the phone.

"Right. They're all pretty small, so no sleeves or anything . . ."

"I gathered that much when you said you had three. Plus, you don't strike me as the kind of person with sleeves."

"Yeah, no sleeves here," I echoed.

"So instead you have . . ."

He trailed off, waiting for me to answer him, and I ran my hands up and down my legs, wanting to ground myself in my surroundings, in my body. Talking to him quieted my mind and made me feel like I was floating, the way you feel right after you've gotten a massage. He made me relaxed, and I hadn't felt anything close to relaxed in a long time.

"Instead, I have a strawberry on my shoulder," I answered.

"A strawberry?" he asked, incredulous.

"Yes."

"Why a strawberry?"

"When I was little, I wanted to be a strawberry when I grew up."

"You did?"

"Yeah. Once when I was six, we all had to come to school dressed as what we wanted to be when we grew up, and we took a class picture, so there were astronauts, ballerinas, scientists, a few pirates, and in the back, because I was the tallest, there was a strawberry." My voice was soft as I said it, remembering the strawberry costume my mom had made for me. I refused to take it off for a week.

"Wow."

"I know."

"That's . . . that's wonderful. I think a strawberry is a very admirable career path to strive for."

"I thought so too."

"So that leaves two more," he said, and after a moment of silence. "Quit stalling. You've got two more, Strawberry."

"Is that my name now?"

"Maggie . . ."

I loved the way he said my name.

"Rob . . ."

I loved saying *his* name.

His voice was singsongy as he said, "I'm owed two more tattoos."

"Right. Well, I've got a line drawing my aunt did of wings tied together with string on my forearm—"

"Which one? Right or left?"

"Does it matter?"

"Maybe not, I'm just curious."

"But you weren't about the strawberry?" I asked, less because I wanted to know but more because I liked making this conversation difficult for him. I'm not sure why, really.

"No, I was, I was just distracted by the visual of a strawberry in a sea of astronauts."

"I see. They're both on my left side."

"Why wings?"

"My aunt's an artist, and she used to draw me these books when I was a kid about a girl named Maggie who would go on adventures and had a pair of wings she could put on to fly away."

"That's lovely," he said, sounding like he really meant it.

"Yeah, it was. So, I don't know, I guess I just liked the reminder that I have the option to fly away? I'm not sure, I didn't think much about it really, I just . . ."

"You wanted your wings."

"I wanted my wings," I echoed, quietly.

I didn't tell him that right then, at that moment, I wanted my wings to fly me over to him, in his house with a deck, where I could curl up next to him.

"What's the last one?"

I hesitated, bringing my fingers to my right shoulder. This was trickier.

"Maggie?"

"Yeah, I'm still here, sorry."

"It's all right."

"The last one's on my shoulder. The right one," I said quickly, hoping we could skim over it.

"And it's . . ."

"The word JAM."

"Jam?"

"Yeah."

"In all caps?"

"Yes," I said, trying to end this part of the conversation.

"Do you feel really strongly about jam, or . . . ?"

I laughed but cut it short. I had rules to follow, and I didn't feel much like laughing now.

"Not that strongly, no."

"But strongly enough to get it tattooed on your shoulder."

"It wasn't always JAM."

"No?"

"No. It was . . . well, I got it with this guy I was seeing, Jackson. So, Jackson is J, Maggie is M, and there used to be an ampersand in there, those pretentious 'and' symbols, but I changed it," I said, letting the words all run together, spaceless.

"I see."

If you're rolling your eyes at the tattoo, know that I get it. I would too. I did the same when he suggested it, actually. It was one of those things where we knew what we were doing was stupid and something only young, dumb, in-love people did, but something about doing it anyway made us feel even younger, and much more in love. We needed that. Things had been hard for a while. Fraught. You'll understand why in a bit, I promise, I just need to work up to talking about him. But I'll say this much for now: we had been happy and in love until we were miserable and in love, and we needed something to try to bring us back together. I think he needed it more than I did. He needed to know that I was on his team, that I was serious about him. I just needed to know that he was committed to me enough to stick around. It's hard to leave someone after you've branded each other with your initials. That didn't stop him from dying, though. I hadn't accounted for that.

"Yeah. But then things . . . things got bad and so I decided I'd rather have my shoulder say JAM than our initials, so, jam."

His voice was soft as he spoke. "I love jam."

"I like it more now."

"I'm assuming you're a fan of strawberry jam, then."

"Of course."

"So you and this Jackson character . . . I take it you're not close?"

If he'd asked me that earlier in the night, when I wasn't so hypnotized by his voice and comfortable under the blankets, I wouldn't have answered. I would've said something snarky or asked him a question hoping to distract him, but I didn't.

"After we broke up? No. No, I was pretty heartbroken by it. He died a few months later, so then there was a second wave of heartbreak and—"

"Oh, Maggie. I'm so sorry," he said, really sounding like he meant it.

I was glad we were on the phone and not face-to-face, because the earnestness in his voice was a little too much for me. So I pulled the covers up over my head and squeezed my eyes shut tight.

"Thanks. It's okay, it was a while ago."

"How long ago did he die?"

"A year."

He let out a big exhale, and I copied him. I hadn't realized I'd been holding my breath.

"Want to talk about it?" he asked.

Yes. No. *Yes.*

"Another time."

"Okay. Of course. So when you said you were sad earlier . . ."

If he had asked me again, I would've told him everything. I would have told him about the fact that for the last year, I'd spent more time crying than doing pretty much anything else. I would have told him about the fact that I still slept in Jackson's old Looney Tunes shirt, the one he'd left behind when he left me. I would have told him about the fact that the first time I had sex with someone who wasn't Jackson, I started sobbing hysterically and the guy, a DJ in what would become a long line of DJs, pulled out and left my apartment as fast as possible. I didn't notice, I just kept on sobbing. But Rob didn't ask again, so I didn't tell him.

"Yeah. I may have left something out. Didn't really feel like boat-party conversation."

"I guess not. Is that why sleep's been hard?"

I nodded but realized that he couldn't see me.

"That's what they tell me," I said through my exhale.

"They?"

"My therapist. And Dani."

"I see. Well, I think they'd be right."

"I think so too. Doesn't make sleep any easier, though."

"No, it doesn't."

We were quiet for a moment, and I wanted to open my eyes and see him in front of me, but I knew I wouldn't, so I kept them closed, stretching my limbs under the blankets.

"When my mum died, I didn't sleep for five days," he said. "I used to go on walks. One night I got as far as West Hollywood and I didn't even realize it. I just needed to be moving, otherwise I'd think about it too much." I put the phone on speaker and set it down by my ear, closing my eyes as he continued. "I wish I could say that it goes away, but I don't think it does. Not all the way, at least. I feel like the whole grieving process is like . . . it's a bit like when you go to the beach, you know? And you get back to your place and you're covered in sand, so you get in the shower, but for days afterward, you're finding sand everywhere. Your hair, under your nails, it's everywhere. But little by little, you find less and less of it. There's still sand, it's just not everywhere."

"Wow," I murmured, floored.

"Was that too pretentious? It felt pretentious as I was saying it . . ."

"No. It was . . . *wow*. You should really write that down. That was . . . beautiful. Super poetic."

"Poetry's more Ingrid's thing," he murmured.

"Right. Of course," I said, hating the fact that I'd brought up poetry, or anything related to you, at all.

"Did all go well with your shoeless friend tonight?" he asked, and I silently thanked him for the subject change.

"Yeah, but she's at Craig's for the night."

"Ah. I see. I didn't know they were together."

"They've been together for about a year and a half," I said, marveling at the reality of that statement. A year and a half of Craig.

"Very sweet."

"Uh-huh."

"You don't sound convinced."

"No, they're very sweet together. I like him, I do. I *love* how happy he makes Dani and he's really good to her, I just . . . I don't know, Dani's so wonderful and Craig's just . . . he's Craig-tastic."

He laughed again, deep and throaty, and I did the nails-into-my-palm thing but it didn't work. His laugh cut right through me.

"I hear you."

"I just feel like almost every heterosexual couple I come into contact with, it's the same thing: the woman's great, and sweet and pretty and wonderful, and the guy's just . . . good. Fine."

"Ouch. You're never meeting Ingrid, then. Can't have you thinking I'm just there," he joked, but I'm still not sure if he was really joking.

We were in agreement: I would never be meeting you. What is it they say about the best-laid plans?

"You know what I mean though, right?" I asked, opening my eyes to stop the room from spinning.

"Absolutely. It's just another thing to hear it verbalized."

"Sorry about that."

"No, it's not a bad thing. You're good at this."

"Good at what?"

"At talking. I like the way your mind works. I like getting to hear the gears turn," he murmured.

He liked the way my mind worked. I was a goner.

"Thanks."

"So I should tell you something," he said, and my entire body clenched. I already knew about the married thing, what was next? Kids? A second family?

"Oh god. What?"

"One of the guys at the party, James or Joe—"

"Joey. I bet it was Joey."

"Short guy? With the coked-up girl?"

"That's him."

"Right, well, Joey told me who your dad is."

Oh. Better than I thought it was going to be, but still not great. When people find out about my father, they either quote his movies to me, explain his movies to me, ask me if his movie *Button Nose* is about me (it isn't—at least I think it isn't), tell me they think he's hot, or ask me about his wives.

"I see."

"And the thing is, I tattooed him the other day," he continued.

Well, this was new.

"What?"

"Yeah. Last week, I think."

"He got another tattoo?"

He had five. One for each wife. He didn't believe in covering them up because he said that "the love was still there." I don't think the wives agreed. I know my mom didn't.

"Yeah, he did," he replied.

I wondered whose name it was this time.

"What did he get?"

"It was a small one. Just a sketch of you and your sister. When you were kids. I didn't know it was you at the time, obviously, but as soon as Joey said it, it made sense. You were a cute kid. He sent me a picture a few months back, so I've been looking at it on and off for weeks," he explained.

So not names, then. I felt unnerved by the idea of my father sitting in his hotel suite, drinking a jack and coke from the minibar as he went over dailies with my face on his body.

"Huh. Where'd he get it?"

"He got it on his left bicep."

"Oh."

"You aren't close, I take it."

"Not really. But that's crazy."

"I know. I'd stared at a photo of you for three hours before we even met. That sounds creepy, I know. I didn't mean it that way, though."

"I know. What picture was it?" I asked.

"The two of you were sitting in director's chairs, your sister—"

"Pearl."

"Pearl. She was laughing at something out of the frame, and you were sitting on the end, staring the camera down."

I knew the picture he was talking about. My mom had taken it when we visited my father on one of his sets somewhere in Europe. Amsterdam, I think. Pearl was twelve and I was six.

Pearl had gotten her period that day and I'd seen my father do coke with one of the actors. Lily. His not-yet-second wife. He'd always loved women with floral names. Ana was his only non-floral wife so far, though he called her Blossom, a pet name that made my skin crawl.

"Oh, yeah. I know that one. I was six," I replied.

"You were feisty. I can tell."

"Can you?" I asked, pleased.

"Between the strawberry thing and the photo, absolutely. You haven't changed much."

"No, I guess not. That picture was taken like four months after strawberry day, I think."

"If I'd known that story when your father came in, I would've put a strawberry in there somewhere."

"I don't think he would've known what you were talking about. I don't think he knows the strawberry story."

"No?" he asked, puzzled.

"I mean, I'm sure he's heard it, he might vaguely remember the story, but he's not the type to remember that stuff."

"What stuff? Stories about his kids?"

He sounded shocked and it made me smile. Something about picturing his incredulity made me feel light.

"Yeah. That stuff," I mumbled.

"Oh."

"Yeah."

"Prick."

I laughed. I couldn't help it.

"Maggie! We have rules, for chrissakes!"

"I'm sorry, I'm sorry! But you're right. He kind of is. Did he tip well?"

". . . Ten percent."

I groaned. Of course he didn't tip well. He'd had one job as a waiter when he was my age, and because of that, he thinks he's "paid his dues." I don't quite know what that means, but he seems to think it entitles him to not tipping well, a quality that never ceases to embarrass me.

He visited me once when I worked as a waitress, and at the end of the meal, he tipped seven percent. From that day on, the line cooks nicknamed me Seven Percent. I quit a few months later. I still tip at least twenty percent, even when I can't afford it.

I should explain something: I don't have my dad's money. I think people assume that I do, which I get, because I would too, but save for the occasional birthday check, his money doesn't belong to me. That was my decision, not his. After he married Lily and then divorced her for someone younger, breastier, I cut myself off from him and his cash. That hurt him, I think, which was kind of the point.

I used to see that as a point of pride, that I was out there in the trenches, making my own way, earning my own money, but every time I don't get cast in a project or a house-sitting job falls through, I seriously consider asking him to send me some money. I'm too proud for that, though.

Ten percent annoyed but didn't surprise me.

"Fuck. What a prick!" I exclaimed.

"It was kind of shitty, but it made for a funny story."

"Well at least there's that, I guess."

"You said that he's in town, right? Where's he based?"

"New York. He moved when he and Ana got married."

"Oh, the sacrifices we make in the name of love," Rob joked.

"Guess how old she is."

He groaned. "Oh no."

"Oh yes."

"Older or younger than you?"

"Older."

"Older or younger than Pearl?"

"Older," I answered.

"Older or younger than *me?*"

". . . I'm not telling."

"Oh god, is she my age?"

"Uh-huh," I responded, fighting an eye roll.

"Fuck. And how old's your dad?"

"Sixty."

"Fuck."

"Yup. Nothing hotter than being married to a man who could very easily be your father, right?"

"Wow," he muttered.

"Yeah."

"That must be shit. I'm sorry."

"It's okay. It used to be hard, but now it's just funny. And sad, I guess."

I didn't want to talk about my father anymore. If we kept talking about him, then I'd have to think about the fact that he must have had phone calls like this one with Lily, while my mom was off tending to me and Pearl. I didn't want to let myself see how similar the situations were.

"I'm trying to imagine my dad with someone my age and it's proving difficult," he revealed.

"What's he like?"

"My dad?"

"Yeah."

I opened my eyes briefly to plug in my phone before putting my head back on the pillows and shutting them again, letting his voice wash over me.

"He's retired now, but he was a baker," he said.

"No way."

"He was. He had his own bakery back home in Manchester, and he'd get up every morning while it was still dark to make the bread and the pastries and set everything up, but he sold the business a while back. It's been franchised now."

"Wow."

"Yeah. He's lovely, really. He's from Romania originally, so he used to speak it around the house, which I used to be embarrassed by, when I was a teenager, but now I'm very grateful. It comes in handy if you want to talk shit or complain, or anything like that. He's incredibly quiet, but a deeply kind man. An easy crier, too, so you'd like him."

"I liked him the second you mentioned bread," I confessed.

"Most people do. Ingrid's gluten-free, and I remember trying to explain it to him when we first started dating. He couldn't wrap his head around it. He still can't, really. He keeps trying to force bread on her . . ."

As I imagined an older Rob, holding loaves of bread in his hands, a slow smile came over me . . .

5

The next thing I knew, I was opening my eyes as sunlight blasted through my too-sheer curtains.

Jackson had hated them. He said they were the enemies of his sloth-like existence, so I bought him an eye mask for when he'd sleep at my place. I still had it. It hung from my lamp, and some nights I'd put it on the pillow beside me, the one on "his" side of the bed back when he'd laid claim to a side of my bed, but I didn't use it. I liked waking up with the sun and getting things done before the rest of the world was awake. It appealed to my competitiveness. That morning was no different. The sun was up, so I was too.

I grabbed my phone to see what time it was, and my stomach flipped. It was eight a.m. I was still on the phone with Rob. We had been on the phone for five hours and twenty-two minutes.

His side of the phone was quiet except for the faint sound of his breathing, which, if I closed my eyes, sounded like he was right next to me. I didn't know when I'd fallen asleep. I remembered him talking about his dad, but nothing more, so I must've crashed somewhere around there. And he'd stayed on the phone.

I wondered if he'd closed his eyes too and imagined me breathing beside him. I wondered how long after I'd fallen asleep he'd done the same. I wondered if I'd snored. He didn't.

I sat, still staring at the phone, trying to decide what to do. I decided it would be weirder if he woke up and I was still on the phone, waiting for him, and besides, I wanted to listen to the latest Maron podcast, so I needed my phone. I hung up. Five hours, twenty-six minutes, forty-four seconds.

I spent the rest of the morning on a hike, listening to Marc Maron talk to an actress I both loved and envied, one I'd seen in at least seven audition rooms, and pretending that he was interviewing me, planning my responses in my head as I walked a trail populated by rabbits and women who ate less than rabbits.

It was eleven a.m. when I got a text from Rob. I was on my porch, neglecting my cereal and making a playlist for the mood I wanted to be in (happy and grief-free—my ideal mood and the name of the playlist; subtlety is not my thing), when my phone buzzed.

Rob had sent me a text. And then another one, just seconds later. I thought about waiting the socially prescribed seven minutes before opening and responding to him but vetoed that quickly because a) I hated playing games, and b) we were friends and friends don't play games. Maybe charades. Or poker. But other than those, no games.

I opened the texts.

> Good morning. I'm hoping you slept well. It sounded
> like you did. I'm off work until this afternoon
> and was wondering if you've eaten.
> Want to grab some food?

> I debated not sending that in the hopes that you
> were still asleep, but I doubt it.

I stared at the text. And at the uneaten cereal next to me. Friends "grab some food" together, right? I texted back.

morning. i'm up, you were right. let's eat.

Two minutes later, I got a call. I waited until the third ring to pick up. "Hello?"

"Good morning," he said, yawning. I smiled. I loved his yawn almost as much as I loved his laugh.

"Morning."

"So how many hours of sleep did you get?"

". . . Four."

"Maggie!"

"What?!"

"That's horrible," he chided.

I grinned, examining my hair for split ends as we spoke. I'd decided that it was better for me, for him, for everyone involved, if I distracted myself while we spoke on the phone; that way I couldn't get too excited about anything he said. It didn't work.

"It's not my best, no. How much did you get?"

"Six. It was heavenly."

I wondered what he meant was heavenly. I hoped he meant me. I rolled my eyes at myself.

"Now you're just bragging," I teased.

"I am. I'm sorry. I'll make it up to you. Breakfast?"

"Yes, please."

"Where are you?"

"My apartment."

"I figured that. I meant where in the context of Los Angeles," he explained.

"Oh. Right. Studio City."

"I'm in Laurel Canyon. Want to meet at Aroma in an hour? It's on Tujunga, do you know it?"

I knew it. It had been one of Jackson's favorite places. He loved their blue velvet cake and ordered it every time we went, mostly because he liked eating foods that were so artificially colored they looked like they would dye your insides, but also because he'd decided the cake was an ode to David Lynch, and, like every other sensitive art boy, he *loved* David Lynch.

"Yeah. I'll see you there."

"Okay. I'd say get some sleep in the interim, but I think that would be a fruitless request."

"It would be, yes," I responded.

"Right."

"Okay. See you there."

"Yeah, see you there."

He didn't hang up.

"Bye," I said, trying to bite back a smile.

"Right. Bye. See you later."

I hung up and walked into the kitchen, dumping my cereal out into the sink. I felt bad for wasting it, but it's not as though I could save already-milked cereal, so I felt justified in the waste. I moved to my room, trying to figure out what to wear. What are you supposed to wear when you meet your married friend for breakfast? I wished Dani were home.

I settled for a white vintage dress of Dani's that she'd stopped wearing and given to me and a pair of Adidas that had belonged to someone before me. Pearl, I think.

I turned on my "happy and grief-free" playlist and started walking towards the restaurant. I could've driven; it would have been quicker, but I needed the extra time to clear my head. Lucy Dacus's cover of "Dancing in the Dark" started and I set off, ignoring the jeers from the pickup truck that idled at the crosswalk as I planned out what I was going to say to Rob, what I was going to order, how I'd greet him.

He was there before me, which I had hoped for but didn't really expect. I am almost always the first person to arrive. It's why I bring books with me everywhere; I don't like absentmindedly scrolling on my phone and I like the idea that whoever is late to meet me (or merely on time) will see me reading, but Rob had been earlier than me, so I wouldn't get to be caught reading by him. Not that time.

He walked towards me and we met in the middle, in front of the gelato place that gives you the free wafers. He smiled with his whole face. I don't know how else to say it. It was contagious, evidently, because I did it too. My cheeks hurt.

"Morning," he said, pulling me in for a hug. He was warm and I wanted to burrow my face into his neck, but friends don't do that, so I settled for closing my eyes and trying to memorize the feeling of him and his warmth. I pulled away first.

"Morning," I said, missing his arms as soon as I pulled back.

"Did you walk here?"

"Yeah. It's not too far from my place, so."

"How far is not too far?"

"Like two miles."

"I don't think I've ever met a Los Angeles native who volunteers to walk more than four blocks," he said, grinning.

"Now you have."

"Now I have."

We walked into the restaurant, grabbing menus. I didn't need one, though. I'd already decided what I wanted. I like looking at the menus of the places I'm going to before getting there so I can know exactly what I want before I arrive. My mom does the same. I'm not sure what it means. That day, though, it meant that while Rob studied the menu, I could study him.

His hair was just as unkempt as it had been the night before, but a little greasier. He'd probably shower later. He still had some sleep in the corners of his eyes, and his shirt had a hole in it, right by the neck. I wanted to poke my finger through it. I didn't.

"Do you know what you want?" he said, leading me towards the barista-waiter to order.

What a question.

"Yeah, I do, but you're not paying."

"Maggie."

"Rob."

"I'm paying. I told you I'd make up for sleep-bragging. I'm buying breakfast."

"But I still feel bad about the whole ten percent thing! You're not buying," I reasoned.

"That was your dad, not you. And besides, if I got hung up over every shitty tipper I've tattooed, I'd never tattoo anyone ever again. Quit being stubborn. Accept the free food."

I stared at him. He stared back. I sighed, defeated. I wasn't too torn up about it, though. I love free food. And the idea that he was buying me breakfast. It implied something . . . definite, I guess. Something shared.

"Fine."

"Good," he said, smiling.

We ordered. Breakfast burrito and a hot tea for him, scrambled eggs and an iced red eye for me. He paid, smirking at me as he paid the bill.

"See? That wasn't so hard, was it?"

"No, I suppose not."

We sat outside, by the fountain that takes up too much space. My chair was rickety and uneven on the ground, but I didn't mind. I took a sip of my coffee and he grimaced.

"What?" I said, taking another sip.

"How do you drink that? It's poison."

"It's not poison, it's coffee."

"It's coffee with espresso, Maggie. That's poison. How many of those do you drink in a day?"

"Of these drinks specifically or just coffee in general?"

"In general. I'm curious. And scared," he joked.

"Probably five? I don't know, I don't really keep track."

That was a lie. I drink at least seven cups a day and keep track of my beverage intake almost religiously on my hydration app, my most used app other than my period tracker and Spotify. I didn't lie for any real reason, though. Five isn't *that* far off from seven. I just didn't want him to realize how much of a mess I was, I guess.

"*Five?* Maggie, no!"

"It's not *that* bad," I muttered, taking another sip.

"The coffee intake or the drink you have in front of you?"

"Both."

"The coffee consumption isn't bad for an all-night trucker, I suppose. But you're not a trucker. And that drink is sludge. You'll never be able to convince me otherwise."

"Try it."

"What?"

"Try it. You never know, you may love it," I said, waving the drink around.

"I will absolutely not love it."

"Come on. One sip."

I held it out to him, and he studied it, eyes going from the drink to the straw to me and back again. He sighed, relenting and reaching over to take the drink from me. He brushed against my hand when he took it, and I looked down quickly, focusing on putting jam (strawberry, of course) on my toast. I looked back up at him as he brought the coffee to his lips. He sipped and gagged, his face scrunching up in disgust.

"You just tried to poison me!"

"It's not that bad." I laughed.

"It is absolutely that bad."

"More for me, then."

I snatched the drink from him and took a long sip, exaggerating how much I enjoyed it.

Rob dug into his burrito; I watched him eat. He was shoving the food into his mouth as though if he didn't eat fast, the food would start to fight him. Did you ever notice that? I'm sure you did. I'm sure you've written a poem about it. I'll have to read it someday.

"So," I said, taking a bite of toast. "Do you just tattoo portraits, or do you do other things too?"

"I do other things, but mostly portraits. Of people, pets, all of it. I gave someone a portrait of their ex's cat the other day. They'd loved the cat, not the girl, I guess."

"Wow."

"I know."

"Was it a cute cat, at least?"

"Not really." He laughed.

"I can't decide if that makes it better or worse."

"Worse, I think. I love the wings, by the way. They're lovely. Your aunt did them?"

He nodded towards my forearm, and I looked down, remembering once again that the wings had not always been a part of my body.

"Yeah. Seventeenth birthday present. My mom flipped out. Didn't talk to my aunt for a month."

"Really?"

"Uh-huh," I said, taking a bite of my under-salted, over-cooked eggs.

"Why? She doesn't like tattoos?"

"No, it's not that. She'd wanted to give me my first tattoo. She felt robbed of the experience, I guess."

"Is she a tattoo artist, then?"

"Nope. A photographer. She liked the idea of giving me a tattoo, though. Thought it would bond us."

"Huh."

"Yeah. She's . . . she's a character," I said, taking another bite of food.

I didn't know what else to call her. I still don't. My mother is what happens if you cross a cast-iron pan with a feather boa. Simultaneously reliable and entirely frivolous.

"How about the strawberry? Can I see it?"

"Professional curiosity?"

"Something like that, yeah."

I looked over my shoulder before lowering my sleeve and revealing the strawberry. I don't know why, I wasn't doing anything particularly scandalous. It just felt intimate. Too intimate for an outdoor patio full of screenwriters and kids waking up from their naps.

The strawberry's small, about as big as my thumbnail, and brightly colored. It looks more like a photo of a strawberry than a tattoo, really. My niece calls it my "shoulder sticker."

"I love it," he said, smiling with his entire face again.

"Yeah?"

"Yeah. It's so realistic. Makes my mouth water," he said, laughing a bit. I clenched my thighs together and forced myself to stare at his ring.

"My niece loves it. She wants to get one when she's older. My sister's still mad at me for that, actually. She says I'm a terrible influence."

She is right; I am, just not in the way she thinks.

"How old's your niece?"

"Harper's four."

I can't say Harper's name without grinning. She is my favorite person in the world, a beam of light and joy and chubby cheeks and always-sticky hands. She's the one who pulled me out of my grief after Jackson, not that she'd know that. Not that I'm done with grieving him. She was the only real distraction I had in the weeks after his death.

"And does she live nearby?"

"They live over in Venice," I explained.

"And what does your sister do?"

"Is this an interrogation now?" I asked, teasing him in what I'd decided was an *extremely* platonic tone of voice.

"No, I'm just curious. Friends should know these things about each other," he answered.

I looked down at the hem of my dress when he said that. Something about hearing him call us friends made me want to cry. I wanted so badly to *want* to be his friend, really, I did, but we both know that I wanted a whole lot more than that.

"Pearl's a stylist."

"Oh, wow. Very cool," he said, sounding genuinely impressed.

"She's ridiculously cool."

"And you're close with her?"

"Very close. Pearl's husband, Jonah, and I are really close, so I'm over there a lot."

"How much do you see them?"

"Once a week."

"Oh, so you're *very* close," he declared.

"Yeah, I guess so. We didn't used to be, but that changed when I was a teenager. What about you, any siblings?"

"I've got three older sisters."

"Three?"

"Yep."

"Wow."

"I know." He smiled and sighed.

"Are you close with them?"

"I'm closest with Anne, she's the oldest. But she's in Scotland with her husband, who's basically right out of *Braveheart*. A great guy, but *very* intense. I'm not too close to Georgia and Beth, but that's just because they don't get along well with Ingrid, so it's tricky now."

Did you know that? I'm sure you did, you're perceptive. That must have been difficult, knowing your husband's sisters didn't like you. I'm sorry.

"Do you get back there often?"

"To Manchester?"

He'd finished his burrito by then, and after gesturing to me whether it was okay, took a piece of my toast and slathered it with jam before finishing it off in three bites.

"Yeah," I responded.

"I get up there about three times a year. Four times if Ingrid isn't on the road."

"Must be nice."

"It's good going back. I miss them, but LA is home now, which I never thought I'd say."

"No?"

"No. I came out here when I was twenty-four. I followed a girl—"

"Really?" I asked, trying not to be jealous of a girl I'd never met.

"Julia Tommins. We'd dated in school, and she wanted to be an actress, so she came out here and I followed."

"What happened?"

"She broke up with me a month later. And then moved to London. She's a lawyer now, I think."

"But you stayed."

"But I stayed. And now here we are," he said, arms stretched out as he motioned around the garden.

"Were you heartbroken?"

"Completely. Devastated. I drank a lot and cried a lot and drew a lot of pictures of her being skewered by Cupid's arrows. They were total shit, but very therapeutic."

"I'm sure."

"Can I see your other one?" he asked, changing the subject.

"My other what?"

"Tattoo."

"Oh. Right. Sure."

"You don't have to, I'm just curious."

"No, it's fine. Just, don't expect anything good, okay? He was pretty fucked up when he did it and he had bad handwriting to begin with, so—"

"He tattooed you when he was drunk?" he stammered, brow furrowed.

"No."

"I don't understand."

I was going to have to tell him the story. I knew I would eventually, I just didn't imagine that I'd be telling him the story over breakfast. Dinner seemed more fitting. Or after a lot of alcohol.

"Jackson was an addict."

"Oh, Maggie." He sighed.

"Yeah. He'd been sober for a little less than a year when we met, but a little after his one-year-sober birthday, he fell off the wagon, which I didn't know until a few months later. But he was high when I got this."

I lowered the other sleeve of my dress and looked down at the tattoo. The J and M were scraggly and uneven, the A clearly done by someone else. Someone with a steady hand. Someone who was sober. It was messy, obviously, but I'd gotten to the point where I'd stopped being able to see Jackson's messy attempts at an ampersand. It was just an A now.

Rob stared at it for a bit before bringing his hand (the right one) up to touch it. He did it quickly, probably unconsciously, but maybe not. I forced myself to stay still.

"How long were you two together?" he asked.

"A little over a year."

"Wow."

"I know it's not that long, but—"

"No, it's long enough. I'm so sorry. I can't imagine what that must have been like."

His hand moved from my shoulder to my hand, which he squeezed before returning his arm to his side of the table.

"Thanks. Thank you. I'm okay—" I stammered, but mercifully, he cut me off.

"You don't have to be."

I looked up into his eyes and temporarily forgot about The Ring and Jackson and my sleeplessness and the kiss and everything else. The world slipped away, and if I were the type of person who wrote songs, I would write a song about it, but I'm not, so this is as close as I'll come. I'd write a poem, but I don't want to take any more from you than I already have.

We parted ways soon after that. He tried to convince me to let him drive me home, but I refused, stubborn as always.

Breakfast had been safe and infidelityless, and I didn't want to push my luck by having any more time with him. I figured getting in an enclosed space with him so soon after he'd touched my skin would be like going to a bar to celebrate your first week of sobriety.

He hugged me goodbye and told me not to drink any more coffee, and I wished him luck with his tattooing, trying to think of something funny and charming to say before putting my headphones in, playing Julia Jacklin, and taking the long way home.

6

When I got back to the apartment, I was greeted by the aroma of essential oils and watermelon vape smoke, Dani's signature scent. I opened the door (she never locks it, something I've tried and failed to train her out of), and found her sitting on the sofa, listening to Joni Mitchell remixes (I know, remixing Joni is horrible, but it's best we move on from that musical monstrosity for the sake of brevity) and eating a muffin. Dani always starts and ends her day with sweet foods. Breakfast is time for pancakes, pastries, and waffles, nothing else. (She says that oatmeal is depressing and refuses to eat it.) This is something I still don't understand, but I've found it best to just accept it.

When she saw me, she jumped up from the couch, squealed, and ran to me, tackling me in a hug that would have seemed excessive even if we hadn't seen each other in months. She was like a dog in that way. Always thrilled to see you, no matter how much time has passed.

"Hiiiiiiiiiiiiii," she said, kissing my cheek and accidentally exhaling vape smoke on my face.

I stifled my cough and hugged her back, kissing her on her cheek before pulling away.

"Hi," I responded, heading towards the couch to grab a bite of her muffin. It was zucchini. No thanks. I handed her the piece, which she happily took, sitting, you guessed it, on my lap.

"Where were you? You slept here last night, right?"

"Yeah, I slept here. I went to Aroma for breakfast."

"Alone?"

She was raising her eyebrows and grinning at me.

"No, not alone," I murmured, looking away from her.

"With anyone I know?"

"Kind of."

I didn't know why she was dragging this out, but I refused to volunteer any information.

"Someone from the party?"

". . . Yes, Dani. Someone from the party."

She clapped her hands, squealing.

"Someone quite tall?" She giggled.

"Yes. Tallish."

"And English?" Dani asked in her worst English accent.

"Yup."

"And broody, maybe?"

"Yep."

"And a tattoo artist?"

"Uh-huh," I said, wishing I knew some way to get out of the conversation.

"Oh my god, I knew it!! I told Craig last night, I said, 'Maggie's about to fall in love,' and I was right!!! I can't believe it!!!"

I paused, debating how exactly to burst Dani's bubble. I was beginning to think that she might be more disappointed by Rob's marital status than I was. Maybe.

"Dan," I cut her off, but she was persistent.

"We can go on double dates and—"

"Dani."

She stopped then, looking at me and not into my future. Her smile faded and she instinctively reached for her vape, her equivalent of a safety blanket.

"What?"

"Rob's married," I declared, less to her and more to myself.

She coughed on her vape. I had to look away to keep from laughing. Or crying. Both, maybe. There'd been lots of cry-laughing in the fifteen hours since meeting Rob. Did he have that effect on you too?

"*What?*" she said, scrambling off my lap and grabbing some rose-water spray.

"Uh-huh. Her name is Ingrid and she's a poet and—"

"Married married? Like with a ring?"

"Yes, married married. With a ring. And a house. And a deck."

"What?"

"Nothing. He's married, though." I sighed and looked down again.

"Happily?"

"I don't know, I think so."

"But . . . but soul mates?"

Her voice sounded small as she spritzed me with rosewater. Apparently, I was in need of some cleansing.

"I think you might have to resume your search. This one's pretty unavailable, as far as soul mates go," I insisted.

"But you got breakfast together."

"Yeah. We're friends."

I could have told her about the kiss right there. In fact, I should have. But at that point, I liked having the kiss as something that only Rob and I shared. If I told Dani, she'd tell Craig, who'd tell Joey, who, depending on how well the rest of the party had gone, would tell Liv, making our brunches all the more awkward for me.

I didn't know if Rob had told anyone, but I doubted it. My story would be a tale of a drunken mistake people in their twenties make. His would be a tale of infidelity and disloyalty. Between the two of us, though, it wasn't a story of anything other than a moment we shared. I didn't want to share it with anyone else. I didn't want to share anything with anyone else, really. Just him.

"Friends?"

"Uh-huh," I said, this time looking at her.

"Huh."

She paused, rosewater spray poised in front of my face, making me squeeze my eyes shut.

"Is that weird?" I asked, knowing full well that it was.

"I mean, I guess not. You guys looked like you got along last night, it's just . . . I don't know, are married guys *allowed* to be friends with other women?"

"I'm friends with Jonah—"

"Yeah, but he's your brother-in-law, that's different."

"I'm friends with Craig—"

"We're not married, though. And besides, you're not *really* friends with Craig. You just get along with him. Like how I wasn't *really* friends with Jackson."

Dani froze, and I bit my tongue. This would happen every once in a while. She'd mention Jackson the way that you'd mention your friends' still-alive exes who'd broken their hearts—with a bit of contempt and dismissiveness. She'd forget that, in his death, he had been sainted, his faults erased, his missteps forgiven. I never knew how to react when she'd do it. She didn't either, I know.

I didn't know what to do about my feelings towards Jackson. He'd died so soon after breaking up with me that I hadn't gotten through my anger in time to throw it away and trade it out for grief, so instead I was left with a grief-anger cocktail that didn't mix well and left my stomach feeling knotted and made sleep impossible. I still didn't sleep on his side of the bed, and I kept his toothbrush in a drawer in my room because I couldn't bear to throw it out. It felt like every day I found something else to mourn when it came to him, his absence. But there was anger, too. So much anger. I'd find myself coming up with things I should've said to him while we were fighting, lines that would've ended the fight with me on top, or I'd just get angry about fights we'd had all over again. Some days I wasn't sure what hurt me most: Jackson's death or the breakup.

"Oh, Mags, I'm sorry. I just meant—"

"I know what you meant. It's fine, I got it," I said, cutting her off.

"You know, now that I think about it, I don't think it's *that* weird for you and Rob to be friends," she reasoned, not sounding all that sure.

"No?" I said, both relieved and guilty that Dani's Jackson slipup had led her to letting me off the hook for my new friendship.

"No. I think it's kind of cool, actually. He seemed cool."

"Yeah, he is."

Dani looked at me for a moment, studying my face—which I tried to school into an unreadable expression, one that belonged to someone who hadn't kissed a married guy just hours before (I failed, I'm sure)—before grabbing the rest of her muffin and practically shoving it into her face.

As she finished her muffin, Dani clambered back onto the sofa, squeezing behind me and prompting me to move onto the floor so she could braid my hair, her second-favorite thing to do other than sit on people's laps and read tarot cards.

Having Dani braid my hair made me feel like I was a little girl again. Something about the touch of Dani's fingertips on my scalp and the sound of her voice as it hummed and trilled around me made me feel as though I were levitating.

I closed my eyes as Dani combed through my hair, gently. She was always gentle with me.

"So," I said, softly, "how did Craig like the party?"

"He loved it. He wants to do the same thing next year, I think."

Fuck.

"Oh, really?"

"Yeah. I know. Not your thing. You don't have to go next year, I promise."

If Dani's hands weren't in my hair at that moment, I would've hugged her. I settled for tilting my head back further into her lap, which she understood, and so she leaned down and kissed my forehead.

Dani and I have known each other since we were kids. We met the first day of kindergarten on a log. The other kids made fun of me for the sushi in my lunch, so I hid, drowning my sorrows in soy sauce. But she marched up to me, sitting beside me as she ate her PB&J. She asked me about my hair, which was pink at the time, and I asked her if I could try her sandwich, as I'd never had non-health-food peanut butter before.

As it turned out, I liked her sandwich more than my sushi, and she liked my sushi more than her sandwich, so from that day forward, we shared food.

I was seconds away from napping, I could feel it, when Dani spoke again, her fingers still in my hair.

"Mags?"

"Yeah?" I said, eyes still closed and tongue thick with sleepiness.

"Just be careful, okay? You and Rob have a connection, but I know you know how things like this play out. And I don't want you to get hurt again. Not after . . . you know."

She didn't have to say any more, I knew what she meant. When you know someone as well as I know Dani, words feel unnecessary.

After Jackson died and I spent a month at Pearl's house, not sleeping or eating, crying every twenty minutes, and watching *Sesame Street* with Harper, I returned to the apartment and went through a series of boys (it's the only correct term for them, despite our often too-large age differences) whom Dani described as "training-wheel rebounds." They weren't ever my type and were always people I knew would never hurt me as badly as Jackson had. People who wouldn't break me when they inevitably left. This was different. I knew it. So did Dani, I think.

I wouldn't have been surprised if she knew about the kiss already, either from reading my thoughts or her tarot cards or my scalp. If she did, she didn't say anything. Dani wasn't a pusher. She was a believer in letting things play out naturally, going with the flow. She was nothing if not on-brand.

"I'll be careful, I promise," I said, half telling the truth, half lying. I knew it, too. I'd abandoned caution bit by bit since kissing Rob. Soon there'd be none left.

My phone vibrated with a text. I opened it, silently cursing the stampede of butterflies that swarmed around my insides and braided my nerves.

> **Breakfast was great, thanks for meeting me.**
> **Any more coffee consumption thus far?**

I smiled, scrunching my face tightly to keep from squealing and repeating the mantra I'd decided on using while on my walk home: *He's married he's married he's married he's married he's married he's married.*

It's funny how sometimes when you repeat a phrase so much, it loses its meaning. The words became Jell-O in my mind, fluid and formless, devoid of meaning or inflection, and I looked back down at my phone, hands poised to respond.

> **thanks for the free food, that always**
> **makes it taste better. no more coffee yet,**
> **but the day is young . . .**

The typing dots came up, and the butterflies went nuts.

> **Maggie. No. More. Coffee.**

> **How's this: if you can go a day without coffee,**
> **I'll buy you lunch next week.**

I even liked seeing my name in print, knowing that he was the one who had typed it. I stared at my name on the screen for a moment longer, before rereading the rest of the text. Another meal. With him. That he'd buy me. And eat with me. Sold. Playing with Fire continued, I suppose.

just a day without coffee? easy. you're on.

You sure?

absolutely. get ready to buy me lunch

I'll believe it when I see it.

As I read the text, I could imagine his smirk and grinned in response. You didn't enter my mind once, I'm sorry to say. Maybe it was Dani's fingers playing with my hair, maybe it was the fact that as long as I wasn't looking at him or listening to him, I could forget that he was married, linked to you. I don't know.

I spent the day texting Rob and trying to read *Anna Karenina,* a book I'd lied about having read since high school. I wondered if he was texting you as much as he was texting me. I wondered if he'd told you about me. I wondered if you sensed something, a change in him, an unnameable distance, anything.

What I'm asking is: Did you know that I was a threat? Could you sense it? Because I don't think I did. Did the scorpion know that it was the villain of the toad's story? I'm not sure. To the scorpion, it's a tale of instinct. To the toad, it's a tragedy.

Funny, the stories we tell. I think I'm the villain of yours; maybe Rob is too. We're both sorry and we're not.

7

Craig came over that night, walking through the door, kicking off his shoes, setting down a bottle of wine, and making a beeline for the Thai food we'd just opened. (Dani'd given him a copy of our key after they'd been dating for a month, which, for her, was a relationship milestone record.) Dottie, unleashed (I've only ever seen her with a leash a handful of times), waddled towards me, where she began licking at the garlic chili sauce I'd spilled on my arm. I pretended that she went to me because I was her favorite, but I doubt it was true.

"Mags," Craig said, lowering himself onto the couch as Dani kissed his temple. He shoved a spring roll in his mouth and spoke around it. "I've got a house-sitting job for you if you're in."

I perked up, but only slightly. Craig had taken the last spring roll, the one I'd been eyeing for the last five minutes. I'd really wanted that spring roll.

"Who is it?"

"A friend. A friend of a friend, actually. She's up in Laurel Canyon and she's off to Toronto for the festival, so it'll be ten days. The pay's good and her house is sick. Pool, hot tub, rain shower—"

"Why do you know so much about her bathroom situation?" Dani said, sounding very un-Dani. She saw me look at her and quickly took a bite of pad thai, avoiding my eyes.

"I've been over a few times."

"You've been over and used her shower?" I said as casually as I could muster. I didn't want Dani to have to ask it. Best she keep up the easy-breezy facade she'd honed in front of Craig.

"No, I was just over when she had it installed. She's married, guys. The interrogation can wrap up." He kissed Dani on the cheek after he said that, and I felt myself softening towards him a bit. Dani did too, evidently, as she fed him some of her food.

He slurped the noodles, and she wiped his mouth for him. I was struck by extreme disgust and jealousy.

"When does she leave?" I asked, focusing my attention on Dottie, who'd fallen asleep on my foot and made it go numb. I wanted to bring the feeling back to it but didn't want to wake Dottie, so I started flexing my ankle, soft at first, then harder.

"Next week. Want me to connect you guys?"

"Yes, please," I said, taking a sip of the wine. It tasted expensive and made me feel like a little kid again, sneaking sips of drinks from around the dinner table. Expensive booze always made me feel childish, as if I wasn't meant to be drinking it.

Craig pulled his phone out and sent my contact to Lucy, the owner of the Laurel Canyon place. A few seconds later, his phone dinged at us. Craig's phone was never on silent. Or vibrate.

He looked down at the screen and smiled.

"She says she'll call you tomorrow."

"Cool. Thanks, Craig."

"Not a problem, Mags," he said as he leaned down to whisper something in Dani's ear.

I wasn't an idiot; I knew that the only reason Craig set me up with these gigs was to get me out of his and Dani's hair for little bits at a time. That sounds bad, I know, but it wasn't. I understood it.

Since Jackson, Dani'd become reluctant to let me out of her sight for longer than a few hours at a time. She didn't want me to ever feel alone, so she tried her best to make sure that I wasn't. It was sweet of her, really, and though I never told her, I appreciated it. I needed it, on a certain level. She knew that. Dani knew a lot without me ever having to tell her.

So it was kind and good and nice of her, but it put a strain on things with Craig. It's hard to have a girlfriend who won't leave her best friend's side. I understand. It's hard to have a best friend who won't leave her boyfriend's side. Craig and I talked about that once.

We'd made Craig host a dinner party for our friends because, unlike us, he had a proper dining room with a table and matching chairs, meaning no one would have to eat on the floor while we drank too much and got full on brie and baguette even before the dinner was brought out.

It was the end of the night, and I'd stayed behind to help clean up before crashing on the couch (I'd had too much to drink, and besides, Dani was still worried about having me sleep alone at the apartment), when Craig came into the kitchen after carrying Dani to bed (she's always been good at avoiding cleanup).

He stood next to me, and we fell into a steady, quiet rhythm, me washing, him drying. We didn't acknowledge each other, except for the brief moments when he'd take a glass from me, but after a while, he broke the silence.

"Dan really loves you," he said, still looking down at the highball glass he was drying.

I paused for a moment, unsure of where this was coming from or what I should say.

"Yeah," I replied, "she does."

"You love her too, I can tell," he said, drying a serving spoon in his oatmeal-colored dish towel.

"She's my best friend," I said simply, though there was nothing simple about what Dani was to me. She'd been my sister, my mother, my therapist, my partner, my competitor, my cheerleader, my stylist, my dermatologist, everything. Is there a term that can sum that up? If so, I didn't know it.

"You guys have just been in each other's lives for so long, you know? Sometimes when I'm around you guys, I feel like you're communicating telepathically or something. Like you have this private language, this world that only the two of you are allowed into."

He said that as if it were nothing. As if he were commenting on the weather, but from the way he refused to look at me, I knew he wasn't oblivious to the gravity of what he said. He wasn't wrong, either. Dani and I used to talk about that. How there were moments when we were sure we were having full conversations in the privacy of each other's brains.

We used to think our connection was like that of twins, because while we weren't related, we had the same birthday. I'm not sure if I mentioned that to you before, but it's true. We were born on the same day at the same hospital. We were just a few rooms apart.

Anyway, I knew what Craig meant. Even more, I could feel the loneliness in his words, and in that moment, I wished I could grant him entry into our world, teach him our language of shared looks and history, but the urge dissipated quickly. Some things are special because they're only shared between two people, you know? Maybe I was being greedy, I don't know. I guess I am kind of greedy. You know that. I'll work on it.

"We kind of do," I said, slowly, measuredly, so as not to sound smug.

"I know! It's great most of the time. I love watching it, actually. It's like watching tennis or something, but I don't know, sometimes I . . ."

"Sometimes you wish you were the one playing tennis?"

"Yes. Yes! That's exactly it. I love Dani, you know? I *love* her. She's fucking incredible," he gushed, grabbing another sip of his drink. I watched him the way you watch little kids when they're being adorably difficult—eyebrows raised, biting back a smile that would only make them self-conscious if they were to spot it.

"She is," I said, trying to keep the endearment out of my voice.

"And you guys are great, you are, you're great, but *fuck,* sometimes I just wish that you guys weren't so . . . so fucking *close.* 'Cause I feel like I'm suffocating trying to get in between you guys."

He was slurring his words a little, so I wasn't sure if he'd remember saying this to me in the morning, but the slurred speech didn't take anything away from the intensity of his words. He was threatened by me. Or maybe not by *me,* but by my connection with Dani. I'd never liked Craig as much as I did when he told me that.

I hadn't realized how much he'd seen. How much he'd understood.

"You don't have to suffocate, Craig," I said, mostly because I didn't know what else there was to say.

"I know, I know, it's just—"

"It's hard, I get it. It must be hard. I never really thought about it, but I get it. Dani loves you, though. As close as she and I are, she loves you."

He looked up at me, his face lighting up.

"She does?"

"Of course she does. It's just different. You guys have your own tennis match going, and I like watching it. Most of the time, at least. I get it."

"You get it," he said softly, almost to himself.

"I know she's been a little attached to me since—"

"You don't have to talk about it," Craig said, putting up a hand to stop me.

"I know. I just want you to know that I know it must be hard. Thanks for being patient."

He smiled at me then and put both of his hands on either side of my face, like a grandparent might.

"It's okay. Take all the time you need. You'll be okay," he reassured me.

Those were simple words, I know, but I knew he meant them. And even more importantly, I knew that they were true. Not yet maybe, but they would be.

That was our best moment, I think. Even more than the dead sister talk. Even more than when he held my left hand at Jackson's memorial while Dani held my right one. Even more than when he sat with me on the porch for six hours, from midnight till the sun came up, in total silence while I cried. He surprises me sometimes.

Anyway, back to the Thai food and sleeping dog and numb leg. Craig ate more of Dani's noodles while I combed my fingers through Dottie's fur.

I watched Craig and Dani for a bit, quietly. I hated and loved being their third wheel in equal measure. Hated it for obvious reasons, I'm sure. Being with a couple only exacerbates the fact that you yourself are not a part of a couple and, depending on how recently you've been dumped, makes you think about your last ex, which, if you're me, makes you think about all your other exes, which then makes you think about every person you've ever been attracted to and rejected by. Not a great spiral, as far as things go.

I loved being around them, though, too. There's something calming in being around two people whose love for one another is so strong that it feels like it's an essential fixture in the room. It's as if their love is as commonplace and dependable as the lights.

It was then that my phone buzzed in my hand. I'd gotten a text. From Rob. A response to one I'd sent earlier that he hadn't responded to. I'd been thinking about it all night, in between eating too much takeout and thinking about *not* thinking about my unanswered text.

It hadn't been notable, really. If it weren't for the lack of response, I wouldn't have given it a second thought, but because my text was met with nothing, his silence became louder and full of shadowy intentions in my mind.

We'd been talking about exes. Not Jackson, because we both knew enough to know that that wasn't really a text-friendly topic. We were talking about DJs and why I found myself dating them so frequently.

DJs?? Really

i know, it's ridiculous. and dumb.

Okay, at least you know it. Why DJs though?
If you think they're ridiculous. And dumb.

idk, I guess I just always liked the idea of dating a musician,
you know? being his muse, breaking his heart,
hearing an entire album written about me full of
inside jokes or secret messages and things

Don't we all? But how do you go from that to DJs?

well the thing is, i don't know that many musicians

And that was it. I'd sent it at 4:35. It was 8:42 now. That meant I'd
been thinking and overthinking and rethinking the text for over four
hours. Not my worst text-related thought spiral, to be honest.

But it didn't matter anymore, because he'd texted back. The butterflies that had been quietly humming in my stomach formed a mosh pit,
stomping on my insides.

Sorry it took so long to respond, I was working.
Your text made me laugh, though.

what was it this time?
another portrait of someone's ex's cat?

No, not this time. You'd like it, actually. It was a turntable.

fuck off . . . no way

I swear to god!

i don't believe you

He sent a picture of his handiwork next. He hadn't been lying, it *was* a turntable. Beautifully drawn, but still, a fucking turntable. I realize that it's hard to be a tattoo snob when you have a poorly covered-up couple's tattoo on your shoulder, but that hasn't stopped me thus far. The irony doesn't escape me, though.

wow, okay, i take it back. not a liar

Thanks for that. Redemption feels good.
What're you up to? Trolling for DJs?

I scoffed and smiled at the phone, as if he could see me.

nooo, not tonight. eating thai food and cuddling a dog

You have a dog?! How has this never been mentioned?

it's craig's dog, not mine

Oh, I see. What's its name?

dottie

Incredible name. What does she look like?

This is where a normal person, devoid of expectations or ulterior motives, would take a picture of Dottie and send it, just like that. Easy. I didn't do that, though.

Instead, I lifted Dottie up despite her heaviness and posed with her, positioning her in my arms as if she'd fallen asleep on top of me. Dottie, being a good Los Angeles dog, was used to being used as a prop in pictures and settled in quickly, falling asleep on my chest, which only made my boobs look better.

I looked down at Dottie and took the picture, hating myself for it, the display of not so carefully hidden narcissism, and after analyzing it intently, double- and triple-checking to see if I looked like I had a double chin in it (I didn't), I sent it.

> she's dead asleep, but makes for
> a great weighted blanket,
> so there's that

I waited one minute. Then two. I checked the picture again, making sure it wasn't deeply unflattering or overtly suggestive.

Dani and Craig cleaned up the leftovers and headed to bed after I told them I'd walk Dottie. I told them that while staring at my phone.

Ten minutes and still no response. I sighed, a deep, heaving sigh that woke Dottie, and she scrambled to her feet (paws?), scratching my chest with her nails in the process. I didn't mind, though. I stood, grabbing my wine and finishing it in three big gulps. If I was going to wallow, I was going to do it right.

I placed my empty glass in the sink and walked to the door, grabbing Dottie's leash, my phone, and headphones before heading out to take her on a walk that I was sure I needed more than she did.

I turned on my wallowing playlist (lots of Mazzy Star and Phoebe Bridgers, of course), and we set out into the night. My street was quiet, as it always is after the sun goes down, and as I made my way along the road, I scanned the houses I passed, houses I'd seen hundreds of times, looking for a distraction.

I was passing my favorite one, a Spanish-style bungalow with an overgrown garden in the front yard, when my phone rang, interrupting "Don't Think Twice, It's All Right."

Wanna guess who it was, or are you through with the guessing games by now? I'm sure you are.

I answered it, too anxious to wait more than one ring before picking it up.

"Hello?" I said, trying to sound nonchalant.

"Hi," he said on his exhale. My chest got tight.

"Hi."

"Hi," he repeated, louder this time.

"You said that already."

"Right. I did, didn't I?"

"Uh-huh. You can say it again if you want, though."

"Thanks for the permission. I think I'm good for now though," he murmured.

"Okay. What's up?"

Dottie peed on the lawn marked with four different signs asking dogs not to pee on it, and I tried to focus on the feeling of my feet against the pavement (I am almost always barefoot, another trait inherited from both Dani and my mother) to ground me to something unrelated to him, his voice, his breath.

"Nothing really. I just got off work and you were on my mind. The picture was great. She's a very cute dog. And an even cuter weighted blanket."

I was on his mind. I was on his mind. *Fuck!* I closed my eyes and repeated my mantra five times before responding.

He's married he's married he's married he's married he's married.

"Yeah, she is, isn't she? I'm walking her right now and she's looking especially good."

"I'm sure she is."

"How was work?" I asked, hating the banality of the question but loving how domestic it felt to ask him that. I pictured asking him that over dinner, over drinks, in bed.

"It was fine. Pretty slow today, actually. How was the rest of your day?"

"Good. Slow too. Just some more reading and then Dani, Craig, and I had dinner."

"Right. With the weighted blanket."

"Exactly."

"So no DJs today, then," he said, sounding so nonchalant that it felt urgent. I don't know if that makes sense, but all I can say is that it sounded like he had put effort into his effortlessness.

"No DJs today. No more DJs for me, I've decided."

"Oh?" he said, sounding relieved. Maybe he didn't, though. Maybe I was listening for that, applying a filter to his tone.

"Yeah."

"And why's that?"

"I'm not sure, really. They just don't interest me all that much anymore."

"Huh," he responded, and I could picture him running his hand through his hair as he spoke. "Interesting."

I dragged my bare feet along the concrete, closing my eyes and trying to come back to my body. He made me float. I didn't want him to make me float, but he did.

"I'm gonna be house-sitting in your neck of the woods soon, I think," I said, less to give him the information and more because I didn't know what else to say.

"Oh yeah?"

"Yeah. It's somewhere on Lookout, I think. I'll be there for ten days."

"Ten days, huh? That's a good chunk of time."

"I know," I said, picking up some of Dottie's shit and heading along the street. "I think it'll be good, though. The house has a pool and apparently a rain shower, which is exciting. Someone in the industry, I guess, 'cause she's going to Toronto for the festival."

"Wait," he said. "Do you know her name?"

"Lucy something. I don't know her last name."

"I bet it's Lucy Brooks."

"What?"

"Her name's Lucy Brooks. Oh my god," he exhaled, and I could hear his breath through the phone.

My pulse got fast; the night air got cold. I kept my gaze fixed on Dottie as she stopped to sniff my neighbor's undermowed grass. I wished I was a dog in that moment. It seemed like a blissfully uncomplicated way to be.

"What?" I asked, still wishing I was a dog, not a person with a crush on a married man whose voice lit me up and settled me down all at once.

"She lives across from me," he said in a tone I couldn't read. The butterflies multiplied. Twice.

"No way."

"Yes. She's a critic, she goes up every year. She's lovely. The house is brilliant, too. Amazing pool."

"That's what I've heard," I said, still trying to sound unaffected by the knowledge that I'd be living across the street from him for ten whole days.

"I'm pretty jealous of it, actually. Especially in the heat."

"Well," I ventured, "feel free to use it whenever you want while I'm there."

I pictured him in the water, his arms slicing through it, the muscles in his back moving, and I silently cursed my overactive imagination.

"I might take you up on that," he said, his voice sounding more hoarse than usual. I bit my tongue. Hard.

"So, neighbor," I said, forcing my voice through the lust-formed lump in my throat, "you'll be happy to know I didn't drink another cup of coffee for the rest of the day today."

This was true, actually; I'd almost caved around four in the afternoon, but I persevered.

"Really?"

"Really," I proclaimed.

"Not one?"

Dottie was pulling on the leash, trying to urge me to go home. Or maybe she sensed who I was talking to, and she wanted to stop me. I don't know. I turned around and brought her back to the house.

"Nope, not one."

"And?" he said. "How do you feel?"

"Exhausted."

He started to laugh, and I put Dottie back in the apartment before heading back out into the world. I needed our conversation to exist outside of the apartment, away from Craig and Dani and their infidelityless relationship. Not that that's what Rob and I had yet, but I wasn't dumb. I knew where our whatever-it-was could go. I knew where I both hoped and feared it would go, at least.

"So, I haven't changed your life then," he said.

"You've just made me very, very tired. You'll change my life with free lunch, though, I suppose. If it's especially good."

"What constitutes an especially good lunch?"

"That's a good question," I said, because I didn't want to say what I was thinking. *You, Rob. If you're there, it's especially good.* The thought made me want to gag. It felt too cheesy.

"Once you figure it out, let me know and I'll make sure it's involved. I figure you're entitled to a reward for your sacrifice."

"Thanks for that."

"Maybe if you're exhausted, sleep will be less of a hurdle for you tonight," he whispered.

I'd thought about that too, but I doubted it. In the weeks following Jackson's death, I'd tried it. Going caffeineless, taking melatonin, everything. It didn't work.

Whenever I slept, he'd be in my dreams. He'd break up with me or ignore me, any number of cruel and hurtful things, but it always ended the same way: he'd leave. The dreams were worse than the sleeplessness. In the dreams, I could never speak. I was voiceless. I'd try to yell, to cry, to reason with him, but I'd open my mouth and no sound would come out. I didn't know what it meant. I didn't want to know.

"Yeah," I said, "maybe."

"It'll get easier."

He sounded so sure, but I wasn't.

People were always so quick to say that it would get better with time. They did the same when Jackson and I broke up. Their logic seemed to be that because, in time, it wouldn't hurt quite so bad, my heartbreak couldn't possibly be as life-altering as I felt like it was. It pissed me off.

More so with the heartbreak than with his death. I tried talking to my sister about this once, when she'd told me that "in time" I'd feel better. I tried explaining to her that heartbreak was the loneliest state of existence, but she didn't understand.

She hugged Harper in her arms before saying, "How can it be lonely when what you're experiencing is a feeling that every person experiences at least once in their lives?"

That's the problem, though. Because everyone has had one—at least one—massive, messy, heartbreak, and moved on with their lives, and they forget how painful it was. They don't remember what it was like, not really. They're just existing in a state of recovery-induced amnesia. The wound has faded and scarred, and they've forgotten the hurt of it. I didn't tell her that, though. I just nodded and smoothed Harper's halo of curls.

I hoped Rob was right, though. I hoped that time would smooth things out, would act like a balm on my hurt, but I wasn't so sure.

"Maggie?" he said. I didn't realize I'd been silent for so long.

"Yeah?"

"Just checking to see if you were still there," he mumbled.

"I'm here."

"Okay. Good."

"Tacos," I said.

"What?"

"Tacos. That's what makes for an especially good lunch."

"Oh. Right. You Californians and your Mexican food," he teased.

"Do you not like Mexican food?"

"No, I love it. I just like how . . . *passionate* you lot are about the stuff."

"Of course we are. It's delicious."

He laughed and I let out a long breath, trying to encourage the butterflies to leave me. They didn't. Stubborn fucks.

"Fuck, Maggie." He let out a groan. "That's Ingrid on the other line. I should take this. I'll call you tomorrow, though, okay?"

"Right. Okay, yeah. Go. Bye," I said, hanging up as soon as the words were out. I wanted to throw my phone into the street and peel my skin off my body, starting with every place he had touched me. Maybe if I did that, I'd no longer feel so drawn to him. Instead, I went back home, sat on the porch, and lit up a cigarette. My second of the day. I'd done well.

8

Not knowing what to do, I tried calling my mom, who, despite being three hours ahead of me, was sure to be up. She's a night owl, always has been. We hadn't spoken in a few weeks, which wasn't normal for us, but wasn't totally unprecedented, either. We were always at our best together when we had catching up to do.

"Hi, babe!" my mom exclaimed when she picked up.

"Hey."

"How you doing, angel?"

"I'm good," I said. "How're you?"

"Doing good! Have you seen Pearl lately?" she asked.

"Yeah. Every week."

"How's she doing?"

"She's good. Tired."

"Pregnancy," my mom responded, as if that explained everything.

"Right," I agreed without really knowing what she meant.

"You'll see one day," she said.

She likes talking about all the ways my world will change when I have kids. *When* being the operative word. She seems to think that my life will not be complete until I have children. She forgets I'm twenty-five; my life has just begun, really. I don't want to complete it just yet; I just want to enjoy it. I want to begin it.

"Maybe."

"Anything new with you, hon?"

"Nope, not really. Just calling to check in."

"Poppy!" I heard someone yell from my mom's end. "Come on!"

"Well, I'm at drinks with Claude and Diane." She said the names as if I should know them, but I didn't. "But we'll talk again soon, yeah?"

"Yeah, talk soon."

"I love you, sweet girl."

"Love you too, Mom."

I hung up and put on some music to drown out the sounds of Dani and Craig's moans and breaths. Mazzy Star. Of course. Patron saints of yearning.

I scrolled through Twitter for a bit, not reading anything, just so I could feel like I was doing something. Then Instagram. Elsie had posted something a few hours before. A picture from her bridal shower. I bristled for a moment, hurt I hadn't been invited, before realizing that we weren't friends and there was no rational reason for me to be upset.

I wondered, not for the first time, if she'd stalked me as much as I'd stalked her. I hoped she had. I pulled up my own profile and scrolled through, trying to look at my public persona, my curated persona, from an outsider's perspective.

I didn't post much, preferring to be a voyeur on the app, but I had fifty-seven drafts, mostly photos I'd never actually post. I just liked going through the motions. After deciding that I seemed cool virtually, I quit the app and pulled up my camera app.

Sometimes when I'm bored and alone, I look at myself in my phone's camera, just to remind myself that I am alive. I'm a person in a body and

I am a part of the world, which exists outside of me and my porch and my brain. I feel like I exist a little too much in my head, and so it helps to remind myself that I'm not just a shapeless blob of thoughts, anxieties, and too many feelings. I never take a picture when I'm in a mood like this, though. I'm too self-conscious for selfies, and besides, I don't know my angles. My father told me that once.

"How is it," he'd asked, "that for someone who grew up in front of a camera, you don't know how to pose?"

I know he didn't mean it in a positive way, but I took it as a compliment. I didn't tell him that even though I desperately wanted to be seen, I was humiliated by the awareness that people were watching me. And they were. Watching me.

I'm beautiful. That isn't something I feel comfortable saying, but my therapist makes me say it at least once a week, just so that I'll believe it to be true. The thing is, I know it's true, but knowing it's true doesn't make it any less embarrassing. I know it the same way I know I'm supposed to pretend I don't know that about myself, like everything on the outside of my body is for everyone but me. And to an extent, that's true. My beauty doesn't feel like mine. I had nothing to do with it. It was my parents. Random genetics.

When I was little, people used to talk about my beauty a lot. My sister's too. I would puff up, but not nearly as much as my father would.

It was in those moments, the moments in which others would acknowledge it, that I could feel him turn and *see* me. More than when they'd compliment my humor or brain or talent. Those weren't his, after all, but my eyes, my lips, those were things marked by his genetic signature. Those were his gifts to me.

My father had tried calling me that day. Around three. I didn't answer, though. I'd been busy texting Rob, and besides, I didn't want to talk to him. He was probably calling because Pearl had made him, or Ana. I didn't know which one was worse.

He'd left a message, but I didn't listen to it at first. I knew what it would say. He was predictable.

Maggie Mae, he'd say, *how are you, darling?* Since living in London for a year with Lily, he'd taken to calling everyone "darling" or "love." Not "blossom," though. That was reserved for Ana. I relented a few hours after I saw the message, listening to it with my eyes closed and my fists clenched.

"It's me, your not-so-old man, just checking in to see how you've been. The shoot's been hellish"—they always are—"but we're just about wrapped up. We leave next Thursday, so if you're around, come to the Chateau. Ana and I would love to see you." That was a lie. Ana never loved seeing me. Or Pearl. She hated any and all reminders of his life before her. I didn't blame her.

I hated any reminder of Rob's life with you, after all. Henry's exes too. Not Jackson's, though. I'd thrill at any mention of Elsie, or Khaite, Jackson's ex before Elsie, who was the only person who could get away with spelling her name that way. I loved thinking about him in those days, the pre-me days, when he was stumbling and fucking and shooting up his way through life, all the while hurtling towards me.

"Before you," he used to say in bed or in bars or in the too-small Fiat, "I was asleep."

I'd believed him, of course. That's what you do when a beautiful boy tells you that you woke him up.

I thought I knew what he meant, but now I'm not so sure. I'd been plenty awake before we met. If anything, meeting him felt like settling into a nap. It was his death that woke me up. Or our breakup. I'm not sure which. Either way, I was awake now, too fucking awake, and all I wanted was to close my eyes and rest.

Rob didn't feel like rest, though. He felt like electricity. He felt like a jolt of caffeine and adrenaline to my system. *Oh*, I remember thinking while we kissed, *so this is what Jackson meant.* Maybe I hadn't been awake all that time after all.

A little before eleven, I headed to bed and fell asleep. I dreamt of Jackson. And Rob. They were singing along to a song I couldn't hear, and I woke up crying. I checked the clock. I'd slept five hours.

I slipped out of bed and put on two sports bras in preparation for the run I was trying to convince myself I'd enjoy, all the while trying to figure out what song they'd been singing. It felt important.

When I got back to the apartment, sweaty and feeling marginally better, Craig was in the kitchen, drinking matcha and eating my yogurt. He was shirtless, as usual.

"Morning," he said, mouth full of yogurt spit.

"Morning."

"Good run?"

"Yup."

"Nice. Bathroom's open, if you were wanting to shower," he offered.

I *had* been wanting to, but as soon as he suggested it, permitted me to do it, I felt ambivalent about the idea. I did it anyway, though.

I got out of the shower right when an unknown number began calling me. Judging by the area code, I assumed it was Lucy. I picked up.

"Hello?"

"Hi," said an Australian woman, "is this Maggie?"

"Yeah. Are you Lucy?"

"What? No, I'm Marley. Marley Frankel. I'm your father's assistant."

Oh. Jesus. He'd gotten a new assistant, then. His last one, Jeb, had been a sweet, soft-spoken boy from Kansas. He always called me "miss," despite my protestations and the fact that he was only a year or so older than I was. I wondered what happened to him.

"Oh. Hi," I stammered.

"Hi. Is this a bad time?"

"No, not a bad time. What's up?"

"Your father was just having me call to confirm that you're on for brunch tomorrow at the Chateau. Is ten good?"

I'd be surprised if I weren't so annoyed. It was so like him, to confirm a plan that hadn't been made. His way of reminding me who had the power. I sighed, wiping the fog from the mirror and looking at my face to see if there were any blackheads to pick at. No dice.

"Yeah. Yeah, ten's good," I said, trying to sound as little imposed upon as possible. It came out pained, though, I know. I could hear it. I'm sure Marley could too.

"Brilliant. He's staying under-—"

"Stanley Kubrick?"

"Yes."

I rolled my eyes. He always stayed places under Kubrick's name. He said it was his way of "paying homage to his hero." I thought it was his way of convincing himself that the two of them were linked. Same difference, I guess.

"Great. I'll be there. Thanks, Marley." I sighed.

"Not a problem. Have a good day."

"You too."

I hung up and wondered how much she was getting paid. I checked my phone and read two texts from another unknown number. Lucy.

> Hi, Maggie. This is Lucy, Craig's friend. I was wondering
> if you were around at all tomorrow to come up
> to the house so I can walk you through the ins and outs.
> Let me know what time works for you,
> I'm around all day.

I responded, still dripping all over the tiles.

> hi! tomorrow's good for me! does 11:30 work?

She responded quickly, which made me like her right away.

> 11:30 is great, thanks!

She sent her address along and I plugged it into Google Maps.

It was beautiful. Spanish, like the house I loved on my street, and sur-rounded by vines of jasmine. I dragged my fingers across the screen, trying to decide which house I thought belonged to Rob. Belonged to you.

I hoped it was the yellow one. It looked . . . delicious. A ridiculous word for a house, I know, but since you're a poet, I thought you'd appreciate it.

9

Rob and I didn't talk that day. Not much, at least. He sent me a photo of another tattoo he'd done, a dog that didn't look anything like Dottie despite his insistence to the contrary. He wasn't too set on it, though. It made me think that maybe he didn't think it looked like Dottie after all. Maybe he'd just wanted an excuse to text me.

I took Dottie on another walk and ate leftover pad see ew standing over the sink while I watched *Almost Famous* for the second time that week, crying and laughing at all the same places I had cried and laughed two days before.

Around five, my phone lit up with a notification. Rob had followed me on Instagram. I squealed despite myself, then scoffed in response, the combination of sudden noises waking Dottie from her nap. She gave me a disgruntled look, as if to say *Pull yourself together, Maggie.* I knew she was right, but I couldn't help myself.

I pulled the app up and went to his profile. He had thirty thousand followers. Wow. Jesus. I scrolled through, hoping for photos of him, but all I found were his tattoos, which, after momentary disappointment, I was glad for. I combed through them, all fine lines and shading. They were so intricate it took my breath away. I didn't know that was possible in a tattoo. They were art. I wondered if you had any tattoos. I wondered if he'd given you any.

I tried searching for you on Instagram, but of course, I found nothing. Of course you weren't on social media. You were too cool for that. I knew it before I even met you. I was relieved that my search for you had been fruitless. If I'd been able to put a face to your name, your claim over him, it would have felt too real. At that point, you were still as shadowy as his tattoos.

10

I woke up the next day with three hours to spare before I had to head out the door for brunch. I'd fallen asleep at three in the morning after scrolling all the way to the bottom of Rob's profile. Twice. Okay, four times.

I got dressed quickly, pulling on a gingham dress Pearl had given to me because apparently my boobs looked better in it than hers did, and a pair of cowboy boots I knew my father hated. They'd been my mom's when she was my age.

I went to the coffee shop on my street, one of those too-expensive places that was built for people who liked taking pictures of coffee more than they liked drinking it, and got a large latte with four extra shots. *Poison*, Rob would say.

I liked imagining that he was watching me as I went about my day, being charmed by my every movement. Thinking of myself through his eyes gave me a sense of love for myself, a sense of tenderness that I hadn't experienced in a while. Not since Jackson.

I showed up to the hotel early, as per usual. Less to spend more time with my father, and more because I knew I'd get shit for having to leave sooner than he'd like, so I could meet with Lucy. He always liked it when things went according to his schedule, as this brunch ambush reminded me.

I walked to his bungalow suite and started the countdown till my escape in my head. Eighty minutes until freedom.

The bungalow was a mess, unsurprisingly. My father had always been a slob who normally married neat freaks, so his slob-like tendencies were kept in check, but Ana was the exception. If anything, she was messier than he was. Clothes littered the floor, empty glasses sat on every available surface. I pitied the housekeeping team, not for the first time.

Ana had answered the door, not my father. He was on the phone. He was always either on the phone or about to get on the phone. Funny coming from a man who didn't allow phones on his sets.

Ana gave me the once-over before saying, "You're early. He's on with Damien." I didn't know who Damien was, and I didn't much care. I followed her into the den of dirty glasses and laundry and sat on the sofa, grabbing a piece of toast.

"You look tired," Ana continued as she poured herself a glass of grapefruit juice. I'd only seen her eat a handful of times. Pearl and I were convinced she lived on celery juice, green tea, and apple cider vinegar. Jonah claimed he'd seen her eat a french fry once, but there was no proof, so we didn't believe him.

"I didn't sleep much," I said while chewing my toast. I always loved disgusting her.

My father came in then, still on the phone. He blew me a kiss, grabbed a Danish, and continued listening to Damien talk about whatever Damien was talking about.

Ana applied lotion to her heavily tanned legs. "You should try melatonin. It really helps."

"I'll give it a try, thanks."

I'd already tried melatonin. It gave me weird dreams.

My father reentered the room at ten fifteen, right as I'd started serving myself parfait.

"Darling!"

"Hi, Dad," I said, not bothering to stand.

"You were early."

That came out more as an accusation and less as an observation. I let it go. Fifty minutes to go.

"I've gotta be out of here by eleven, so I figured I'd come early."

"Eleven? Where are you off to?"

By this point, Ana had moved to the bathroom, presumably to apply a face mask. Or snort a line. Both, maybe. I'd seen her do it a few times, and since then, I always associated the two.

"Laurel Canyon. I'm house-sitting up there. Lucy, the woman who owns it, is heading up to Toronto—"

"Going for the festival?" he supplied.

"Yeah. She's a critic. Goes every year."

My father scoffed, taking a bite of the Danish. I shouldn't have mentioned Toronto. He hated the festival, which he insisted had nothing to do with the fact that his films had never been selected to premiere there. He instead said that it was a knockoff Sundance, Cannes, and Venice all rolled into one "sycophantic, poutine-filled orgy."

When he got on those tirades, it was best not to remind him that poutine was a Montreal thing, not a Toronto thing. I loved the festival up there. I used to go with my godmother every year, despite my father's complaints. My godmother had five films premiere at the festival. She, it seemed, was loved by the sycophantic, poutine-filled, orgy-goers.

My father continued to scoff about the festival, mumbling something about why anyone would want to waste their time in Toronto as he pulled his phone out from his robe pocket.

I stared at the parfait in front of me, trying to think of something to say, a question to ask him. I felt like I was on a bad date whenever we were together. I guess I was. I never knew how to approach him. My sister had the same problem with him, but now that she had kids and Jonah, she had buffers and go-to conversations. My dad always asked about Harper's poop and what her first word had been, as if she were permanently an infant.

"Hey, my friend said he tattooed you the other day," I blurted.

My father slowly looked up from his phone, as if I was pulling him away from something he'd wanted to invest his attention in. More so than the brunch he'd forced me into attending, at least.

"That guy's your friend? The guy with no ink?"

I ignored his ink comment, replying, "Yeah. Rob. We met a while ago through Dani's boyfriend."

I didn't want to give my father any more details than were necessary. I hated that I'd even mentioned Rob, actually. I didn't want him anywhere near my father.

"He's a little old, isn't he?"

"He's like thirty-two," I said, bristling at my own defensiveness, "and besides, he's just a friend."

"Hmph," he breathed out, staring at me for the first time since I arrived. I rolled my eyes at him, at the whole situation. The way he'd decided to play the involved and concerned parent now, after everything.

"Can I see it?"

He stopped staring and puffed up a bit as he pulled at the sleeve of his robe, showing me his bicep.

"Sure. He's talented, that friend of yours."

I reached out over the smorgasbord to touch the tattoo. This was the first time my father and I had touched in a year. Not for any real reason, I just hadn't seen him much.

The tattoo was stunning, and this one packed a punch the others hadn't. Maybe because it was of me and my sister, but it took my breath away. It felt like a living, breathing piece of art. I stared at my ink-self, open-mouthed. There was life in those eyes, I swear.

My eyes filled with tears, as they often do when I see photos of myself as a kid. My therapist tells me it's because they make me wish I could be the parent I never had to that version of myself.

I looked at the ink version of Pearl and my chest got tight. He'd nailed it. He'd gotten Pearl's discerning eye and inherent warmth. In ink. How did he do that?! It still awes me to this day. Were you as impressed with his ability? Was it what drew you to him? Do you know about Rob's tattoo? I'm sure you do by now.

Ana returned, dewy from her face mask and amped up from her line. I always liked her more right after she'd done coke; it loosened her up and made her forget that she didn't like me. She was much more charitable in those moments. Once, she'd given me a coat of hers that cost at least a month of rent, just because I told her I liked the fabric. I'd felt weird about it, but Pearl told me that it was the least Ana could do and besides, "You don't return free Gucci." I'd only been brave enough to wear the coat out twice. It felt like playing dress-up.

I was eyeing the contents of her suitcase, wondering what I might be able to walk away with this time, when she took my hand in hers.

Ana fixed me with a stare before she opened her mouth, head cocked. "And how is Baby doing?"

When she was drunk or high or tired or a combination of the three, she alternated between three nicknames for me: Baby, Littlest, and Cheeks. I preferred Littlest, because it made me feel dainty and young, much younger than Ana, even though she's only seven years older than me. Cheeks was good too, though. It made me think of that gangster, Babyface something.

"Baby's good, Ana. How're you?"

"Baby doesn't seem so good. Dark dark circles and chapped lips! Pop, look at her," she said, twirling a strand of my hair on her finger.

She called my father Pop, which disgusted me just as much as him calling her Blossom did.

My father looked at me, his face tightening when he took in the boots. His eyes shot back up to my shoulders, focusing on the JAM tattoo that had only become visible because my sleeve slipped. I tried to hide it. I thought I'd been careful. I'm still not sure why I felt like it was something I needed to hide, but I did.

"What's that?"

"What, the tattoo?"

"No, the dress. Yes, the tattoo. What is it? Is it new?"

"I got it like a year and a half ago," I explained.

"When?"

"Like, March."

"And what is it?"

"The word jam."

"Jam?" he sneered.

"Yes."

"Why jam?"

"I don't know, Dad, I just like jam, I guess."

My father scoffed again; I dug my nails into my palms to keep from crying, from throwing my parfait at his head and screaming at him.

The more time I spent with him, the more I felt like I was slipping into becoming him, or Ana, or some combination of the two. I sat and watched the two of them as Ana made my father a plate and he looked at his phone, aggressively typing something to someone, Damien, maybe. I didn't want to be either of them. I didn't want *Rob* to be either of them, but the more I watched them, the more I worried that I was watching what Rob and I could turn into, if things went the way I wanted them to.

The rest of brunch was fine, I think. No one was really paying much attention to each other, but that's standard procedure for us. My dad went back and forth from his phone to the food, Ana dashed in and out of the bathroom every few minutes or so, and I just spent the time staring at the space between my father's eyes. He didn't even notice.

Before I get to my trip to the canyon, to Lucy, let me say one thing about my father: I don't hate him. I'd like to make that clear. I'm sure you don't believe me, but it's true, I don't. I don't feel much for him, really, other than disappointment. And embarrassment. And sorrow. Okay, so maybe I feel a *few* things for him, but hatred isn't one of them. Not anymore. It was, for a while.

I was nineteen then, and I went through a phase that is surprising to no one and mocked by everyone: I dyed my hair, wore too much eyeliner, and decided I'd spend the year hating my father and sleeping with men who were emotionally unavailable, too old for me, or both.

I found a journal entry of mine from that year. It read: *It's been four days since my last cigarette, and I miss them. Meanwhile it's been fifty-one days since I spoke to my father, and I don't miss him. AT ALL.* The entry was undated. *AT ALL* was underlined five times. You know, in a completely undramatic way.

The problem was, my therapist told me, I had no respect for him. When she'd said that I rolled my eyes, because that's what you do when someone you pay obscene amounts of money to says something you already know. She smiled softly, cocked her head, and waited a bit. I burst into tears.

Back to the canyon. I arrived a little before eleven-thirty and parked in front, looking to the delicious lemon house, which I guessed was yours based on Rob mentioning his love of the color yellow, to see if I could spot him before realizing I didn't know what car he drove and my attempts at detective work would be fruitless. I knocked on Lucy's door and was typing out an additional "here!" text, just in case she hadn't heard me, when she opened it.

I wanted her hair. Badly. Red red *red* and those curls?! I mean, you've seen them. They're phenomenal. But I was really taken with her eyes.

What's it called when they're different colors? Heterochromia? Fuck. It's astonishing.

"You must be Maggie," she said, pulling me down into a hug. Her shortness made me feel weird about my boot selection. I hated highlighting my height around other shorter women. It made me feel anti-feminist, for some reason.

"I've heard so much about you!"

"From Craig?" I asked, surprised. I tried to imagine what Craig would say. I couldn't think of anything other than our tennis talk, but that didn't feel like a thing you'd share with a friend of a friend. Or anyone, for that matter.

Lucy laughed a bit.

"No," she chortled, "from Rob. My neighbor? Apparently, he's a friend of yours!"

There was no accusation in her tone—she sounded genuinely happy about my friendship with Rob—but I felt my face go hot and I had the sudden urge to apologize, walk out the door, and drive over a cliff. In that order.

"Oh yeah," I said, running my hand through my hair and getting stuck on a tangle, "he's great."

"The greatest. He says you're lovely. Very responsible. He was singing your praises when we talked."

I nodded because I had no idea what else to do, but my ears were ringing, and I had to bite back a hysterical and entirely too-girlish giggle.

"Right!" she exclaimed, clapping her hands and startling me out of my fugue state. "I'll show you around, shall I?"

The tour was nice, all glass walls and chrome accents and open floor plans, but I was distracted, thinking too much about Rob telling others about my loveliness. I tried imagining the look he'd have on his face as he thought about me. I wondered if he'd gotten red in the face too.

At the end of the tour, Lucy gave me the key, a piece of paper with all the ins and outs of the house, and a jar of jam she'd made. (Did you ever get some of her jam? It's really good.) I was to move in on Sunday morning and I'd stay for ten days. I walked back to the Fiat, too distracted by thoughts of rain showers at night and TV in bed to notice the figure approaching me from the lemon house.

"Maggie!"

It was him. I stayed surprised for a moment before realizing this was exactly what I'd hoped would happen, what I'd pictured the night before when I was trying to make myself sleep. Maybe I'd manifested it. Dani was always manifesting things; maybe her talent for it had rubbed off on me.

"Oh," I said, trying, once again, to sound nonchalant. "Hey!"

He got to me in three steps and wrapped me in a hug, picking me up a little. Not much, no swinging around or anything, but the tips of my toes were all that remained on the pavement. I was a goner.

"Did Lucy give you the stamp of approval?"

He put me back down and I stepped away.

"Yeah, she did. Apparently, a neighbor of hers told her that I'm quite responsible. Thanks for that."

He blushed, looked down, and brought his hand (the right one) up to the back of his neck.

"Not a problem. I just needed access to the pool, didn't I?" he asked, teasing.

I took in his appearance. He was in that striped shirt, the one that makes him look like a hot sailor, and those jeans with the tiny holes at the knees. As I said, I was a goner.

I saw him take me in too. Or felt it, really. I had to look away. Not because of the intensity of it, though. It felt . . . tender in a way I wasn't used to.

Jackson had once said that I was good at being objectified but bad at being observed and accepted. I punched his arm and started to cry. He kissed the top of my head and grabbed my right breast, squeezing it. I laughed so hard I thought I'd stop breathing.

"What's that you've got there?" Rob said, bringing me back to the present. He nodded his chin at the jar.

"Oh. It's jam."

"She gave you jam?"

"She did," I responded.

"Did she see the tattoo?"

"No, she just handed it to me before I left."

He laughed a bit.

"What kind is it?"

"Guess."

"It's not—"

"It is," I answered, grinning.

Rob laughed harder this time, clapping his hands for emphasis.

"That's too fucking good," he said, still laughing.

"I'm a little convinced you put her up to it."

"I didn't, I swear!"

"Likely story."

We stood there for a bit, just looking at each other. And smiling. Like total fucking idiots.

"Where are you off to? Any big plans?"

"No plans," I said. "I was just gonna go back to the apartment and eat too much jam. What about you? Are you working today?"

"No, I'm off. I was just heading out to run some errands. Want to come? I'll buy you tacos. And maybe even a coffee."

I paused, less out of hesitation, and more to convince myself that I needed to be convinced. It's pitiful how quickly I would have agreed to anything he proposed to me.

"Sure," I said, "I have nothing better to do."

"That's the kind of unbridled enthusiasm I'm looking for in an

errand-running partner," he quipped, as he walked towards the pickup.
I swallowed my groan and got in, immediately wishing I had offered to
drive or simply driven myself home to eat too much jam and listen to
sad music.

It smelled like him. Like sweat and lemons and ginger and smoke . . .
I was so overwhelmed by it that I had to hold my breath for a moment
and close my eyes, repeating, once again, my mantra.

He's married.

Rob climbed in next to me and the smell intensified.

He's married.

Rob turned to buckle himself in and I did the same.

He's married.

He turned the truck on and pulled out of the driveway.

He's married.

He handed me the aux cord as he made his way down the canyon
road.

He's married.

"Really?" I asked. "You want me to DJ?"

"Yep. Copilot's job."

"I thought a copilot's job was navigation."

"That too, but I don't need navigation help. Besides, I want to know
what music you like," he explained.

He said that so simply, but it felt huge. To me, the idea of sharing
my music with him felt about as personal, as intimate, as talking about
Jackson. Or my father. Or whatever I was feeling right then, with him,
in the truck. In his scent.

I scrolled through my Spotify playlists, trying to decide which of my
deeply specific ones would best fit the mood. I hadn't thought to make
a playlist for sitting in a truck with a married man you like so much it
feels like you're choking. I'd have to make one soon, though. The feelings
needed to be set to music.

After debating for a moment between "music to impress the training wheels with," "for when you're so sad you're happy," and "does yearning count as exercise????" I settled for the latter, choosing "I'll Be Here in the Morning." I didn't want to play anything too overt, and I figured Townes Van Zandt's drawl could make the subtext a little cloudier, which I wanted. As soon as it started, Rob's eyes lit up and he glanced at me, smiling.

"Townes Van Zandt?"

"Uh-huh," I said. I knew it was a good pick.

"Good choice," he supplied before beginning to sing along.

His voice? Christ.

It's not like he was a professional or anything, he was gravelly and unpolished and a little out of tune, but he sounded so raw that it made me clench my legs together and force myself to stare out the window. I couldn't look at him when he sounded like that.

He's married, I repeated in my mind, trying to drown him and Townes out. I was unsuccessful.

"Suzanne" by Leonard Cohen was next. Rob shook his head in appreciation and launched in along with Lenny. If you can't beat them, join them, right? I joined in, quietly at first, my head stuck out of the window like a dog, but the wind was whipping my hair against my face, so I withdrew back into his scent, singing all the while.

"You have a beautiful voice," he murmured as he made a right while resting his wrist on the steering wheel.

"Thanks," I said, trying not to reveal just how much I loved him saying that.

The Eels were next. "I Like the Way This Is Going." Rob grinned.

"You are quickly becoming my most favorite copilot slash DJ," he gushed as he slowed for a yellow light. He was a good driver. With him, I didn't feel the constant need to brace myself for hypothetical potential impacts as I did with Craig, with Dani, with my father, with Jackson. I felt safe.

I used to fear the car. I'm not sure why, really. I've never been in an accident or anything; I was always just very aware of the fact that any time I got into a car, I was essentially putting my life in the hands of every other person on the road. Jackson used to think it was funny to make quick stops and change lanes without signaling. I used to yell at him, and he'd laugh, reaching over to tousle my hair like I was a kid or something. I hated it. Even when I pretended to be charmed by it, I hated it. But with Rob, it was different. Almost everything was different with Rob, actually. The driving was just another thing, another marker of just how different he was from Jackson.

I kept singing along, alternating between trying not to release any of my own thoughts and feelings into the song and pouring them all out in the hopes that maybe I wouldn't feel it all so intensely if I did. I was so distracted by the thoughts swimming around my mind, I almost missed the way Rob was staring at me. We were at a red light. I was singing, he was staring. Gaping. Gawking. Whatever.

I didn't know if I should stop singing or continue, but I felt that if I stopped, he'd compliment me or talk to me, and that felt too much like something I wanted, so I pretended not to notice him and kept on singing. Some of the best acting I ever did was in the moments I pretended not to notice your husband.

I watched him from the corner of my eye as I stuck my arm out the window, letting the wind push against my fingers. He stared for a bit longer before shaking his head and laughing softly to himself.

We pulled into the grocery store parking lot right as "A Case of You" started. He parked and I made to get out of the truck, but he stuck his arm out, stopping me.

"We've got to wait at least until she gets to the chorus," he said. "I love this song."

I settled back into my seat, smiling. I understood. I loved the song too.

Joni got to the chorus and we got out of the truck, heading into the

Whole Foods, a grocery store I only went to when Craig was buying or else when I was feeling ridiculously frivolous.

"So," I asked as we made our way in, past the flowers and samples of thirty different types of kombucha, "what're we getting? What's on the list?"

"Just the essentials. Eggs, tea, some fruit. Almond butter, milk—"

"Regular milk?"

"As in cow's milk? Yes, regular milk."

"Huh," I said, placing a dozen eggs in his basket. I looked around at the other shoppers and wondered if they thought we were a couple, doing the shopping for the home that we shared to be eaten in the life that we shared. I hoped they did.

"What?"

"Nothing," I responded. "I just don't think I know many people who still use regular milk."

"And what," he said as he grabbed a few avocados, "would you have me drink instead? Hemp milk? Flax milk? Rice milk? I could go on. I think there are as many milks here as there are weight loss supplements."

I laughed and he shook his head, at me or at himself I'm not sure, but he was smiling ruefully, and I shook my head back at him, smiling just the same.

"You're ridiculous," he teased, still smiling. I don't think he was complaining.

"And you're walking right past the milk."

He stopped and rubbed his eyes for a bit before resting his hand on my face. He pretended to consider the various milks. He was right, there were more kinds of milk than there were reasons for, and for a moment, I thought about Jackson, who used to predict that years from now, the new milk fad would be "beef milk," and people would be quick to dismiss oat and almond and hemp and the like. I almost said it to Rob, passing it off as my idea, but that didn't feel kosher to me. Not that any of this was kosher, I guess.

We got back into the truck after only twenty minutes or so, and before we pulled out, Rob said we made a good team. I flushed with pride and busied myself with trying to pick what song should be played next. I wound up settling for Prince's "Nothing Compares 2 U." Subtle, I know.

We pulled up to a taco truck a few songs later. I wasn't hungry, but it didn't matter. I'd eat anyway. Anything to get more time with Rob.

"Hungry?" he asked, parking and grabbing his wallet.

"Starving," I lied, hopping out.

We ate over the hood of his truck, and even though he ordered four tacos and I only got two, he finished before I did. Jackson used to say I ate slow enough that by the time I finished breakfast, it was time for lunch. I never told him that when I was with him, I purposefully ate slowly just to take up that much more of his time. Maybe I was doing the same thing with Rob.

"What's next on the list?" I said, downing the rest of my taco in one bite.

"Bookstore. I've been wanting to read more, and I figure if I spend too much on books, I'll be forced into reading them."

His logic was sound. We headed back into the truck, and I grabbed my cigarettes from my purse. I gestured, wordlessly asking if it was okay for me to smoke inside, and he nodded, reaching out to grab one for himself. He snatched my lighter and lit his own before reaching over to light mine for me. I looked up at him as I leaned over the flame. His eyes darkened, and I leaned back quickly, scared of how much I wanted to kiss him in that moment.

Screw subtlety. I played Laura Marling's "For You" and pretended it was shuffle's fault. If Rob had any doubts, they didn't show as he smoked while driving us to Skylight Books. My stomach lurched as we pulled up in front, where, majestically, we found a spot. I hadn't been there in months. Thirteen months, to be exact.

We piled out of the truck and into the shop, where he made a beeline to the employee recommendations and I went to the back, where I knew no one would see me. Not yet anyway.

I browsed the shelves, grabbing another copy of Rob Sheffield's *Love Is a Mixtape*, a book I already had seven copies of, and the latest Murakami, before Rob found me reading the back of a book about modern-day feminism.

"Anything good?" he asked, gesturing to my pile. He had six books in his hand. How he fit them all in one hand, I didn't know.

"A few," I said, still looking at the book. I finished the description and added it to the pile. I was sure it would have something to say about my whatever it was with Rob.

"Are you even old enough to know what mixtapes are?" he asked, gesturing to my Sheffield.

"I'll have you know I'm a deeply nostalgic person," I responded, adding a book I wasn't all that interested in to my pile, "even for things I wasn't alive for. And besides, he's amazing."

"If you say so. Who is he?"

"This music critic I'm obsessed with. I've read this a bunch. I think you'd like it. This can be yours," I offered.

"I can't take that from you."

"You can and you will. I have seven copies at home. I doubt Dani will let me bring an eighth into the house."

"Seven copies of one book?! That's obsessive, even for you," he teased, and I puffed up a bit at the idea that he knew about my obsessive tendencies.

"What can I say? He's incredible. You're taking the book, though. Consider it a thank-you for the free meals."

"If I knew I'd get books out of the deal, I'd have bought you at least four more meals."

"Well, now you know," I retorted, trying not to imagine more time with Rob spent eating food he'd bought. Kind of like a date . . .

"Fair. I'm buying you a coffee as a thank-you, then."

"You already promised coffee. You're gonna have to spring for dinner if you really want to thank me."

The words were out of my mouth before I realized the boldness they carried. I would have taken them back if it weren't for his smile, I promise you.

"Touché. Dinner, then. Tomorrow? I don't work till late."

"Tomorrow's good," I said, trying to sound unaffected by the plans we were making. "Do you have everything? I'm in need of caffeine."

"Lead the way." He gestured towards the checkout with his books.

I headed to the counter, forgetting for a second why I'd been nervous to be back until I saw who was behind the counter. It was Peter. Jackson's friend.

I'd been worried that Mary would be working, the girl I'd been convinced was into Jackson despite his insistence that she was gay, or bi at the very least, but it was Peter.

I hadn't seen him since the memorial, when he'd played "River" with his band and acted surprised that I had shown up. When he saw me, he raised his eyebrows slightly and his brow piercing got crowded by his forestlike eyebrows.

"Maggie." He sneered, reaching for my books. "It's been a while."

"Yeah," I said, trying to seem casual, "how've you been?"

"Fine. Just working. How are you?"

His voice was full of pretend concern, and that made it worse. He had never liked me. Jackson told me that once, and I pretended that it didn't affect me, but it was a lie. We both knew it. I wasn't good at not being liked by people.

"I'm okay. Working a lot," I mumbled.

"Clearly not enough to curb your social life," he said evenly, nodding his chin towards Rob. He finished ringing me up. "That'll be sixty-two ninety-eight, by the way."

"He's just a friend," I said, feeling my blood rush to my face. I wondered if I sounded believable. To him *and* to Rob. I slid my debit card towards him, and he rolled his eyes at the strawberry-covered card, just as he had the first time I bought a book from him.

"Another Sheffield? I guess Jackson really *did* influence your taste," he let out, handing my card back to me.

"Yeah, I guess so. It was good to see you, Peter."

"You too, Button Nose."

Peter calls me Button Nose because of my father's movie. You might've seen it. It's his most popular one, the one that got him his awards. He made it when I was eight. It's about a man and his daughter, who he calls Button Nose, and his struggle to remain close to her despite the fact that they no longer live together. Before you ask, it's not about me. At least I don't *think* it's about me. But Peter's always been insistent that it is. He also knows how much I hate when people think that, and how much I hate being called that.

I walked out with my books then, forgetting I had come in with Rob until I saw the pickup parked in front of me. I set the books on the hood and practiced the breathing techniques my therapist had given to me. Rob came out after I'd breathed seven times.

"You okay?" he whispered, unlocking the truck and grabbing my books for me before putting them all on the passenger seat.

"Yeah," I lied, trying to compose my face into what I thought was a casual smile. "I'm fine."

"Are you sure? That guy was a dick."

"Yeah, I'm okay. He was fine. It's fine. He was . . . he knew Jackson," I confessed, my eyes closed. I wasn't going to cry. Not there. I dug my nails into my palms.

"Oh," he said, putting his hand on my back.

"Yeah," I responded, opening my hands and getting my face into an actual, not totally fake smile. "It's okay, though. I'm fine. Coffee?"

"Coffee," he agreed, still looking at me.

I guess now that we're here, I should talk a little about Jackson. Seeing as the bookstore was where I met him. It'll be quick, I swear.

I met Jackson long before Rob and I went on our errand run. I'd had a good audition (another victim, this time a funny one) and celebrated by going to Skylight to buy myself too many books.

I'd been browsing the aisles, overwhelmed by just how many books I was interested in, when he approached me. Jackson. I felt him before I saw him. I'd been reading the back of *Saving Fish from Drowning*, a book I'd been interested in but not enough to drop fifteen ninety-nine on, when he spoke.

"You don't want that," he said, seeming self-assured.

I looked up at him. I want to say that I knew he'd be important right away, it sounds good, but I didn't. I knew that he was cute, though.

He was tall and pale and buzzing with an energy I was drawn to, and that's before I saw his eyes. Green and gold and with pupils that were so big I'm impressed I saw the other colors.

"No?"

"No," he echoed, grabbing a book off the shelf while staring at me. Jackson didn't gawk. Or gape. He stared. At me.

I warmed, trying to draw myself up to my full height, but that wasn't enough, even in my boots. I always liked tall guys, sue me.

"What do I want, then?"

"You're asking me?"

"Yeah, I am. You seem to have an idea, based on your deep knowledge of me," I teased.

"Well, because I know you so well, I'll do you a solid," he said. He handed me the book in his hand. You guessed it, Rob Sheffield's *Love Is a Mixtape*.

"Really?" I said, glancing at the title. "I'm a little young to remember the days of mixtapes."

"So am I. Doesn't matter. It's about love and music and grief. You'll relate."

I stared at him and he stared back. My stomach lurched. I didn't look away, though. A staring contest with a boy who'd prove to be the death of me. It's becoming clear to me that I have a pattern.

"I'll take it into consideration," I replied, taking the book from him. He grinned at me and I smiled back, rolling my eyes at the satisfaction emanating off him.

"I'll tell you what," he offered, grabbing it back from me, "I'll buy it for you. Read it. If you don't like it, let me know and I'll buy you the fish book."

"And if I do like it?"

He grinned even more, showing me his chipped front tooth.

"Then you'll give me your number."

"I'm not really in the habit of giving strangers my number."

"Then let's stop being strangers. I'm Jackson," he said, extending his hand. It was pale and veiny and what can I say? I'm a sucker for hands. I shook it.

"Maggie."

"Well, Maggie, do we have a deal?"

"Yeah," I said, trying to sound—you guessed it—relaxed. Cool. "We do."

"Great. I'll be right back."

He walked behind the counter and bagged the book for me. I pretended not to watch him as he wrote something on the back page. Instead, I plucked a book off the shelf and held it in front of me, not bothering to read the description on the back or the title of the book.

Jackson sauntered towards me and handed me the bag.

"You'll like it, I swear," he promised, still smiling.

"I'll hold you to that."

"I hope so. I have a lot riding on this, after all. It's not every day you have a date depending on someone's opinion of a book."

"I don't remember agreeing to a date," I teased, careful to make my voice sound calm and measured.

"You didn't," he said simply, "but if you do like it and give me your number, I'm going to ask you on one, so . . ."

This was the first time he hadn't sounded so cocky. This was when I felt something other than the initial attraction. Something about the uncertainty in his voice made him sound like a kid, and . . . I don't know.

"I better like it, then," I replied, smiling to let him know that there was no need for nerves. Not anymore. He smiled back at me and my heart skipped a beat.

Someone coughed behind me and I turned to see Peter. I didn't know him by name yet, but it was him. Same eyebrow piercing. Same air of self-importance. Jackson straightened up and grabbed a book at random from the shelf, pretending to work.

"So, miss," he said, putting on his working voice, "this is an incredible piece of writing. Personal, emotional, really beautiful. I would highly recommend it."

He winked at me and I grinned, turning in time to catch Peter sigh and walk away, back behind the counter.

I read *Love Is a Mixtape* that night and, as Jackson predicted, loved it.

I turned to the very end and saw, in Jackson's messy handwriting, a note: *I'm hoping if you like this you'll give me a call. Or if you didn't like it and want to fight about it, call me. Either way, I'm hoping I get a call. No pressure, feel free to rip this out, but just in case, 555-859-7630.*

I called him and it went straight to voicemail, an occurrence that would come to be routine. "Hi, you've reached Jackson. I can't get to the phone right now, or, more accurately, I'm doing something on my phone and am not in the mood to talk. Either way, leave me a message. I'll get back to you."

I still remember my message, only because Jackson played it back to me after we'd been dating for a month. He'd kept it, a small, wildly insignificant gesture that I put everything into.

"Hi," I muttered, my smile audible, "it's Maggie. From Skylight. I finished the book. *Love Is a Mixtape.* I'm only saying the title 'cause I'm almost positive this is a move of yours, putting your number in books you buy for girls, but either way, I finished it. I'm not telling you what I thought of it, though. Not on a voicemail. Hope you're having fun doing shit on your phone. Bye."

When I woke up, I had a message from him. This was before sleep was hard. I used to be good at sleep, actually. Not that it's a skill, but I was good. I'd get eight hours every night. I didn't need coffee, I was energized. And rested. And things were easier. But I woke up to a message that I deleted after listening to and then undeleted and have since re-deleted and re-undeleted at least fifteen times.

"Maggie. It's Jackson. Hi. Not that you have any reason to believe me, but that's not a thing I do, actually. The number-in-books thing. Although now that I know it's effective, I may have to adopt it as one, I don't know . . . In any case, I want to hear your thoughts about the book. You have a good poker face. Or poker voice, I guess. Anyway, let's meet up, if you're game. I have Tuesday off if you're around."

I'll get into what happened when we wound up meeting up, but before that, I should get back to coffee and errands and Rob. That's what you're here for.

"You sure you're okay?" Rob asked as we filed out of the coffee shop. "You're having decaf. You never get decaf."

"I'm already caffeinated enough. Besides, I thought you'd be impressed by my lack of caffeination," I said, sipping the iced decaf.

"I'm impressed, I promise. Just surprised, is all."

We walked in the direction of the truck in a settled kind of silence that only comes when you're comfortable with someone. I loved my silences with Rob as much as any of my conversations with him, I think. They soothed me.

"Any other errands?" I asked, breaking the silence.

"Yeah, but I think I've bored you enough. I can take care of it later."

"What is it?"

"I was going to get the truck washed, but like I said, I can just—"

"I love the car wash. Let's do it," I insisted.

"Yeah?"

The way he was looking at me was as if I'd told him I was part unicorn or something. Like I was otherworldly.

"Yeah. The full thing or drive-thru?"

"Drive-thru. Obviously. I like watching the spongy thing."

"Good. Let's do it."

I hopped in the truck, moving the books from my seat to the center console, and queued up some drive-thru songs. "So Far Around the Bend" by the National and "peace" by Taylor Swift. (I refuse to justify my love of her songs to you. Besides, as a poet, I'm sure you get it.)

He navigated his way through LA traffic easily, with his left hand on the steering wheel. His right hand rested on the books, and it took everything in me not to reach out and take it. I stared at it, though. That felt like a fair compromise. Still, it wasn't enough.

We were quiet as he pulled into the drive-thru and put the truck in neutral, giving the car-wash tracks control. Matt Berninger crooned to us as we looked through the windshield, watching the machines go to work as if we were watching a fireworks display, or something at an aquarium. I relaxed into the seat, letting the lyrics and the hypnotic movements of the sponges and wipers wash over me. I let my arms rest, not realizing how close our hands were until they brushed up against each other.

I looked down at them, marveling at how a brush of skin so brief and insignificant could set me on fire. I glanced at Rob, but he was staring straight ahead, so I did the same, willing myself to ignore the millimeters of air between our skin until I felt his fingers brush against the back of my hand. I looked back down at Rob's fingers tracing invisible circles onto my skin. He was still staring straight ahead.

My skin felt hot; my heart was beating so fast it felt like my blood was vibrating. I willed myself not to move a muscle, not to disturb the moment, even though all I wanted was to turn my hand and have him trace the lines of my palm.

I didn't want the car wash to end. I prayed that the machines would break down, leaving us stranded right there, in the middle of the tunnel, perpetually stuck in that moment, his fingers on my hand, my heartbeat louder than the music. It didn't, but one of my prayers was answered: as we neared the tunnel exit, his thumb found my palm and lightly traced the lines. I looked down. So did he.

We finished the wash and he brought his hands back to the steering wheel while I looked out into the sun, trying to process everything that had just happened. If I were a girl in a Taylor Swift song, I would have kissed him, but, as I was all too aware, I was not a girl in a Taylor Swift song.

We stayed silent as he navigated us up into the canyon. I tried to regulate my breathing and bring feeling back into my hand without moving it. If I moved it, the moment would really be done. I wasn't ready for it to be done, though.

"So," Rob said, pulling up to his—to your—house, "dinner tomorrow?"

I paused, trying to remember when we'd agreed on dinner, still stuck in shock from the car wash.

"Yeah, sounds good."

"Do you want to go somewhere, or—"

"We could eat at the apartment. I don't want you to keep having to buy me food," I said quickly. I didn't know how to function with him outside, around people. Plus I knew that Dani would be at Craig's. She usually spent every other night with him, so it was easy to plan around her absences.

"Are you sure? We can eat up here too, or—"

"No, let's do the apartment. I'll be up here for a while, so we can do that later or something."

What I didn't say was that the idea of doing anything in your house made me feel unclean, and I didn't want anything to dirty my time with him.

"Okay, then. Your apartment it is. I'm excited. I've been trying to picture it, and all I've got is the image of a bunch of espresso machines and ashtrays," he joked.

"I don't know if I should be flattered that you've tried to picture my place or offended that you basically just think I'm a chain-smoking caffeine addict."

"Flattered, definitely. Can I bring anything?"

"Nope. I've got it."

"Okay. What time do you want me?"

"Seven?"

"Seven it is," he echoed.

He parked and I got out, taking my books and handing him the Sheffield.

"Are you sure you want me to have this?"

"I'm sure. You'll like it, I think," I said, realizing I didn't know what kind of books he liked. I hated the reminders of all the things I didn't yet know about him.

"Thank you. I'll get started on it tonight."

"You don't have to, just read it whenever."

"Maggie."

"Rob."

"This is important to you. I'm gonna read it."

As he said that, he did the thing where he freezes you with his eye contact. You know what I'm talking about, right? Where the feeling of being *seen* by him is so intense that you feel transfixed.

"Okay," I said, relenting.

"Okay."

"I'll see you tomorrow."

He took a step towards me, pulling me into a hug. I held my breath and closed my eyes, reveling in the feeling of being surrounded by his warmth, his heartbeat, his smell. I don't know how long we stood there like that, but it felt like years. We broke away and I smiled, waving as I got into the car. It wasn't until I pulled past the house that I let my breath out, gasping.

I reached for my phone, wanting to call someone, to talk about what had just happened, before I froze, realizing who I'd wanted to call.

In the weeks after he'd died, I used to call Jackson all the time. I'd leave messages: long, rambling ones; short ones. Sometimes I'd call just to hear his answering machine before hanging up and dialing again. That went on until his parents cut off his phone.

So it was Jackson I'd wanted to call and talk to about Rob. Messy, I know, but what about this hasn't been messy? I knew what Jackson would say, too. He'd shake his head at me, laughing, and, in a scarily accurate impression of my father, say, "Maggie Mae, you seem to have found yourself in quite the shit-show, huh?"

He'd wag his finger at me and reach over, tousling my hair before kissing me once, twice, three times on the forehead. Then he'd hold my shoulders, stare me down, and say, "You're really in it this time, kid. It'll be okay. It'll be fine. When have you ever been drawn to easy, anyway?"

He used to say that to me when I'd cry to him about him. He'd shake his head as if it was obvious, and say, "Yeah, it sucks. I'm not easy to love, I know. But when have you ever been drawn to easy?"

I used to wear that as a badge of honor. It wasn't until my therapist suggested that maybe it wasn't my love of complications but my masochism and martyr complex that made messes appealing. I've never in my life hated someone more for being right.

That's what I missed most, I think. Not the sex or the laughter or the days of being able to sleep. I missed talking to him, being heard by him, and hearing him talk. I missed our conversations, even the dumb ones, the ones about what we should eat for dinner or what movie we should pretend to watch while hooking up. I missed fighting with him about whose turn it was to do the dishes. I wished I had recorded it all. The memories of us played in my head the way old songs do, where you remember almost all the lyrics save for the bridge, and so you just keep repeating them in your mind, hoping that the more you repeat them, the clearer it will all get. I did that with our conversations, only the bridge never got clear. I still had the voicemails, though.

Jackson loved voicemails. He hated texting, which I told him was pretentious and he said was justified. But he loved voicemails. He'd leave long ones. Full of pauses and sighs and rueful laughter. I always suspected that he made them long on purpose, just so he could ensure he was taking up that much more of my time. I didn't mind, though. I would've listened to hours of them if I could.

I pulled into my parking spot and sat in the car, still buckled in. I did that sometimes, just sat in the car, staring at nothing, gathering myself for something I didn't know was coming. My mom used to do the same thing, when Pearl and I were little.

She'd call them her "strategy sessions." I never knew what she was strategizing about, though. Pearl and I always stayed still. We wanted to strategize too. Sometimes we'd play chopsticks while my mom sat and stared, other times we'd copy her, wondering if we were doing it right.

I pulled up my voicemails and played one Jackson had sent me at three a.m. a month after we'd started dating. It was three minutes long. Like his Instagram, I had the message memorized, but playing it in my head wasn't the same as hearing his voice, so I played it.

"Hi. It's late, I know. You're sleeping. I know this because I just snuck out of bed to call you. Weird, I know. You're probably gonna laugh at me in the morning when you get this. You're definitely gonna laugh, actually. I don't blame you, it's a weird thing to do, but I just . . . I wanted to talk to you, but you looked so peaceful sleeping and I didn't wanna wake you up and risk you biting my head off or something. Dani got in a while ago and she lit the incense that smells like shit, so now your apartment reeks, not that you'll notice. You're a deep sleeper, it's insane. I probably could have called you from bed and you would've stayed asleep. I'll try that next time, maybe. But anyways, I don't really know why I called, actually. I didn't really have anything I wanted to say, I just . . . I wanted to talk to you. I'm such a girl, it's fucking ridiculous. You're turning me into a girl. I wanted to tell you tonight that I like you. A lot. Obviously. It's stupid, I know, but this past month, I've been happy, I guess, and . . . and I haven't been happy in a while, so thanks for that. God, this is dumb. Whatever. I'm gonna go back to bed and pretend to sleep till you're up, so . . . bye, I guess."

I woke up that morning to the message and listened to it while Jackson showered. When he came back into my room, still dripping and pink-cheeked, I started laughing.

He grinned and shook his head at me. "You're lucky you're cute, or else I'd be outta here."

He didn't leave, though. We didn't leave my room for the next two days, except to grab yogurt and water and for the occasional smoke break. Dani called it "joint hibernation." She stayed at Craig's that week and I forgot to miss her.

I took a deep breath and got out of the car, walking into the apartment. Dani was asleep on the couch, surrounded by self-help books. Her computer was open, still playing *Pride and Prejudice,* her go-to lazy day movie. I sat on the floor beneath her, watching Keira Knightley jut her chin while Matthew Macfadyen pined over her. The volume was too low for me to hear anything, but it didn't matter. I'd seen it enough to know what was going on.

11

I woke up and it was dark outside. Dani was still on the couch above me, but she was awake, watching *About Time*. I stretched, feeling more rested than I had in a while, and looked up.

"Hi you," Dani cooed, smiling wide.

"Hi. What time is it?"

"Eight. You slept for a while. I woke up at five-thirtyish and you were out cold."

"I was?"

"Yeah. You must've been tired. Big day?" she asked.

She moved over and I sat next to her on the couch. The two of us pretzeled our legs together and I laid my head on her shoulder.

"A bit. I saw my dad."

"Fuck."

"Yeah," I agreed.

Dani put on her robe, a gauzy white number she'd embroidered tarot card imagery on, and burrowed into it, staring at me.

"How was he?"

"The same. It wasn't too bad, I guess, just . . ."

"Just the usual amount of bad?"

"Yep."

"Was Ana there?" she asked, rolling her eyes.

"Of course."

"And? Did she eat anything this time?"

"Of course not."

"Right, what was I thinking?"

We laughed for a bit, and then I settled back into Dani, letting out a sigh. She ran her fingers through my hair.

"Well, he's going back to Brooklyn soon, right? You won't need to see him for a while, at least."

"He leaves soon, I think."

"That'll be good, right?"

"Yeah. I guess so." I sighed.

"You okay, Spoon?"

Dani's been calling me Spoon for so long that neither of us remembers where the name came from.

"Uh-huh. Just a little . . . I don't know."

"What's up?"

She paused the movie and turned to face me, our legs still entwined. I looked into her eyes and took a deep breath, looking away as I let it out.

"I hung out with Rob today," I confessed.

I tried to make my voice sound light and airy, as if what I'd just said wasn't at all unusual, but I'm not sure I was successful. My voice sounded thick with sleep and guilt. I looked down at my hand, the one Rob had touched, branding it with his fingertips. I tried to remember the feeling of his skin on mine.

"Oh yeah?"

"Yeah. We ran some errands and got lunch. I'm gonna be house-sitting right next to him, so we just ran into each other."

"Huh."

"What?"

"Nothing." She waved me off, but I pushed her.

"Dan."

"Mags."

"That doesn't sound like nothing," I said, nudging her.

"No, it's nothing. It's just . . . you're spending a lot of time with him, that's all."

"Not a *lot* of time with him. I've only seen him twice this week."

"Okay, but—"

"Dani. He's my friend. We're friends. I like hanging out with him, that's all. Stop worrying, okay? You'll get wrinkles."

She stared at me for a bit, but I held my ground, insistent. Maybe if I could get Dani to believe it, then I would too. Rob and I were just friends.

"Okay," she said, letting a breath out and squeezing my hand. I thought of Rob, and our hands in the car wash. I felt my cheeks flush and I got up.

"I'm gonna take a bath and try to get some more sleep."

Dani looked like she was going to protest, but she stopped herself. She was, after all, always telling me I needed to sleep more.

"All right, sleep well. I'm going to Craig's for a few days, but I'll see you when I'm back. Wanna go on a hike or something?"

"Yeah, sounds good. Love you," I replied.

"Love you more."

"It's not a competition," I shouted as I headed into the bathroom.

"You only say that 'cause if it was one, I'd win!"

I smiled as I turned the taps on, making the water as hot as I could stand it. Jackson used to say I was like a lobster with how hot I made my baths.

When I got into bed, my skin still pink from the scorching water, I retraced the patterns Rob had made on my hand, closing my eyes and willing myself back to sleep.

I woke up six hours later, at three thirty. The sky was still dark. Before I grabbed my phone, I thought I'd only slept about half an hour, so I was relieved to see I was wrong.

Fifteen and a half hours until Rob would be here, in the apartment. That thought energized me more than the sleep had. I climbed out of bed and started cleaning my room. There wasn't much to clean; I pride myself on being neat, but I organized and reorganized my books, folded the last of my laundry, and laid out an outfit to wear for dinner: paint-stained jeans and a red shirt Dani said made me look like a girl on an album cover.

I moved to the kitchen, putting dishes away and sweeping up the strands of Dani's and my hair. We were both shedders.

Dani woke up at eleven to a spotless apartment. I still hadn't changed out of my pajamas and was sitting on the porch, drinking coffee, smok-ing, and listening to Stevie Nicks: I needed her guidance.

Dani left a while later, a piece of toast in hand. I was happy to see her go and then immediately felt guilty for my happiness.

Rob and I didn't text much leading up to dinner. I texted to ask him if he was allergic to anything and he said he was deathly allergic to any-thing and everything vegan. After threatening a tofu-filled meal, I put my phone away and closed my eyes for a bit, enjoying the feeling of the sun on my face.

12

Rob arrived at six forty-five, bottle of wine in hand. When he knocked on the door, I took a second before opening it, taking a deep breath and sniffing my pits to see if they smelled. They didn't. It was time to face the music. *It's just dinner*, I remember thinking.

His eyes widened when I opened the door, and we both stood there for a moment, looking at each other and smiling stupidly. We started laughing at exactly the same moment.

"Hi," I said through my grin.

"Hi."

He was frozen, still staring, still smiling. I shook my head, trying to knock some sense back into my body. I was going to need all the sense I could get, judging by how our hellos had gone, after all.

"Wanna come in, or were you just gonna drink on my doorstep?"

"I was debating it, but inside is good," he agreed, smiling.

I stepped aside, making room for him, and he entered, looking around at the books and plants and photos on the walls.

"Wow," he said, turning his head every few seconds. His eyes were wide, like he was trying to take everything in.

"It's not a bunch of espresso machines and ashtrays, but—"

"It's beautiful. It's great," he said.

"Yeah?"

"Yeah. Much better than coffee and ashtrays."

"Okay, good." I sighed and smiled some more.

I walked into the kitchen, and he followed, still looking around like a kid in a candy shop.

"Do you want anything to drink? Water? Wine? Oat milk?"

Rob scoffed. "As tempting as oat milk sounds, I'd love some wine, thank you."

I opened the wine and poured him a glass, grabbing some water for myself. I knew that I needed my wits about me for the moment.

"So, can I see the place?"

"The apartment?"

"Yes, the apartment. Can you give me the tour?" he asked, grinning.

"Sure," I said, wiping my already-sweaty hands on a dish towel before ushering him out of the kitchen and into the hall. "So you've seen the main area, common space, whatever . . ."

"I have, yes."

"And the kitchen."

"And the kitchen," he echoed.

"So, this is the hall," I said, pulling ahead of him and trying not to sound like a realtor, before realizing in that moment that I *was* being a realtor, in a way. I was trying to sell him on myself, sell him on this home Dani and I had built. I wanted him to want to call this place home.

"Feels very hall-like. I like it."

"Find anything interesting in there?" I asked, nodding my chin in the direction of the drawer he'd been perusing.

"An extraordinary number of bobby pins and several decks of tarot cards."

"Dani's," I explained. She had at least four different decks that she'd use according to what phase of the year she was in when she did a reading. This seemed like overkill to me, but it worked for her, so I tried not to question it too much. I made a mental note of the bobby pins, though, as I have a tendency to lose them constantly.

"What's next?"

I opened the door to the bathroom and walked in, trying to look at it as if for the first time. Rob followed me in. I don't think I'd ever realized how small it was.

Dani and I'd spent lots of time in the bathroom, taking baths together that lasted hours and resulted in trips to the fridge for more wine or, on occasion, snacks; brushing our teeth side by side and pushing each other to try to spit first, like kids do; or just chatting, like when she'd sit on the toilet as I did my makeup for auditions.

We'd lived in that space together and it had felt like there *was* space, but right then, in the bathroom with Rob, whatever space there had been disappeared. I could feel my heartbeat in my fingertips, and I tried in vain to take slow, steadying breaths. I could feel the heat of him, even as I stayed in the corner.

He looked around and I tried not to look at him, focusing instead on the tiles, which I could never decide if they were birds or fish. The brushstrokes were bold and unclear.

"I love the fish tiles," he said. "Very on-theme."

So they were fish, then. As he said it, it became obvious. They were fins and scales, not feathers. How could I have ever seen anything other than fish?

He turned to face me, and we were so close I felt like if he breathed too hard, I'd tip over. I looked at his lips and saw him look at mine, and then it was feeling a little bit too much like that night on the boat, so I straightened up and cleared my throat, clenching my fists.

"Next stop?" I asked, trying to sound flighty and unaffected.

"Next stop."

I escaped the fish room and Rob followed, trailing after me as we headed to my room. I felt the butterflies leap and jump and fuck with every step, and I tried to focus on my breathing. Realtors don't get butterflies when they show people bedrooms, do they? I didn't think so.

"This," I said, stepping in, "is my room."

Rob paused for a second, maybe less, before stepping over the threshold and into the room. I wondered if the pause had been deliberate or not.

He laughed softly, more to himself than to me, I think, and touched the photos on the walls, brushed the spines of the books on the shelves, and peeked into my closet.

"You like organizing things by color," he stated, with his head still in the closet, "the books, the clothes, everything . . ."

"I just like the way it looks. It makes sense to me that way. Is that weird?"

"Not weird, just interesting."

"Oh. Okay."

We got quiet again, then, and Rob went back to touching everything. Every time I saw his fingers touch something of mine, I felt my blood heat up and my cheeks flush.

"You don't have any pictures of yourself up here," he observed, looking back at the photos on the wall. He was right, I didn't.

The wall was littered with photos of Dani, Pearl, Jonah, Harper, my mom, Dottie, Craig, my dad even, but it was free of photos of me.

There was an empty space on the wall where a picture of Jackson used to live, but I'd taken it down a few months before. It felt like it wasn't my place to have him up there anymore. The photo was tucked into the copy of *Love Is a Mixtape* he'd bought me, still on the shelf, just a few feet from Rob.

"Yeah, I know, I just always felt weird having pictures of myself on display."

"Why?"

"It just feels so narcissistic. Like, I know what I look like. I don't need a constant reminder of what my face looks like, you know? It's hard enough walking by mirrors and—"

"You don't like looking at yourself in the mirror?" he asked.

"God no. Why, do you?"

"Oh. I mean it's not my favorite thing, obviously, but I don't dislike it. I'm old enough to feel settled in my face, I suppose," he reasoned.

"Well maybe I'll get there one day. Until then, though . . ."

"That makes me sad." He sighed.

"It does?"

"Yes," he said, looking at me with an earnestness that felt too intimate and unwelcome, despite being exactly what I wanted, what I needed. "You have a lovely face. It's a shame you don't appreciate it."

"Right, well . . ." I trailed off, and he kept looking at me for a bit, but I had to look down at my hands, forfeiting that round of our ongoing staring contest.

I felt skinless in that moment. Something about having him in my space, in the room where I'd talked to him on the phone and thought about him and dreamt about him and masturbated while thinking about him, it all felt real.

Real the way that our hands in the car wash tunnel had been real. Real the way the kiss on the boat had been real. Real the way the phone call we fell asleep on had been real.

I looked up at the ceiling, hoping to find something there to center me, to make me feel shielded somehow, but I found nothing.

"I love it," Rob said, startling me out of my reverie.

"You do?"

"Yes. It's just so . . . you. It's wonderful."

I turned and walked back towards the kitchen to hide my smile. It was cartoonish, I'm sure. I waited to hear Rob's footsteps following me, but they didn't come. I glanced back and saw him sitting on my bed, staring at the photos on the wall. I considered going back in, but thought better of it, pouring myself a glass of wine and pulling the ratatouille out of the oven.

I had racked my brain for hours that morning, trying to figure out the perfect meal to cook that would be impressive without being showy. Ratatouille felt right. And easy. And French, which is inherently romantic and . . . shut up, Maggie. Shut. The. Fuck. Up.

"Something smells good," Rob declared from the doorway, taking a sip of his wine.

"Ratatouille."

"Impressive!"

". . . of the oven, maybe, not me. I just chopped some things," I mumbled.

"Well you chopped them beautifully, then."

"Great, thanks. If this whole acting thing doesn't work out, maybe I'll just chop things for a living."

"Almost as admirable a career path as being a strawberry."

I laughed, not bothering to stifle it. I didn't want to think too much about rules that night.

"How can I help?" Rob asked, pouring himself a little more wine and refilling my glass.

"If you grab the bowls for me, that'd be great. They're in the—"

I broke off because Rob had already located them, handing them to me. It's small and stupid, I know, but I'd always said that the mark of really knowing someone was knowing exactly where to find things in their kitchen and he had. It felt like he'd been here hundreds of times before, drinking wine and grabbing forks and bowls and glasses and being at home in my home. It heated me up.

I spooned chunks of eggplant and peppers and onions into the bowls and nodded my chin towards the door to the porch. Rob took both bowls and walked out as I grabbed the wine and took two steadying breaths. They didn't work.

"This is delicious," Rob said around bites of his food. I grinned, hiding it behind bites of my own. We were sitting close enough that if I wanted to, I could reach up and brush his hair back, away from his face. I *did* want to, but I stopped myself, sitting on my hand to make touching him all the more difficult.

"Do you cook a lot?" Rob asked, taking a sip of his wine.

"Yeah. I started when I was a kid. My mom made me and my sister each responsible for one dinner every week, so I've been cooking since I was eight or nine."

"And what did eight-year-old Maggie make for dinner?"

"Pancakes."

"Pancakes? For dinner?"

"Every single week. And not just any pancakes, pink pancakes. I was a little obsessed with pink foods, so any time I could make my food pink, I did," I explained, remembering plates of pink mashed potatoes.

"That's adorable. How were they?"

"The pancakes?"

"Yeah."

"Phenomenal. They're still one of my standbys. Pearl makes me make them for her every time I go see her."

"Oh, so they're actually good. Not just pink and adorable," he reasoned.

"Yeah, they're pretty amazing. Dani's obsessed with them too, but I make them purple for her. Or orange. The color varies based on whoever I make them for."

"And what color pancakes would I get if you were to make them for me?"

I looked at him, cocking my head to the side and pretending that the question required more consideration than it really did; I was just using it as an excuse to blatantly stare at him.

"Green," I said, taking another sip and wishing I had taken longer to make my decision, if only to have the excuse to stare at him for a bit longer.

"Why green?"

"They'd match your eyes," I explained without thinking, as if it was obvious, which I guess it was.

He was quiet for a moment, letting my admission hang in the air. He bit his lip and saw me glance from his hands to his eyes to his lips, and I shouldn't have done it, but I couldn't look away, not yet.

"I'd like that," he said quietly. "Green pancakes sound great. You'll have to make them for me next time."

"That can be arranged," I replied, finally looking down. A strand of my hair came down and mercifully covered my face, but I didn't have much time to take refuge in the shield before his hand came and brushed it back behind my ear, the way guys do in movies before they kiss the girl.

Shockingly, I didn't freeze when he did that. My body relaxed, feeling buzzed on his touch rather than the wine.

"You keep hiding," he said, hand still cradling the side of my head, "leaving the room and changing the subject and peeking out behind your hair and it's driving me nuts. What're you hiding from?"

I wanted to punch him in the face. And then smash his face into mine. And scream and hit him and throw The Ring over the side of the porch and make *him* cry and moan and throw The Ring over the side of my porch himself. Instead, I looked up at him and stared him down, doing everything in my power not to back down or look away.

"You," I confessed, "I'm hiding from you."

"Why?" He sounded genuinely pained, and I had to close my eyes for a moment.

"You're married," I said, hating the words and the truth that they carried.

"I know that. I know, I know, but—"

"But what?"

He sighed, a deep, infuriating sigh. As if my question was dumb, or childish. As if I was asking to be cute, which, for the record, I wasn't. Nothing about this was cute. I suppose that's not exactly true, though.

He was cute. That's part of why we were in this situation to begin with.

"But I don't feel that way when I'm with you," he said simply.

I wanted to scream. I'm sure he did too. You should ask him.

"So how do you feel? When you're with me?"

He groaned. "Don't ask me that."

"Why not?"

"Because there's a line, and if you ask me that and I answer it, I'll be crossing the line."

"You're saying that as if you haven't crossed the line yet."

"I know."

We sat in silence for a moment. I stared at my hands. He stared at his bowl.

"Fuck you," I said. It kind of flew out of my mouth.

"What?"

"Fuck you."

"Why fuck me?!"

"Fuck you and your marriedness and you sitting there, acting like all of this has been aboveboard. And acting like I'm forcing you to cross lines, like all of this . . . *this* is you taking cues from me. Fuck that," I snapped.

"Maggie—"

"I'm not doing this for fun, you know. I don't like this. I don't like sitting here with you and your ring and your invisible lines we can't cross and—"

"I know you don't, I'm sorry if—"

"I don't have the power here, you know."

"Don't you?"

I looked up at him then, but he'd already been looking at me and I could see that the question had been genuine. In that second, I felt like I was seeing myself through his eyes and what I saw was . . . power. It's a beautiful thing to see yourself through the eyes of someone who looks at you that way. I wonder if that's the way he used to look at you before the night of the party. Before me.

"No," I said, "I don't think so."

"Then who does?"

"Your ring," I answered, though I'd really meant what The Ring represented. I'd really meant *you*. Rob laughed, looking down at his ring and twisting it and twisting it.

"Don't take it off," I pleaded, before knowing if I meant it or not.

"I won't," he promised, though he continued twisting it, looking out past the porch railing and into the night sky.

We sat in silence again, and in that moment, I started thinking about that letter that went viral a few years back, the one written by the woman on her deathbed, trying to appeal to women who might fall in love with her husband, who could bring him new love once she'd passed. I wondered if you'd do the same, if you were ever in her position. I wondered if that was noble and loving of her or merely deeply masochistic. I wondered how her husband felt about it.

"I'm sorry," he said, and his voice startled me out of my reverie.

"What?"

"I'm sorry. You're not pushing me to cross lines, that wasn't fair."

"None of this is fair."

"I know. I know. I'm . . . I'm sorry."

"Me too," I responded.

There's this poem by Anne Sexton, aptly named "For My Lover, Returning to His Wife." I've been thinking about it a lot. Understandably, I'm sure. I don't remember the first time I read it. I know it was before all of this, and I'm not sure why it struck a chord with me, but it did. Maybe I was having preemptive déjà vu, or maybe it made me think about my father, I don't know. I left the tab open on my phone, though, and I used to look at it every now and again. I've been reading it a lot recently, and all I can say is that there's this through line, this fundamental thought, that she, the unnamed wife, the cast-iron pot, the fireworks in February, is as much a part of Anne's relationship with her lover as he is.

Anne wouldn't have loved him as she did if he hadn't come to her with the life and love he had built with his wife. His wife molded him into a man Anne could love. Unintentionally, but she did it all the same. I wonder if in loving Rob, I was really loving you, and the way you loved him.

"So," I said, holding my glass of wine just to have something in my hand that wasn't his, "what do we do?"

"What do you mean?"

"I mean there's a line and a ring and what do we do?"

"Are you asking me what I *want* to do?"

"No, but . . . yeah. Yeah, I guess I am." I sighed.

"So ask me."

I put the wine down and stared at him. He licked his lips and stopped twisting his ring.

"What do you want to do, Rob?"

"This," he said, stretching over the table and kissing me.

I'd forgotten how soft his lips were. Maybe that's not true, but it's like when you purposefully remember someone to be uglier than they were, just to make not loving them easier. I'd tried to think of his lips as chapped and inexperienced, but that flew out the window the moment he kissed me again. Can I really say "again" when I'd been the one to kiss him first?

I remember wishing that I knew how to hold my breath for minutes on end, just because I didn't want it to stop.

I wondered if anyone ever died from being kissed, from kissing with too much of themselves. It wouldn't be a bad way to go if you think about it.

His hands tangled themselves up into my hair, then came to the sides of my face, then my neck, the back of my head, my shoulders . . . it was like he couldn't decide what he wanted to touch. I knew, though.

My hands stayed on his head, in his hair. I wished he could swallow me whole. I wished I could live inside of him, see everything through his eyes, taste only what he chose to feed himself with, live as an extension of him.

He got up, still in the kiss, crouched and awkward, and came around the table so that there was nothing between us. He knocked the table a bit and one of the glasses tipped over, spilling wine. We laughed into the kiss, not bothering to give in to the interruption.

He tried to join me on my chair, but it was too small, so I broke the kiss for a moment.

"Hold on," I said, breathless, "I have an idea."

I got up and sat on the porch railing, my legs wide enough for him to stand between them.

"You're a genius," he murmured as I reached up and pulled him to me by his shirt.

The kiss felt more like sex than most of the sex I'd ever had. I don't know if that's an endorsement of Rob's kissing skills, an indictment of the lack of sexual prowess of all the boys I'd been with, or both. I didn't care.

I just knew that my entire body was awake and Rob had woken it up. I knew that I wanted to live in that feeling. I wanted to glue our lips to each other, but I also wanted his lips to be on every part of my body. I wanted him to kiss my teeth, my nails, my hair, all the dead parts of me, waking them up too.

I wanted all those things, but I pulled away, gasping for breath. His lips chased mine and I laughed. He did too, before kissing my chin, my jaw, my neck.

In the past, I'd always felt that when boys kissed my neck, my shoulders, my breasts, they were trying to claim me. They were marking me as something that belonged to them. It wasn't like that with Rob, though. It felt like with every kiss from him, I was claiming myself. There's something very poetic about that. Triumphant and sad all at once.

He brought his hand between my legs and swallowed my gasp with his mouth before pulling away.

"Fuck," he said under his breath, less to me and more to himself.

"Fuck," I agreed, thinking of the first kiss on the boat. These were good "fucks." Messy ones, but good.

"I have to go soon, I have—"

"Work. I know."

"I want to take my time. I don't want to rush—"

"You can rush," I said quickly, breathlessly. He laughed. I did too, still breathless.

"We should clean the wine up," he responded, his hand still between my legs.

"I'll get it later."

"It'll stain."

"I don't care."

He laughed again.

"You're ridiculous," he teased.

"And you're wasting time that could be spent rushing."

"Touché."

We didn't have sex that night. It reminded me of my first date in high school when I was dropped off at home and spent the rest of the night with a thrumming between my legs and my fingers on my mouth, trying to hold onto the feeling of someone else's lips on mine.

Rob insisted on doing the dishes as I cleaned the spilled wine, and we kept looking at each other in the reflection of the kitchen window, sporting matching smiles.

When it was time for him to leave, I walked him to the front door, holding his hand, and he turned at the door, smiling.

"So," he said, trailing off, his unoccupied hand reaching up to touch the back of his neck.

"So."

"I don't really know what to say."

"What's your first instinct?"

"It's stupid."

"I'm sure it is," I teased.

"Enough of the sass."

"Sorry, sorry. I like stupid, though. Tell me."

"This was nice, right? I'd . . . I'd like to see you again. Soon."

"I'm relocating right across from your house for several days. You'll see me. Soon."

His smile got bigger.

"Okay, then," he said, scratching his beard.

"Okay."

"So, I'll see you?"

I covered my smile with my hand before he moved it away from my face.

"Yeah," I said, "you'll see me."

"Good."

"Good."

He shook his head and leaned down, kissing me once more. I ran my fingers through his hair and leaned into it, deepening the kiss. He pulled away for a second.

"I've got to go," he said, not moving.

"Then go," I responded, kissing him again.

"Okay, I'm gonna go. I'm leaving," he said, kissing my neck again.

"Leave, then," I replied, tilting my head back, giving him more of my neck to see, to touch, to kiss.

He groaned, pulling away.

"I really have to go now."

"Nothing's keeping you here," I teased.

"I'm not sure if that's true."

"No?"

"No. I'd say there are a number of things keeping me here."

"Really?"

"Yes."

"Wanna list them?" I asked, grinning.

"Yes. No."

"You don't sound very sure. Maybe you should stay till you figure it out," I offered, teasing him some more.

"No, I'm sure. Let's just say for brevity's sake that the list begins and ends with you, all right?"

"All right. Now get out of here, would you?"

"Fine. Fine. I'm leaving."

"Good."

"Good."

He didn't leave, though. Not right then, anyway. He just looked at me, his eyes crinkling at the corners, his features soft. I wanted to peek inside his brain right then, see what he was thinking. He shook his head again, and I closed the door.

"Go work," I yelled through the door.

"Yes ma'am," he said, and I could hear his steps towards the gate. "I'll see you later."

I heard him open and close the gate, and I turned, my back resting against the door, fingers to my lips, still smiling wide. My cheeks hurt.

13

I slept for six and a half hours that night, which, for me, is unprecedented. I didn't even remember trying to sleep, just the moments before
unconsciousness that were spent with my fingers tracing the path his lips
had made from my mouth to my jaw, down my neck and up again. When
I woke up, I turned towards my bedside table, picked up my phone, and
saw a new text from Rob, sent at 1:42 a.m.

> If I keep smiling this much tonight, people are
> going to start asking questions.

I giggled, thrashing my body around in my bed like a madwoman.
Maybe I was. Love is a kind of socially accepted insanity, after all.
I wrote back, too excited to draft anything cool and aloof.

> you sound very eager for someone who was rushing
> to get your ass out the door last night . . .

I put my phone away and walked to the bathroom, looking at myself in the mirror. I wanted to see if my appearance had changed somehow.

It hadn't, but I sported two seminoticeable hickeys on my neck. Once I saw them, they got warm. It was like my pulse lived in them, those two faint juvenile marks. Proof of my time with Rob. Proof of his mouth. Proof of my body, my desirability.

I didn't bother covering them up as I went on my hike. If anything, I craned my neck out, daring all I encountered to notice them.

As I wrapped my hike up, my phone rang. It was Pearl. I picked up after the second ring.

"Hi!"

"You sound happy," Pearl said over the sounds of Harper singing in the background.

"You're supposed to start phone calls by saying hi back, Pearl."

"Hi back. You sound happy." The way she said it sounded both like an accusation and a sigh of relief.

"That's because I *am* happy. Is that so hard to imagine?"

"Yes. No. A little bit."

"Jesus." I groaned.

"No, not hard, just . . . it's good! It's great!"

"Yeah. It is. What's up?"

"Harper's forgetting what her favorite aunt looks like and I'm forgetting what my little sister looks like, so we're inviting you over for a tea party."

"A tea party?"

"Yes. Jonah bought her a tea set the other day, so now she's in a phase," she explained.

"So she's out of the fairy phase, then?"

"Nope, they're coming to the tea party too."

I tried to imagine Harper drawing pictures for her fairy friends, leaving snacks and notes for them, not knowing that it was Pearl and Jonah who'd leave her things in return. She'd spend hours once she'd gone to bed drawing elaborate pictures of their invented fairy world. Our mom had done the same for me and Pearl when we were kids, until my dad left. My fairy notes stopped coming for a while after that, until Pearl took up the mantle. When I was eleven, she told me it had been her who wrote the notes. I didn't speak to her for a week. It wasn't until I got older that I realized how kind it had been of her to do that for me, to keep the magic alive for a six-year-old girl whose family had exploded and whose mom had been plunged into a world of anger and hurt.

"Oh good. What time?"

"Two? Does that work?"

"Yeah, I can be there. Should I bring anything, or—"

"Just you. Wear pink. It's the new tea party rule."

"I didn't know tea parties had rules," I mused.

"Harper's do."

I laughed, picturing my niece ordering my sister and the fairies around, surrounded by teacups and stuffed animals. That seemed far away as I sat down in my cluttered car full of receipts for purchases made months ago and bottles half filled with sunscreen, lotion, mouthwash.

"Okay, I'll be there. In pink."

"Good."

"Good."

"Mags?"

"Yeah?"

"It's good to hear you happy," she gushed.

I smiled. It was good to *feel* happy, but I didn't want to say as much. Not yet. I didn't want to jinx anything.

"Yeah, yeah. I'll see you later," I replied, dismissing what she'd said.

As soon as I hung up and started the car, I got another call. I answered, assuming it to be Pearl. She was famous for calling, hanging up, remembering she'd forgotten to tell you something, and calling again seconds later.

"Is there another tea party rule you forgot to tell me?" I asked, smiling.

"If by 'another' you mean 'a first,' then yes," Rob said.

"Oh." I let out a breath. "It's you."

"Yes, it's me. Who'd you think it was?"

"My sister. She just called, so I figured it was her, but . . . never mind. It's you."

"It's me. What'd she call about?"

"I've been invited to a tea party," I answered, pulling my hair out of its haphazardly done ponytail.

"Very posh."

"Yup. Nothing's classier than a tea party with a preschooler, some imaginary fairies, and two grown women."

"You're in very high demand, it would seem."

"Am I?"

"I'd say so. I was calling to ask if I could see you today, but it seems a four-year-old beat me to the punch," he explained.

"She did," I said, still smiling, "but she goes to sleep early, so I'm not *completely* spoken for."

"Good. I was moments away from letting myself be jealous."

My cheeks warmed up and my skin erupted in goose bumps as I took in what he'd just said to me. I felt desired; I liked that feeling. I was no longer a sweaty, rumpled person in a too-full car, I was someone worth spending time with. Someone desirable.

"No need for that."

"I'm glad to hear it. Want to grab a drink when you're done with tea?"

I grinned. "Yeah, okay. Seven thirty good?"

"Yeah, I'll be done with work early today, so that's good."

"Okay, cool. Want to meet at . . . Oil Can Harry's? It's close to mine."

Rob started laughing so loud, it startled me.

"Of all the bars in LA, you pick Oil Can Harry's?" he asked, incredulous through laughter.

"It's close by! And it's cheap. And I like the name."

"All right, your logic is sound. Let's do it."

"Yeah?"

"Uh-huh. I'll see you there. Have fun at the tea party, you."

"You" had never before sounded like a term of endearment, but right then, with the accent and the moment of crippling vulnerability and all of it, it sounded more endearing than any pet name I'd ever heard.

"Okay," I responded, my voice soft.

"Okay."

We stayed on the line, silently, for a bit.

I could hear his smile. I wanted to devour it.

I didn't hang up. Neither did he.

"Did you get any sleep last night?" he asked, breaking the silence.

"A bit," I said, softly.

"Good. You need it."

"Yeah, I know."

"I don't know what else to say."

"Then hang up," I teased.

"I don't want to. I like hearing your voice."

He said it so simply, it shocked me. *I shouldn't be allowed to drive when I'm on the phone with him,* I remember thinking. *He's too distracting.* I had to force myself to focus on the cars next to me, ahead of me. The traffic lights, too.

"But I wasn't talking," I responded, feeling giddy.

"That's okay, I like your silences too."

I groaned.

"What?" he asked, laughing.

"It's just that you have this incredibly annoying tendency to always say the perfect thing."

"You say that like it's a bad thing," he exclaimed.

Yes, I thought, *it is.* I didn't want this. I didn't want to be on the phone with a married man, laughing about nothing while feeling . . . everything. I wanted to feel nothing for him, but everything he said made that seem impossible.

"Maybe it is."

"Okay," he said quietly, the smile still audible.

"Okay, go."

"I'm serious. I'm hanging up now."

"So you've said."

"Right."

"Right."

"I'll see you tonight, Maggie." He said each word with such gentleness, it felt like he was hugging me over the phone, which is . . . it's dumb, I know it is, but that's the only way I can describe it.

"Yeah, I'll see you."

I hung up then and sat staring at the road ahead of me, trying to keep the soft, easy quiet we'd shared just moments before.

14

I got to Pearl's wearing pink, as promised. Harper opened the door for me, decked out in light-up sneakers, a tutu, a Spider-Man shirt, and pink butterfly wings. Her hair, a frizzy blond halo of curls, held a tiara, also pink. Just your average tea party ensemble.

She jumped up into my arms and I scooped her up, trying not to crush her wings in the process. She put her mouth to my neck and squealed.

"Hi, bug," I said into her hair, spinning her around.

"Hi," she whispered into my neck.

"You got tall, cutie!"

"I know," she said as I put her down, "I growed."

"You certainly did. It's all the tea you're drinking, I bet."

Harper giggled and we walked into the house.

Pearl and Jonah's house is perfect. Going there always feels like meditation, or at least the only meditation I feel capable of doing. It feels like coming home.

After Jackson died, I moved in for a while, sleeping in the guest bedroom that Harper had renamed "Magzie's room." She'd even painted a plaque saying as much, which Jonah and Pearl nailed to the door. The plaque's still up, a monument to the week and a half I spent not eating or sleeping, instead watching hours of *Sesame Street* with Harper and crying every twenty minutes or so.

We walked onto the deck to find Pearl and Jonah sitting at the "tea table," a small, white table with six just-as-small chairs. Pearl and Jonah sat between a stuffed lamb named Mops. I'd given it to Harper for her first birthday, and she used to walk around holding it by the ear.

"Magzie's here," Harper announced, chest out, proud to be able to make such a declaration.

They looked up and smiled at me. Jonah stood first, walking over and wrapping me in a hug as tight as the one I'd given Harper seconds before. I'd known Jonah for years. Before he and Pearl even met, actually. He was a cinematographer, and we'd shot my first movie together. I actually wasn't playing a victim that time.

It was incredible. Everything you'd want your first job to be: a group of underpaid people low on time who are all so passionate about telling the story they're telling that they don't mind the sixteen-hour days, working through weekends, changing into costumes behind camera equipment, etc. It was all a weird, fast-paced circus act. Jonah was the only one who was steady during the shoot. He was calm while the rest of us whirled and spiraled around him. He was the anchor we all needed.

We got along well, bonding over a love of karaoke and a shared, secret dislike of Patti Smith, and so when the shoot was done, I introduced him to Pearl and the rest is history. This is all to say that Jonah feels as much a part of my family as Dani does.

"Hey, Mags," he said, cupping my face in his hands the way Craig did.

"Hi, Jo."

"It's been a while."

"I know, I'm sorry, I've just been—"

"It's okay. We get it."

"I don't," Pearl declared from behind Jonah, smiling despite herself.

Pearl is . . . she's wonderful. You'd like her, I think. Everyone does. She can make a meal, give sage advice, tell an offensive joke that'll leave you laughing till you cry, and braid Harper's hair in the span of thirty minutes. She's a superhero.

She had Harper naturally, at home, and a few hours after she'd delivered, she was in the kitchen making breakfast for everyone, including the midwife.

I stepped away from Jonah and burrowed into Pearl the way I have since before I can remember. There's something about her smell that instantly soothes me. Sweat and leather and lilacs and something else I've never been able to place but that is so deeply, profoundly *hers* that I wish I could wrap myself in a blanket of it.

"Are you gonna tell me about the hickeys or are we gonna pretend they don't exist," she whispered to me.

"I'll tell you later," I answered, and Jonah laughed. He'd said once that if the two of us were to start a band it should be called I'll Tell You Later, on account of the many occasions on which we'd whisper it to each other at dinner parties before sneaking off into the bathroom to debrief.

We all sat at the table and Harper poured us tea (water), asking us how many "lumps" we wanted with it (I took two lumps). After tea was done, Harper went into the garden to chat with her fairies, and Jonah, Pearl, and I went into the kitchen, where Pearl prepped dinner while Jonah and I drank coffee with no lumps.

"So," Pearl asked, chopping an onion, "is it later yet?"

"Yeah, we can talk about it," I said, taking a sip of coffee.

"What are we talking about? Mags's hickeys? World politics? The weather?" Jonah quipped, grabbing a cracker from the bowl Pearl had put out earlier.

"I'm thinking the hickeys, but we can get into the rest of it later, hon,"

Pearl answered. He smiled at her the way people sickeningly, beautifully in love with each other do.

"What do you wanna know?" I asked.

"Everything," Pearl and Jonah said at the same time.

They love hearing the stories of my love life. Jonah says it makes them feel all the luckier for not having to go through it again, for being settled in the knowledge that they're through with the days of blundering through dates, while I'm still tripping in too-small and too-uncomfortable shoes and falling on my face in front of cute guys (one of Jonah's personal favorites in the chronicles of my love life).

"Well, his name's Rob and—"

"Rob what? Do we know him?" Jonah asked.

"No, you don't, but he actually tattooed Dad, P."

"He did one of the names?" she asked, groaning.

"No, he got a new one. It's of you and me when we were in Amsterdam. The one with the—"

"With the chairs?"

"Yeah," I said.

"Huh. That's . . . oddly sentimental of him."

"Uh-huh."

"Is that how you met?" Jonah asked.

"No, I met him at Craig's birthday party on the boat."

"Oh, the Hell Ship?"

"Yup," I answered.

"So," Pearl prompted, "what's he like?"

I grinned despite myself.

"Oh my lord," Jonah crowed, "she likes this one!"

"Shut up," I yelled, still grinning. "I do *not*."

"You do!!"

"Shut up, Jo," Pearl said, smiling before turning to face me. "But you absolutely do, don't you?"

"Yeah, I do. He's just . . . I don't know, he's sweet and smart and funny and . . ." *And married* is what I was thinking but didn't say out loud. How could I talk about ruining a marriage in front of the only two happily married people I knew?

"How old is he?"

"He's older . . ."

"How much older? Dad's age?"

"Gross, no! He's like your age-ish. He's thirty-two."

"Hey," Jonah said, "I'm *forty-one*! Are you calling me old?"

"No, I'm calling you old*er*, Jonah. There's a difference."

"Right," he said, "carry on."

"I don't know, I just . . . he's kind of annoyingly fantastic. It's a problem."

"How so?" Pearl asked.

"It's not, really, I just . . . I haven't felt anything close to this in a while, you know?"

Pearl nodded. She knew.

"Does he know about Jackson?" Pearl asked, speaking with this measured tone she usually reserves for Harper.

"Yeah, he does."

"Well, that's good," Pearl said, still using her Harper-voice on me.

"Uh-huh."

Pearl looked at me for a moment, her face impassive and still before it broke into a smile, and she shook her head, laughing softly as she wiped tears out of her eyes.

"What is it?" I asked, startled by her reaction.

"Nothing. I'm just . . . god, it's so good to see you *happy*. You seem lighter. You seem younger. It's beautiful."

My heart swelled and I got teary too. Sometimes I forgot that while I was mourning Jackson, everyone who loved me had to sit and watch me suffer. I don't like thinking about it, if I'm honest.

It makes me feel guilty and like I should apologize for my pain, for the pain that my pain caused. I got up from the stool and walked over to Pearl, arms out. It was she who burrowed into me this time, holding me tight. I looked over her shoulder at Jonah, who was also teary-eyed, smiling wide as he watched our embrace.

Before I left, I walked out into the garden to visit Harper and her fairies. She was sitting on the grass, drawing pictures of cupcakes, but she looked up when I sat down next to her.

"I like your dress," she said, putting her crayons down. "It's pretty. You look like a princess."

"I'll save it for you and you can have it when you're older, okay? It'll go in the Harp Box."

The Harp Box is just a trunk of all the clothes in my closet Harper has reserved for herself.

Harper smiled and looked at the dress as if she was imagining how she'd look in it.

"How're you doing, bug?" I asked.

"Good. I missed you."

"I missed you too."

"Are you still sad?"

I was thrown by the directness of the question. I'd forgotten kids' ability to shift the conversation from princess to one's emotional well-being in seconds.

"Mom said you had to take space because of you were oppressed," Harper explained.

"I was what?"

"Oppressed. That means sad," she continued, climbing onto my lap, still facing me. I tucked one of her curls behind her ear before I spoke, trying to imitate Pearl's Mom voice.

"I think you mean *depressed*, Harps. *That* means when you're really *really* sad."

"Are you really really sad?"

"Not anymore. I was for a while, though," I answered.

"Because of Jackson-who-died," she'd said it so simply, it knocked the wind out of me.

"Right," I said, slowly, "because of Jackson."

"Who died."

"Yeah, he died." I sighed.

"I think that's sad."

"Me too, bug."

"A lot of people die sometimes, you know?"

"Yeah, they do, that's true," I said, not sure if I was going to laugh or cry.

"But I think that's okay sometimes."

"You do?"

"Uh-huh," she declared.

"And why's that?"

"Well because," she said, sounding *very* serious as she tried to tuck a strand of my hair behind my ear, accidentally ripping out a few in the process, "the dead people who died aren't dead all the time forever, you know."

"No?"

"No, silly! They used to be *not*-dead people who died, like us! And so it's not forever all the time."

I looked at my niece open-mouthed, trying to figure out how a four-year-old's deeply misguided and convoluted ruminations on death could be so comforting. Instead, I hugged her, squeezing her around her butterfly wings. She squeezed me back as tight as she could.

15

I got to Oil Can Harry's with five minutes to spare and walked in to find Rob already sitting at the bar, a pint of beer in front of him and a gin and tonic in front of the stool he'd saved for me. He looked up when I walked in, and stood, grinning.

"Hi," he said, pulling me in for a hug and kissing my cheek. I felt my pulse move to my hickeys.

"Hi," I said, sitting down next to him, "what're you drinking?"

"Newcastle," he answered, still smiling. "You'll hate it."

"Will I?"

"Probably. Try it," he said, pushing the glass closer to me.

I took a sip and, sure enough, hated it, wrinkling my nose in disgust. He laughed.

"Told you," he said, still laughing.

"It's foul!"

"It's an acquired taste."

"Right. So is lighter fluid, I'm told," I teased.

"More for me, then," he retorted, taking a big sip.

Some of the foam lingered on his top lip, and I reached out to wipe it away. I didn't even think about it. I just reached out and touched him. Like it was nothing. Like it was something I'd done thousands of times before. He ducked his head, grabbing my hand and kissing it. I dissolved.

"So," I said, "how was work?"

"It was fine. The usual. I was a bit distracted, though." His smirk couldn't have been bigger if he tried.

"Oh yeah?"

"Yeah."

"I'm sorry to hear that," I said, not at all sorry.

"I'm not," he said through a grin. "As far as distractions go, it's a good one."

"And what is this good distraction?" I asked, grinning back at him.

"This woman I know. Kind of embarrassing, actually. I can't stop thinking about her; it's like I'm a teenager or something."

"I see," I said, trying to keep my voice even and murder all the butterflies in my stomach, "and what's this woman like?"

"Well," he continued, taking another sip, "she's funny."

"Is she?"

"Oh, yeah. Very. She's bright and kind and painfully beautiful and she does this thing when she's being complimented where she kind of ducks her head down and covers her forehead with her hand, kind of like what you're doing now," he said. I moved my hand from my forehead, looking up to meet his eyes.

Everything got louder. Everything got quieter. I don't know how both things can happen at the same time, but they did. He smiled at me and the volume changed again, making everyone in the bar seem far away. I stared at him as he drank me in. I didn't know my ego was big enough for me to be turned on while being complimented.

"She sounds like quite the girl," I responded, taking a gulp of my drink. I had to force myself to swallow; it was like my throat was locked up, frozen, as I watched him watching me.

"Oh, she is."

"Hmmm," I said because I didn't have anything else to say.

"What about you? How was the tea party?"

"It was good."

"Yeah?"

"Yeah. Very cute."

"And pink, by the looks of it," he said, motioning towards my dress.

I looked down and touched the fabric in my hands, needing a reminder that I was a person in a body in the world. Something about Rob, and his eyes and hands and accent and . . . everything, made me forget where my body ended and the world began.

"I'm going up to Lucy's to house-sit tomorrow," I said, remembering just as the words fell out of my mouth.

"How long are you up there again?"

"Ten days," I answered, trying to sound as casual as someone talking about the weather.

"Does that mean I'll get to see you for ten days straight?"

"Do you *want* to see me for ten days straight?"

He gave me a look, which I did my best to return.

"If I'm honest, I'd like to see you every day, but I'll take ten," he confessed.

Rob took another sip of his beer just as his other hand came down onto my knee. I looked down at his hand, trying to find some anchor to tether my body to the stool. I felt like a balloon, floating and bobbing a few feet above the ground; my only link to the world of the physical was his fingers, which now traced the hem of my dress.

"You look very beautiful tonight," Rob said softly. "Have I said that to you yet?"

"No," I answered, "you haven't."

"Well, it's true. I've been thinking it."

His hand didn't move until I shifted in my seat, trying to get his hand higher on my leg. It worked; his hand came to rest mid-thigh, and I could feel the waves of heat coming off him, coming through his palm and into me, my body.

"Do you work tomorrow?"

"Not till eight," he said, brushing a strand of hair behind my ear.

"And before that?"

"Before that, I've got nothing."

"Oh," I said, "interesting."

"What about you?" he asked, eyes trained on mine.

"I've gotta be at Lucy's at noon, so I guess I'll just pack before I head over there, and then hang out. I've got a script to read, so I'll do that," I said.

We fell into silence again for a moment. I looked around at the other patrons, taking them all in for the first time that night. A man in a feather boa singing "Like a Virgin" on the karaoke machine as his friends cheered him on, drinking from glasses bigger than their faces. A woman looking towards the door every few seconds; she'd been nursing a glass of white wine since I walked in. I wondered if they'd all clocked me and Rob, his hand on my leg, my heart in my throat. I wondered if any of them knew you.

I was startled out of my reverie as Rob started tracing circles on the palm of my hand. He was looking at me with an expression I couldn't name.

"What?" I asked, raising my eyebrows at him.

"Nothing, I just like looking at you while you're watching everyone. I like seeing the gears turn in that head of yours. It's wonderful," he confessed.

"You're doing that thing again," I said, wishing that I wasn't so affected by him.

"What thing?"

"Saying the perfect thing thing."

Rob laughed, throwing his head back. I wanted to lick his neck. I wanted to kiss him. I wanted him to kiss me.

He stopped laughing and met my gaze.

"Do you wanna—" he started, but I interrupted him.

"Let's get out of here."

He nodded and put down a twenty, then grabbed my hand in his as we walked through the door and out into the night. It had gotten cold, and Rob wordlessly removed his jacket and put it around my shoulders. I grabbed his hand again, and he looked down at me, eyes shifting from my eyes to my lips.

"Is Dani home?" he asked, still looking at my lips.

"No, she's at Craig's."

"Good. Meet you there?"

"Yeah," I said, before pulling his head down and kissing him, thankful for Dani's absences and the quick drive ahead of us. I pulled away and he tried to chase my lips with his, but I turned away and walked towards my car.

"I'll see you in a second," I said, grinning as he ran his hands through his hair.

16

I've been trying to figure out how I should talk about this part of the story with you. You said you wanted the details, I know, but I'm not sure how detailed I should get here. I'm trying to be sensitive.

With that in mind, I'll just try to give you the facts, then. As sensitively as I can. You know where this is going, though. You know what we did that night.

I got to the apartment first and ran to the bathroom, hastily reapplying my deodorant and swirling some mouthwash around my mouth before I heard a knock at the door. I spit the mouthwash out, hurried to the door, and opened it. He was standing there, the look in his eyes even hungrier than before. I'm sure I had the same hunger in mine, but I didn't have much time to think about it because the second I opened the door, he stepped over the threshold and kissed me, grabbing my face between his hands.

We were breathless, breaking apart for a few seconds to try to get more air, but neither of us could stay away from each other for very long— until he brought his hand to my waist and I felt the cold, steel weight of his ring on my skin. Even through the material of the dress, I could feel it. Maybe that's not true, though. Maybe I'm only saying that now, to you.

Either way, something about the awareness of his ring made me freeze, and so he stopped.

"We shouldn't do this," I said, wishing that I didn't mean it.

He brought his hand up to his head, running his fingers through his hair the way I'd been doing seconds before.

"Right. You're right," he agreed, clearing his throat.

"I think you should—" I started to say, but he cut in.

"I should go. Before we do something . . ."

"Stupid," I supplied, trying not to look at his lips.

"I was going to say something else, but I guess 'stupid' works," he said, rubbing his face with his hands.

"Okay," I mumbled, straightening the sleeves of my dress, trying to seem nonchalant, "you should go, then."

"Right," he echoed, opening the door. "I'll see you later, then, okay?"

He exited the apartment just as soon as he'd entered it and I stood there for a moment, my hand on my lips, staring at the closed front door, my ears ringing and my heart pounding through my chest.

I'd done it. I'd stopped myself before we'd done anything . . . stupid. Like a good person might. But if what I'd done was good, why did it feel so shitty?

I didn't have too much time to think about anything, though, because just a few seconds after the door closed, it opened again.

"I should go," he said, his voice hoarse, "I should go, I know I should go, but I don't want to. If you want me to go, though, I can—"

He didn't finish that sentence, though, because I launched myself at his face, grabbing him by the collar and trying to put everything that was running through my mind into our kiss.

Our hands were everywhere as we backed down the hallway and

into my room. On the way, I tripped over the carpet and he caught me, laughing into the kiss. We didn't let my momentary clumsiness stop us, though. We got to my room and I shut the door, more out of habit than anything else, as he kissed my neck.

"You smell so good," he murmured into my neck, through and around kisses.

"Thanks," I said, too distracted by his mouth and his hands and his warmth to come up with anything remotely witty to say.

"What is it?"

"What do you mean?"

"I mean what are you wearing that makes you smell so . . . good?" he asked as he buried his nose further into my neck, taking a deep breath.

"Nothing," I answered, floating on air, "it's just me."

"Fuck." He moaned and resumed his attack on my neck as I pulled on his shirt. My dress came off next, and I sat on the bed in my bra as he stared down at me.

"This is pretty." He hummed and fingered the straps.

"Thanks."

"It's gotta go," he said. And it went.

I'm not sure I should tell you the rest, Ingrid. I know you said you wanted to know . . . okay, here goes . . .

We fucked.

That night was the first time.

And the second.

And the third.

PART II

An Affair to Remember

17

We were in bed, panting and sweaty and tangled up in the sheets and each other, when his phone rang. He picked it up and it was you. I stopped floating right then. And stared at his hand with the ring as he stared at the phone. He waited for one, two, three rings before he silenced the phone and put it back on the bedside table.

We sat in silence for a while, but this wasn't the easy quiet of before. There was an elephant in the room in the shape of you that sucked all the easiness away.

"Do you want to talk about it?" Rob said carefully, and I hated him for his delicacy at that moment.

"Talk about what?" I asked, feigning cluelessness.

"You *know* what."

"I'm gonna go for a smoke. I'll be back in a minute," I said, getting up and throwing on his T-shirt as I ambled down the hallway and out to the porch.

I sat on the chair and lit up, trying to ignore the buzzing in my bloodstream and the ghost of Rob on my skin. Instead, I looked out over my porch, straight ahead into the night sky, and tried not to cry.

The door to the porch opened and Rob came out, in briefs and his jacket. He sat silently in the chair next to mine before he reached over and took a puff of my cigarette.

"I'm sorry," he said simply, and I knew that he was.

"You don't have to apologize. You didn't do anything."

"I know, but I'm still sorry."

"Where does she think you are?"

"Work, probably. She won't be suspicious if that's what you're asking," he reassured me, but it wasn't all that reassuring.

"I wasn't," I said, though that's exactly what I'd been asking.

"Do you want to talk about it?"

"Not really."

"Okay."

We were quiet for a bit and he reached over and took my hand, squeezing it and kissing it once, twice, three times.

"How'd you guys meet?" I asked.

"You really want to know?"

"I don't know. I think so," I said, crossing my arms in the cold.

"I'd just been dumped by Julia, and I was feeling sorry for myself, but a friend invited me to a party, so I went. That's where we met. At a party."

"On a boat?"

"No, not on a boat. It was a party in Los Feliz and we were seated next to each other and we met and started talking and then . . . that was it."

"That was it," I echoed, unsure if hearing about you was making me feel better or worse.

"I'm sorry," he repeated, squeezing my hand again. I squeezed back.

"You guys have been together for a while, then," I said, still not looking at him.

"Ten years. We got married young. Too young, maybe," he said, trying to make a joke, I think, but it wasn't funny. Not to me.

"And you love each other?"

"Maggie . . ."

"Have you done this before?" I'd wanted to ask him this so many times, but before that moment, every time I'd tried to, it felt like the words got lodged in the back of my throat. I'd finally done it, though. I'd asked the dreaded question.

Rob's eyes got wide and I couldn't tell if he was shocked, hurt, or angry; all I knew was that it was hard to look at him and even harder to look away.

"No," he said, his voice thick. Maybe now *he* was the one whose words were getting lodged in his throat. "Do you really think that this is something I do? A regular thing for me? You think I'm a person who just . . . has affairs?"

He wasn't angry. He was hurt. I'd hurt him.

"No," I said quickly, trying to fix it. "I just didn't know."

"I've never done this before," he responded. "I didn't *plan* on doing this. I didn't want to do this, to be this person, to put you in this situation, none of this was planned."

"Okay," I said, because that's all I could think to say.

We sat for a bit, alternating between looking at each other and looking out past the porch at the blue-black sky and the bats soaring through it, but my words, once thick and stuck in my throat, were ready to pour out of me that night.

"Why me?" I asked, almost more scared of the question than the answer. Almost.

"What do you mean?"

"I mean, why me? Was I convenient or easy or, I don't know, just there or something?"

"No." He said it firmly, louder than anything he'd said before. "Look at me."

I did, trying to blink back the tears I felt gathering in my eyes.

"First of all, don't ever think I'm here with you out of anything other than my wanting to be with you, okay?"

"Okay," I echoed, hating how uneven my voice sounded.

"I didn't want to feel this way, I didn't expect it, but we met and you were . . . you were *you* and—"

"And you 'forgot yourself,'" I said, echoing what he'd said to me that night on the boat. The night things started.

"And I forgot myself."

"But why?"

"Because," he said, his voice raw and thick, "I've spent the last three years alone in a marriage that is supposed to a partnership, but it isn't. We live next to each other, you know? Not together. I think when we met, Ingrid and I, we had all these ideas about what marriage was supposed to be, what our marriage was going to be, but they weren't real. And we weren't ready, we were young, *so* young. I met Ingrid when I was new here and missing my family and not knowing what my life was going to be and I needed someone safe. And she'd just gotten out of a relationship too, a long one, and she didn't know how to be alone. She didn't *want* to be alone. And neither did I, so we just . . . clung to each other, but I wasn't happy. Not really. I told myself it was fine, *I* was fine, and for the most part, I believed it. And then *you* showed up, rambling and funny and kind and . . . and I remembered what it felt like to be happy. You make me happy, and I wish you didn't, it's not fair to you and it's not fair to Ingrid, but you do. I don't regret any of this. Do you? Because if you do, I'd understand. I can go and—"

"No, I don't want you to go." I felt myself becoming surer of that as I said the words out loud.

"You don't?" he asked, sounding relieved, which made my answer easier.

"No."

"Okay, good. I'll stay, then."

"Good."

"I'm sorry." This was the third time he'd apologized to me that night, but it was the first time I could feel myself take the words in.

I stood and extended my hand to him. "Let's go to bed."

He took my hand and we walked back to the bedroom, which, just minutes before, had been entirely blissful. The threat of you still hovered in the room, but it was smaller. Rob wrapped his arms around me and kissed me on the forehead, my cheeks, and my lips. Quick, tender kisses.

We climbed into bed and he wrapped himself around me as I let the warmth of him seep into my bones.

I don't remember my dreams from that night. I know I had them, some startling enough to wake me up in the middle of the night, but I forgot them. They drifted out of my mind the second I opened my eyes and saw Rob, sleeping soundly, legs twisted in between mine, arm stretched out over my body.

I looked at him for a moment, still wrapped in the cloud of sleep, and felt something inside of me settle.

When people talk about falling in love, often they'll say things clicked into place. I didn't have that. It was more like things relaxed. Everything I'd been holding on to was suddenly filled with air, and I didn't feel quite as crowded as I had before. My thoughts get quieter when I'm in love, I guess.

It's like when you're looking at a picture of a busy street, filled with cars and people and all their lives and worries and thoughts, and at first, it's overwhelming, it's too busy for you to see anything but the sum of its parts, but once you zoom in, everything gets clearer. Suddenly the blurs you were looking at aren't blurs, they're people, and you feel a connection to it. The bigness doesn't seem so big anymore.

I traced his lips with my fingers gently, so as not to wake him, and closed my eyes, drifting back to sleep.

I think about that moment a lot. There was nothing deeply profound about it; we were in bed and only one of us was conscious (and barely conscious, at that), but it was one of the first moments I'd felt peaceful in a long time. I felt grounded in my body, there in my bed that was too small to fit the man sleeping soundly beside me.

I never told him about that moment. I didn't know what there was to say about it, but I wanted to share it with you. Funny, the things I never felt like telling him but I want to share with you.

I woke up again later, once the sun was up and shining through my curtains. Rob was still sound asleep, his breath tickling my face. I looked at the clock and let out a laugh; it was well past nine a.m. I'd slept for eight hours. Like a regular, healthy person. Like I used to every night before Jackson.

18

Rob mumbled something in his sleep and I looked down at him again. My mouth watered and I got up, quietly so as not to wake him, and walked into the kitchen, looking out the window, trying to contain my grin.

"Morning," I heard Rob say behind me. I froze.

"Hi," I said, turning towards him. He smiled and I smiled back.

Rob walked over to the kettle to start making tea. He smiled a lazy smile that made my stomach flip.

"Morning," he repeated.

"Hi."

"You look beautiful," he said, and I laughed because I was sure that wasn't the case, but the way he was looking at me, all soft and lazy, I got the sense that maybe he thought it was.

"You don't look too bad yourself," I replied, and it was true. If anything, it was an understatement. He was rumpled and smiling and he looked entirely edible.

I walked over to him and he kissed me quickly, gently.

"Did you sleep at all, or am I experiencing you on your usual five hours?" he asked, mouth still pressed against the crown of my head, the very top of me.

"Actually," I said, grinning, "you're experiencing me on a full eight hours today."

He laughed and his smile was too big for his face. He looked like a kid, right then at that moment.

"Really?"

"Uh-huh."

"Maggie, that's . . . that's amazing."

"I'm feeling a little weird by just how excited you are to hear I slept an entirely normal amount," I said, grabbing some water from the fridge.

"Normal for most people. Not for you, though," he responded, pouring the now-boiling water into his mug. "That's good. I'm happy for you."

"Me too," I said. "You were too warm to stay awake next to, so I think this victory belongs solely to you." I tried to make it sound casual, but there's nothing casual about telling a married man he's the only reason you got any sleep the night before.

"I'm flattered." I knew he meant it by how softly he said it.

"Don't let your head get too big, though. You talk in your sleep and it woke me up."

"I do *not*!"

"Okay, maybe not, but still, no need to get too pleased with yourself. I was tired, it could've been a fluke," I reasoned, stubborn as ever.

"Maybe," he agreed, though I knew he didn't believe it. Neither did I, but I needed to hide behind something; it had been a while since I was good at being open and vulnerable first thing in the morning with a shirtless guy in my kitchen.

Jackson used to stay up most nights; he said it was a holdover from his pre-sobriety days. At night he'd come to bed with me and stay there until

I fell asleep, either reading or telling me stories he'd make up. I never asked him what he did when I was asleep and he never told me. Craig said he used to see him on the porch some nights, listening to music and reading book after book.

In the mornings he'd crawl back into bed, finally falling asleep around six, right when I'd get up. I tried to stay up with him a few times, but every attempt always ended the same way: with me falling asleep on the couch as he sat, nocturnal, reading.

I didn't think much about the fact that since his death, I'd taken on his sleep patterns, probably because the concept was too sad and too difficult for me to stomach, but it was impossible to completely ignore.

"Do you want breakfast?" Rob asked, heading to the fridge. "I'm starving."

"You don't have to cook, you know," I said, hoping he wouldn't take me at my word. I wanted the domesticity that came with him cooking me breakfast. I wanted it more than breakfast.

"I know I don't *have* to. I *want* to," he said, pulling the eggs out of the fridge. "Eggs good?"

"They're great."

"Okay, go back to bed."

"What?"

"You heard me, back to bed!"

"Why?"

"Because I want to serve you breakfast in bed, that's why," he answered, grinning.

"But why?"

"Because it seems romantic and I'm in a romantic kind of mood. Indulge me."

I sighed, pretending to be disadvantaged by his sudden romantic urge, and walked back to bed, crawling under the blankets that were still warm and, more importantly, still smelled like him.

I closed my eyes, inhaling the scent, wishing I could turn it into perfume and laundry detergent and air freshener.

He came in ten minutes later, with a cup of what I knew to be too-weak coffee and a plate of scrambled eggs.

"Wow." I didn't know what else to say.

"Eat up," he said, "I've been wanting to do this for a while."

"Have you really?

"Yes. For longer than I care to admit."

I hadn't realized how love starved I'd been until that moment, when we were on my bed in rumpled sheets, barely clothed, still smelling like each other and eating food he had made for me, for us. There, in my room, on my bed, we were an "us." You didn't exist. Jackson didn't either. Our us-ness rendered everything and everyone else invisible.

19

I couldn't stop looking at him. I wished, for the first time ever, that my room was full of mirrors, so that I could look at the two of us, in bed, staring at each other. I couldn't decide if I liked the feeling of his eyes on me better when I was looking at him or when I wasn't.

He stayed on the bed as I packed for Lucy's. I packed slowly, luxuriating in the feeling of his eyes on me as I folded shirts, dresses, packed bras and underwear that had never felt as sexy as they did right then at that moment, as he watched me hold them.

We left the apartment at the same time, arm in arm, and he walked me to my car, where he kissed me twice on the forehead and once on the mouth. I watched him out of my rearview mirror as I drove away, smiling so wide I thought my cheeks would fall off my face.

The first thing I did when I got to Lucy's was get in the shower, even though I didn't want to rinse any trace of the night before off my body.

I did, though, letting the water wash over me before getting out, toweling off, and going straight into the pool, which, while counterintuitive, felt like absolutely the right thing to do.

As I swam, I thought about how much I wanted to go across the street, poke around your house, rifle through your things, and gather details about you. Your perfume, maybe, or deodorant. Or at least find out what kind of clothes you wore. I had this idea that if I knew more about who you were, who you *are,* I would feel less haunted by the ghost of you. I didn't snoop. But I remained haunted by you. The mystery of you.

When I got out of the pool, Dani called. I answered, instantly feeling like I was in trouble for something.

"Hello?"

"Are you at the canyon house?" Dani asked airily.

"Mm-hmm."

"How is it?"

"Incredible. I may never leave."

"Don't make promises you can't keep." She laughed.

"Yessir. What's up?"

"Nothing, just miss you. What'd you do last night?"

It was an innocent question, a question I'd been expecting, but as soon as she asked, I was struck by a wave of panic. She knew. She *must* know, otherwise why would she have called, right?

"Nothing," I lied, "went to Pearl's, grabbed a drink, went home."

It wasn't exactly a lie; I'd done all those things. And besides, an exclusion of one *minor* detail wasn't exactly a lie, so I felt okay about it. Kind of.

"Nice," she said, meaning it. I wanted to throw up.

"Yeah. Nice. Uneventful," said I, the liar. "What about you and Craig? Anything fun?"

"Not really. We had dinner with Joey and watched a movie."

"Anything good?"

"I'm not sure. I fell asleep ten minutes in."

"Shocking," I teased.

"It was late, don't start! Anyway, I was just calling to check in. I miss you."

"I miss you too. I'll see you soon. I might be back to grab some stuff tomorrow, probably," I mumbled.

"Good. I'll see you then."

"Love you."

"You too."

I hung up and jumped back into the pool, trying to swim the guilt of my lies away. It didn't work. So, tired and wet and guilty, I wandered into the kitchen, in search of food heavy enough to drown the guilt living in my stomach.

Rob called me after I'd finished a pizza. And had some beer. And some ice cream. And pita chips. And watched six hours of a show whose plot I refused to follow.

"You're supposed to be working," I said, smiling as I picked up the phone.

"Let's try this again. You're meant to say hi when you answer the phone, Maggie."

I sighed through my grin. "Hi."

"Hi."

"You're supposed to be working," I repeated, still grinning.

"My next client's not for another twenty minutes. I've got nothing but time."

"You've got twenty minutes of time."

"You know, if you keep talking about how little time I've got, I may start thinking you don't want to talk to me," he chided.

"No, I do."

"You do?"

"I do."

"Good. How's the house?"

"It's wonderful. Very cozy." I sighed, hiding my face in one of the many beige pillows on the couch.

"Have you used the pool yet?"

"I have."

"And?"

"I'd live in it if I could."

"You're making me jealous now," he said, and I could hear his smile.

"Jealous of what? Me or the pool?"

"Both," he answered.

"How's work?"

"It's good. It's fine. I just gave someone a portrait of Bill Hader on their thigh, which was . . . interesting."

"Their thigh?!"

"Mm-hmm. A big one, too."

"The thigh or the tattoo?"

"The tattoo," he said, chuckling.

"Hmm," I murmured, "staring at Bill Hader for an hour sounds idyllic."

"You wound me," he cried, not sounding at all wounded. "You like Bill Hader more than me."

"I wouldn't go *that* far." I paced around the house, trying to decide if it was worth getting into bed yet or if I should wait it out for another few hours. "What time are you off work? If I can't get Mr. Hader, I guess I'd settle for you."

"I'm off at two, so it's a late one. Will you be up?" he asked softly, and my heart warmed up.

"Probably," I said, yawning.

"Maggie."

"Robert."

"You're yawning."

"Only a little bit," I said, yawning again.

"You're tired. Get some sleep. I'll see you tomorrow, yeah?"

"I'm not *that* tired," I lied, trying, unsuccessfully, to suppress another yawn.

"You are. Go sleep. Call me in the morning. I'm not working tomorrow till five, so I'll be around."

"But—"

"You need sleep, Maggie. Get some rest."

"Fine," I replied, "maybe Bill's around. I'm sure he lives somewhere over here."

"Yes," he said, smiling, "go call up your man Mr. Hader and have him entertain you."

"Maybe I will."

"Goodnight, love."

I grinned.

"What?" he asked.

"You called me 'love.'"

"I did. Do you not like it?"

"No, I . . . it's nice. I like it," I confessed.

"Goodnight, love," he said again, stretching the *love* out long and loud.

"Goodnight."

I hung up, still grinning, and walked into the guest room, where I fell asleep ten minutes into a movie about men with communication issues. I don't remember the title, but I think it was a movie my dad loved.

20

I woke up a little before three a.m., crying. I'm not sure why. I don't remember my dream, but I'm sure Jackson was somehow involved. Or Rob. Or you. Or some combination of the three. But I found myself awake, and I figured Rob was too, so I called him. He picked up on the second ring.

"You're awake. Why are you awake?"

"Well, I fell asleep for a bit—"

"And then?"

"And then I woke up," I answered.

"I see. Hader didn't come over, then?"

"No. Are you home?"

"I am."

"Are you tired?"

"Nope," he said.

"Wanna—" I started but was interrupted by the sound of the door-bell. "Hold on a second," I said, getting out of bed and going towards the door.

I looked through the keyhole and was met by the sight of Rob, still in his clothes, phone to his ear.

"Are you gonna let me in or what?"

I opened the door, the phone still to my ear.

"Hi," I breathed out.

"Hi," he answered, hanging up, then crossing the threshold and kissing me softly.

I put my phone down and brought my hands up to the sides of his face, breathing him in. We broke apart after a while and he took his shoes off.

Then he took my hand and kissed my cheek, and we walked into the guest room. He pulled me onto the bed and into his body, where I curled up, trying to get as close to his neck as possible.

"How was the rest of the night?" I asked.

"It was fine. Just a few small tattoos tonight."

"Mmm," I murmured, soaking up the warmth of our closeness.

"You really slept?"

"I did."

"You promise?"

"I swear," I said, crossing my heart. Rob smiled, taking my heart-crossing hand and kissing it once, twice, three times.

We woke up around the same time; the sun was streaming through the windows we had forgotten to block with Lucy's blackout curtains. My back was to Rob, and I closed my eyes, pretending to be in a deep, steady sleep. I'm not sure why, really. I just wanted to see what he'd do when he thought I wasn't yet awake to the world.

He shifted up, humming and stretching. The sheets moved with him, falling from my arms, but he pulled them back up over me, tucking me in. I felt him prop himself on his elbow and, by the heat of his eyes, I could tell he was staring at my back. I made my breathing steady and even to keep my little ruse up, and as I did so, he leaned down and kissed my bare shoulder softly, so as not to wake me. His fingers ghosted over my outline, and I felt the edges of my body bleed into the air, trying to rise up to meet his skin.

When I was with him, I felt like my molecules forgot that they were hemmed in by the physical boundaries of my body. Borders didn't seem to exist with him. Or maybe they did, they were just further away. The borders weren't at the edges of my body, they existed someplace in the space between us.

I'm not sure how much longer we went on like that, with him lightly touching and stroking my skin and me pretending to be asleep, but by the time I opened my eyes again, the sun had risen higher in the sky and the birds outside had quieted their morning lullabies.

I keep coming back to that moment, that morning, the two of us quiet and private in small, nonverbal declarations of love, meant just for ourselves. There's something vital within that moment. Everything not said, maybe, or else it's the fact that we were both experiencing private moments of intimacy, moments not meant to be shared with anyone but that happened right next to each other, under the same roof and in the same bed that smelled so much like . . . *us.*

I'm not really sure why I'm talking about it right now, actually. I just wanted to share it with you. You asked me to spare no details, so I'm trying my best. Besides, you are as entitled to hearing about our private moments of intimacy as you are our public ones, I suppose. I haven't even told Dani about this. Or my therapist. Or Pearl.

I had a feeling that keeping all of this, keeping *us,* a secret was what made it special. It was just ours, something that was kept safe from a world full of people with opinions and worries and judgments. There were no double dates or social media posts or exposure to the outside world. We do have two Polaroids, though. No one's seen them; they weren't taken for anyone, just for us. We took them at Lucy's, actually. In that guest bedroom with the blackout curtains. Neither of us is looking at the camera; we're both looking at each other, grinning with our bed heads, naked.

21

Ours was an isolated, insular love, and for a while, no one was the wiser. It was just us. The presence of you had somehow faded. Although that's not the case anymore.

At Pearl's wedding, my mom made a speech. She was drunk and mad that my father had brought Ana, so the speech was full of barbed jokes and comments about how she hoped Jonah wouldn't run off with a "newer, shinier model." But she did say one thing that stuck with me: "Love shouldn't be kept from the world, it should be displayed and celebrated. Real love doesn't diminish everything else. It adds to the beauty of the world. It doesn't make other people feel more alone, it enriches them. It warms them. It gives them hope. How can love do that if it's not shared?"

I keep coming back to that. I'm not sure if I've ever had that kind of love. The kind that doesn't feel threatened by prying eyes. The kind that warms and enriches those who aren't central to it. I want it, though.

I want the steady kind of love Pearl has with Jonah, or Dani has with Craig.

Instead I keep finding these men with their addictions and demons, and I try to make it into that kind of steady love, but it hasn't worked yet.

It's like trying to squeeze your foot into a shoe a half size too small. You can walk around in them, but by the end of the day, your feet are tired and sore and blistered, and your walk is strained, unnatural. I am tired of living in discomfort and pretending to everyone, even myself, that I am fine.

For a while I thought that my time with Rob was all slow kisses and steady sleep. Until I put my finger on the truth: even while I was blissfully, deeply in love with him, there was a pulse of anxiety. He wasn't mine, not really. He was yours. Or maybe that's not true, maybe he was entirely his own person, but while I was handing him my heart on a silver platter, he was giving me morsels of his love, and it was good, it really was, but it wasn't enough. How could it be, when it was a love we couldn't share with anyone? And as long as he was with you, I knew it was all only temporary.

He gave me all the time and attention and affection and love that he could. But he couldn't give me everything, because he'd already given it to you. The love he had to give was yours. You were entitled to it, I wasn't. I'm not bitter about it, though, because everything we shared was sweet and good and felt like *mine*. It wasn't enough, but I think the truth is, it was all I could handle at the time.

In recalling it all to you now, in telling you this, *our* story, I'm only just now discovering what it is that I want, and what love, *real* love, looks like. Now that I've seen it, had moments of it, morsels of it, I don't want anything else.

22

I didn't enter your house until I'd been at Lucy's for a week. Rob had moved in too, and so I ducked Dani's calls and told her I was "super busy with auditions."

It was a lie, of course. Another in a string of lies I'd told her since that first night on the boat. I didn't have any auditions that week, actually. I spent my days in the pool, or else in bed with Rob.

We cooked and ate our meals on the deck or in bed, and I started falling back into the pattern of sleeping regularly. I didn't dream about Jackson once.

Then on the seventh day at Lucy's, we were in bed, and I was sitting in between his legs, my back to his chest, when I said that the only thing missing from Lucy's house was a bathtub.

"A bathtub," he marveled, "really?"

"Yes, really. I love bathtubs. I'd live in a tub if I could."

"Hmm," he said, "interesting."

"Is it?"

"A little," he said, and I could feel him smile into the top of my head. "You know, I've got a tub at the house."

"Do you?" I asked, unsure of where he was going.

"I do. A big one."

"Quit bragging."

"I was actually about to offer it to you, but if you aren't interested . . ."

I tensed up. He'd said it so casually, as though there was nothing strange about my entering his house, *your* house, to take a bath.

I started to laugh. There was nothing else to do, in my eyes. How was I supposed to react to my married boyfriend inviting me over to the house he shared with his wife for me to bathe?

"What?" he asked, a little defensively. "It's there, it's not being used, you want a bath. It's not *that* funny, is it?"

"No," I said, still laughing, but less so than before. "It's definitely not funny."

"You don't have to use it, I just . . . I don't know, I thought that I'd put it out there."

"You thought you'd just casually invite me to your wife's house?"

"It's not *just* her house. I live there too, you know," he said it gently, like a parent might when explaining something to their child.

"Right. I know that, but—"

"It's weird. It's weird, I get it. Forget I said anything, yeah? We don't have to go there. We don't have to talk about it," he muttered.

I realized then that he wanted me to go there, to your house. He wanted me to see his world, his home. He was trying to share another part of himself with me, and I was too consumed by thoughts of you to realize it.

"No," I said, "it's not that weird. I mean, it is a little bit, but let's go. I'd love to see it."

"Yeah?"

"Yeah."

"You're sure it's not too—"

"No, let's go. Show me the tub."

So we stood and padded over to the house, not bothering to put shoes on. We didn't have much of a journey, so shoes seemed unnecessary. I could feel my palms sweating as we left Lucy's house. I locked and relocked the front door, trying to stall for time.

I know it sounds absurd, but the whole time we walked across the street, with Rob a few feet ahead of me, looking every which way to see if your neighbors were out before motioning to me that the coast was clear, I expected to find you in the house, sitting on a couch, drinking tea in a robe and writing a poem. I was almost disappointed when Rob opened the door and revealed that, as expected, there was no one home.

I'd never seen so many books in one space before. They were everywhere; it was like you lived in a library. Rob took my hand and led me through the rooms, not giving me nearly enough time as I'd have liked to soak it all in, but I understood his rush. He was as nervous as I was. His hands, typically dry and calloused, were clammy.

I'd have my chance to drink it all in later, anyway. I just didn't know it at the time.

He led me down the hallway and into the bathroom, which housed, as promised, a tub. Not just a tub, though. *The* tub. You have the platonic ideal of a bathtub: deep and big and claw-footed. It took my breath away. It turned me on a bit, actually.

"So," he said, voice gravelly, "this is the tub."

"Wow. It's beautiful," I whispered.

He laughed, a big, open-mouthed laugh, and I felt my heart burst and contract and melt and freeze up all at once.

I wanted to kiss him, but kissing him there felt sacrilegious. At least it did at the time. Funny the boundaries we make for ourselves, and then, as quickly as we make them, cross them out.

"I've never seen someone look so awed by a tub," he said. "You're utterly bizarre."

"It's an awe-worthy tub," I said.

"Want to use it?"

"*Now?*"

"Yes, now. We came for the tub. I didn't realize you'd be fine just looking at it."

"Right. Okay, yeah. Is that okay?"

"I wouldn't have offered it if it wasn't okay, love," he said, turning the taps on.

He came back to me, kissed me on the cheek, and watched me as I watched the tub fill. Being there, in your bathroom, a room where you'd been naked, bathed, brushed your hair, your teeth, it felt like I'd finally crossed a line I wasn't meant to cross.

Sleeping with your husband was one thing, but using your bathtub? That felt somehow more personal. I stood still and kept my eyes firmly planted on the water's slow rise. I wanted to look around, I wanted to know what brand of toothpaste you used, or what scent you wore, but I couldn't bring myself to look around too closely yet. Instead, I stared at the water, holding Rob's hand and half listening to him as he talked about work and the process of decorating your house. I let his voice wash over me, hoping that I was nodding and smiling at the right times, when, in reality, I just wanted to lie back in the water and submerge myself.

The water stopped rushing. Rob had turned the taps off. The bath was ready. I forced a smile and tested the water. The temperature was fine. I was fine.

"Are you sure you're all right?" Rob asked, a hint of concern to his voice that hadn't been there before. Or maybe it had been, I just hadn't noticed it.

"Yeah," I said, taking my hair out of its ponytail and shaking my head, trying to get rid of the thoughts that had found their way into my brain. "It's just a little—"

"If you don't feel comfortable here, we can go back," he said, kissing my shoulder, "we can always just go back."

I don't think he realized the weight his words had. All I know is that standing there, in your bathroom, with your husband, I wasn't sure if we could ever go back. I was right, of course. And wrong.

"No, it's fine. It's your house too, right?"

"I can go grab the lease for you to prove it, if that'll help," he offered, smiling softly.

I laughed, and I heard him sigh with relief as I took off my clothes.

I stood there in your bathroom, naked, and looked at Rob before climbing into the water. He gave me a nod and a smile, another declaration of permission. *It's his house too, it's his house too,* I repeated to myself as I let the water lap around my body.

"Do you want some privacy, or—"

"Could you stay?" I asked, trying not to feel too much like a child. "I'm okay, I'll be okay, I just . . . I don't know."

"I'm here," he said, sitting on your—*his*—stool next to the tub, "I'm right here."

"Okay," I said, "good."

I dipped even lower into the water, then, letting it cover my face. I kept my eyes open, looking up through the water at Rob, who sat still, watching me right back. Something about the water and his stare made me come back to myself. I'm still not sure why. I raised myself and, head bobbing above the water, wiped my eyes and smiled.

"What?" Rob asked, confused.

"You were right. This is a really good tub."

Rob smiled too, and I felt myself dissolve into the water as the ghost of you and everything you represented faded from my mind.

"I told you so," he said.

"You sure you're okay just sitting there? If you have work or something—"

"I'm good right here. I promise," he said, leaning down to kiss me.

I should be less open about how much my sense of security comes from whether or not the men in my world are attracted to me, or how much they desire me, but I'm not. Not all the way, at least.

All I can really say is that Rob settled me in a million ways, but perhaps the biggest one was in his desiring of me. I'm sure my therapist would have a *lot* to say about that, but I wouldn't know, I still haven't told her about this. I guess that's a good marker of how much shame I still feel about it all. You know it's bad when you won't tell your therapist about it.

I think I have this feeling that my sexuality, my desirability, isn't for me. It's for other people, namely men, to track. It's for them to hold, to touch, to look at, to fantasize about. That's a problem, isn't it? That's something for me to think about working on. I'll get to it one of these days.

We left your house pretty much as soon as I was out of the bath. My hair was still wet when we made our voyage back across the street to Lucy's, me ahead of him this time, where we crawled back into bed and stayed there for a while.

Rob called in sick the next day, and we lazed around in bed, leaving only to make tea and get snacks for sustenance. I'd stopped drinking coffee around Rob, sneaking it when he wasn't around the way I imagined Jackson had done with his drugs.

I didn't ever want to leave that bed. I didn't ever want to leave the canyon. The second I did, I knew that the reality of the situation would sink in. In the bed in the canyon, we were just like any other couple, spending our days tangled up in each other, talking about everything and nothing, trying to soak up every minuscule detail the other revealed, but back out there, in the real world, the truth would show its ugly face to me.

You were coming back soon; I knew that, so did Rob, but we didn't talk about it, not yet. The inevitability of your return loomed on the horizon, but we distracted ourselves with sex and swims and mugs of tea.

I kept ducking Dani's calls, trying to put everything that existed apart from the canyon, apart from our tiny, beautiful world of two, in a box far far away, where it couldn't reach us.

It worked, for the most part. We lived blissfully, peacefully, until every night at five thirty, when Rob would go outside to the deck to take your call.

I should've been thankful for the routine of it, but I wasn't. It could've been worse, I suppose. You could've called when we were fucking, or laughing, or just lying in bed, staring at each other the way Dani and Craig sometimes did. That used to make my stomach turn until I had someone to do it with myself. I wasn't, though. Thankful.

Your calls, always on time, always at least thirty minutes, turned my insides to lead and made me want to storm across the street and break all your dishes and rip up your clothes. I wanted to pick up the phone myself and tell you that Rob couldn't talk right now because he was busy with *me,* the person he actually, *truly* wanted to spend his days with, not you.

I wanted to tell you that he was lying when he said that he missed you. He didn't at all. He was too busy falling in love with me to miss anyone. I wanted to say you should just extend your trip indefinitely. Go ahead and file for divorce already, because as far as Rob and I were concerned, it was over between the two of you.

Your calls brought out the worst in me.

I never asked Rob what you talked about and he never told me. It wasn't for me to know; it wasn't about me. Whatever you both talked about on your calls existed in a world that belonged entirely to you, and while it may have been naive, at the time I believed the same could be said of my time with him. That's not true, though. It never was. My time with Rob was stolen, not sacred.

23

I can count the number of times we said "I love you" on four hands. Two pairs. His and mine.

I said it first, but I'm not sure if it should count, because he was asleep. Does a confession of love count if only the person confessing it is awake?

It was late and I woke up from a nightmare that you and I were naked, standing in a ballet studio side by side as Rob assessed us both, clipboard in hand. I woke up panting and sweaty and decided I wouldn't eat that day, hating the feeling of being in my body. I sat up, and Rob, still half asleep, tried to pull me back towards him, breathing steadily into the space my chest had occupied on the mattress a second before.

I looked down at his face, a wide-open book of rest and ease and dream, and it just . . . slipped out. Quietly, and in a hoarse, sleep-filled voice, I said it. "I love you."

Rob slept through it and I was glad for it; the words felt girlish and silly, like they belonged on conversation heart candies and not in my mouth, but I said it, and once those words are out there, it's hard to take them back. You know that, though.

Jackson was the first one to say "I love you" when we were together. It was early in the relationship, too early, probably; we'd only been dating two months or so, but we were in his bathroom, a tiny shoebox of a room barely big enough to fit him, let alone both of us at once. If we wanted to brush our teeth at the same time, one of us (most often me) would have to stand in the shower, spitting the toothpaste out down the drain.

It was one of the few rainy nights of November, and Jackson's tin roof picked up the sound of each raindrop as it fell, a sound I loved and he tolerated, and we'd spent the day on the couch in silence, each of us reading books we thought would most impress the other, but it was late and dark and time for bed, so we were in the bathroom.

I was in the shower, in one of his T-shirts, some too-big novelty thing he'd bought as a joke and that I wore when I wanted to feel like a girl-friend, and he was at the sink.

I don't remember what he was wearing; I always seem to picture him in the same thing when I try to remember what we were like when we were a we. So in my imagination, he was in blue jeans and a shirt he'd bought from Art's Deli, his second-favorite restaurant in LA.

We were both brushing our teeth, and when I looked up, he was staring at me. I looked away; then, curious, looked back up. He was still staring.

"What?" I asked, my mouth full of foam.

He spat into the sink before he said, "Nothing, it's nothing."

"You sure?"

"Yeah, I'm sure," he said, still staring.

"If you insist," I said, looking back at the drain.

"I love you," he blurted out, and I looked back at him, my ears ringing.

"What?" I asked.

"I love you. That's why I was staring. I . . . yeah. Love you."

It was my turn to spit. The toothpaste foam fell right down the drain, a perfect shot.

"You love me," I echoed back to him, looking up at him through the half-drawn shower curtain.

"Yeah. You don't have to say it back or anything, that's not why I said it, I just didn't want to keep not saying it, you know?"

"Yeah," I said, slowly, "I know."

"Okay," he said, clapping his hands and laughing a bit, "so that's that, then."

"That's that," I echoed again, dumbfounded.

We didn't talk about his confession that night. He didn't push me to say it back, and I didn't, at least not for a while.

I waited a few weeks, not for waiting's sake, just because I wasn't sure if I felt it until I knew that I did.

I said it to him after we'd gone to see Pearl and Harper and Jonah for what they said was just a regular lunch, but I knew it to be a ploy for them to finally meet Jackson.

I drove and he sat next to me, trying to seem calm, but he was nervous the entire car ride there; I could tell by the way he kept rubbing his hands up and down the legs of his jeans, up and down, up and down, a rhythm that seemed to calm him while driving me nuts. I hated the sound of it, but I knew it settled him, so I turned up the music and focused on the road ahead.

He did well, that day with Pearl and Harper and Jonah. He listened to Pearl's stories of our youth, laughing at all the right moments, and he and Jonah bonded over their love of Murakami, but that wasn't what made me sure. It was the way he was with Harper that did it.

After lunch, Harper took his hand and dragged him wordlessly to her bedroom, where she made him read her story after story, and he did it, giving each character a voice, providing commentary when he felt it necessary, taking time to point out things he liked in each illustration. I only know this because every once in a while, I'd poke my head in to see it, before Harper kicked me out, stating emphatically that this story-time session was for her and Jackson only.

"Yeah, Mags, this is just for the cool kids," Jackson stated, and Harper glowed at hearing that she was, in Jackson's eyes, cool.

Something about seeing him with Harper, so game and kind, did it. I knew. I knew that this feeling I had swimming inside me was love, real and actual love, not infatuation or attraction. I didn't realize how I hadn't known it earlier, and, after realizing it now, I wanted to get us back into the car, away from Pearl and Jonah and Harper, so I could tell him.

I said it as soon as we got in the car, only an hour after I'd been kicked out of story time. Jackson wasn't even all the way in the car, actually, when I said it.

"I love you," I exclaimed, and Jackson stilled, one foot in the car, the other on the pavement.

"I love you," I repeated, slower this time, relishing the way the words sounded. Jackson looked at me, expressionless, before getting in the car, taking his time.

"What?" I asked, defensively. "You said it too. You said it before me. Am I not allowed to say it too?"

I made to put the car in drive, but Jackson reached a hand out, stopping me.

"I love you too," he said, softly, "obviously I do. I was just surprised. You caught me off guard."

"Well, I didn't mean to. You caught me off guard that time too, you know. And I didn't think it was unexpected or anything," I said.

"You are absolutely allowed to say it too. You're actually required to, now."

"Okay, then," I said, putting the car in drive. Jackson didn't stop me this time. "I love you then."

"Good," he responded, laughing.

"Quit laughing at me!"

"I'm sorry, I'm not. You're just funny."

"What's so funny about me loving you? It doesn't feel funny."

"It's not, you just sounded so . . . *frazzled* when you said it. *That* was funny, not the words themselves."

"Oh," I said.

We sat in silence on the 405 for a bit before we pulled off the freeway into a quiet, residential street, where we proceeded to fuck in the Fiat, and he had to drive the rest of the way back because my feet were numb and my heart was full and I couldn't stop laughing.

24

Before I told a not-sleeping Rob I loved him, I'd almost said it to him several times. The almosts don't count though, do they?

A list of things I knew I loved about Rob before I told him I loved him:

1. The way he looked at me. It made my heart pound and I wanted to sit in that feeling forever.
2. His pet names for me. Every. Single. One. Of. Them.
3. The way he sang along to songs in the car, with his beautiful, raw voice and his love of Van Morrison, who I'd decided was a genius.
4. His kindness. Henry hadn't been kind. Neither was Jackson, really. Kindness was much hotter than dickishness.
5. The way he said my name.
6. The way he kissed me.
7. The way he touched me.
8. That thing he did with his mouth right below my ear.

The first time Rob said it to me, we were at the beach on one of his days off. We'd driven there early in the morning and packed a bag with beers and iced teas and chips. It was right as the sun was starting to set, and we'd both been in and out of the water between naps and kisses and skimmed books, our hair salt soaked and our scalps warm.

We were on the sand, and Rob was stroking my sea-tangled hair, gently undoing knots and lulling me into an almost sleeplike state.

"This is nice," I murmured, my voice just loud enough for him to hear.

Rob hummed in agreement, still stroking my hair.

"I love it here," he said.

"Me too."

"I really love it here. I love . . . I love you," he confessed, and I turned, looking up at him from my spot between his legs.

"You do?"

"I do," he said, smiling wide, "I love you most of all."

"More than the beach?"

"More than the beach."

"More than the sunset?"

"Much more than the sunset."

"More than . . ." But I trailed off, not wanting to let myself say the one thing I wanted to know. *More than your wife?* is what I wanted to ask, but I didn't. Instead, I said, "I love you, too."

Rob's smile got even wider and he leaned down to kiss me, but our smiles were too big and our glee too consuming for the kiss to be one worth describing. Rob loved me and I loved him, and the sun was setting and the ocean was churning and in that moment the world was ours, just ours.

That day was my last one at Lucy's. I would be returning to the apartment and the world that lingered outside its walls. I went back to Dani and he went back to you.

PART III

Love with You

25

Dani greeted me at the apartment with open arms and new incense sticks that reeked of body odor and saffron.

"I feel like I haven't seen you in centuries," she cried, opening the door and grabbing one of my bags.

"I know," I said, trying to feel happy to be home. "I know, I'm sorry," I added, because I didn't know what to say, didn't know how to tell her that right then, I was absolutely, positively not where I wanted to be.

"These are new," she said, fingertips brushing a few not-faded-enough hickeys on my neck.

My cheeks flushed. My heartbeat quickened.

"Oh," I said, trying to figure out just how to lie quickly and lie well. "Yeah. Bad date."

"With who?" she asked, pulling me onto the couch with her. For once, she was not on my lap but on her own cushion.

Fuck. Follow-ups. I should've prepared for that. I should've practiced answers and looks of nonchalance.

"No one. No one. Just some guy. No one important," I said, you know, like a liar might.

"And what's the deal with this one? Another training wheel?"

I forced out a laugh, but it came out choked and hacking, more like a cough than anything. Dani looked at me, cocking her head.

My hands were sweating. I'd forgotten how to be around her. I'd forgotten how to be around anyone other than Rob.

Let's not get into how thoroughly pathetic that sounds.

It was true, though. At the time, at least. I felt totally, entirely unmoored without Rob.

I forgot how to be a person who wasn't being touched constantly, or else gazed at or whispered to or held. I didn't remember how to spend my days if they didn't begin and end in bed with Rob and his smell and his hands and his constant, steady breathing.

I didn't know that yet, though. It was my first day back. All I knew was that I couldn't look Dani in the eyes, and all I wanted in the world was just up the hill, back in the canyon.

"Mags?" I heard Dani ask me, her voice sounding far away.

"Yeah? What did you say?"

"I asked if it was another training-wheel guy. You okay, Spoon?"

"Yeah! To both. Training wheel and the other thing. I'm good," I said, remembering the feeling of coming home from parties in high school when you're drunk and talking to your parents, not hearing a word they say, just focused on stopping the room from spinning and sounding normal. I don't think I ever did a good job of that.

"All right," she replied, eyebrows still furrowed. I reached out and smoothed the creases in her forehead, a thing I remember my dad used to do to my mom sometimes. I don't think I'd ever seen him do it with the other "flower girls."

"I missed you," I said, and as soon as the words were out, I knew that it was true. I hadn't remembered that she was a person to miss until she was right in front of me, with her cocked head and furrowed brow and unsmoothable forehead creases. I'd missed her.

"I missed you too." She smiled, pulling me into her for a hug.

The second I felt her arms around me, I burst into tears. I don't know why. I really don't. Right there on the couch with Dani, I felt like my heart lived inside my throat and that every feeling I'd ever had in my life was surging and swelling inside me, and I wanted those feelings to get the fuck out of my body and my heart and my brain.

I was exhausted.

Figures that after over a week of sleeping more than I had in months, I'd be exhausted, right? I was, though. Tired. Bone-tired.

I wanted so many things, Ingrid. I still do, but my wanting feels more like an engine than an anchor these days. You can use that for a poem if you want to. It seems like the kind of sentence that would show up on a poetry Instagram, which I hate, but it doesn't make it any less true.

Dani stroked my hair and asked me what was wrong, but I used the magic word that was a surefire way of getting her to drop the conversation, which, as I'm sure you've guessed, is Jackson.

I know it was a shitty thing to do, pretending to be crying over my dead ex while in reality, I was crying about everything, including my very married boyfriend. I still don't know what to call him. Maybe *that's* what I was crying about.

26

Rob called me that night after I'd convinced Dani I was okay, or okay enough to be left alone, and I picked up almost instantly.

"I miss you." He groaned into the phone.

I grinned, forgetting about my tears and listlessness.

"I miss you too."

"Come back."

"Lucy's home, I can't."

"Not to Lucy's, come here. Come to mine."

"I can't do that," I said, feeling the tears return.

"Why not?"

"Because Dani'll get suspicious. She's already suspicious, I think. I have to be here. For tonight at least."

He groaned again, stretching it out for dramatic effect, and I sank into the armchair, trying to pretend that this was just like any of our other phone calls. It wasn't, I knew that, but it was a little easier to pretend when he was the one doing the talking.

"Fine," he said, "but I'm afraid I'm going through withdrawal. I'm not used to sleeping without you."

I closed my eyes, repeating what he'd just said to myself over and over, letting the words form a chain in my head, forcing the tears back down.

"Me too" is all I said, my eyes shut to the Rob-less room around me.

"Tomorrow?"

"Tomorrow what?" I asked.

"Can I see you?"

"Uh-huh."

"Good. I love you."

"I love you too," I said. "I've gotta go now."

"Okay," he said, "then go."

I didn't hang up. Neither did he. We stayed that way, reveling in each other's silence for a few minutes. I know how that sounds, but that's just how we were, I guess. We loved each other when there were things to say and we loved each other when there was nothing to say.

27

A list of places I told Dani I was going to, when, in reality, I was seeing Rob: the movies, an audition, my sister's house, running errands, dentist appointment, doctor's appointment, boxing class, a hike, lunch with friends, a date, a house-sitting job.

I went from being a person who couldn't get enough time with her best friend to someone who avoided her constantly. I didn't know how to keep secrets from her; she was the one person I never kept anything from, and so I kept my distance to keep my secret.

If we spent time together, *real* time together, I knew she'd get it out of me one way or the other, and I wasn't ready for that, so instead I avoided her by sneaking into the apartment when I knew she'd be sleeping or doing yoga or at Craig's, avoiding her calls, and faking headaches when we found ourselves alone in the apartment.

I felt horrible about it, but I also felt, in a way, that I was protecting her from it. Maybe that's not true, though. Maybe I was just too scared of what her reaction would be, and so my avoidance was strictly selfish.

I do know that, as much as I wanted to share this with Dani, I felt like I didn't deserve to have anyone share in my guilt, my happiness, my anything when it came to my relationship with Rob. I was doing a bad, horrible thing, and so I deserved to be alone in it.

In the two weeks before you returned to LA, I used each and every one of these lies multiple times, disappearing for a few hours some days or the entire night on others. In reality, though, I was at your house. With your husband. You know this. Dani didn't.

I'd gotten over the fear of being in your house after my third time there. What is it people say about when you draw a line in the sand and get closer and closer to it, until one day you've crossed it, and you've gone so far from the line that you turn your head, look back, and think to yourself, *Didn't there used to be a line somewhere over there?*

That's what happened with me. My first few times, I walked in slowly, trying to take up as little space as I could, trying not to let my eyes linger on any one thing for too long, other than Rob and his mouth and that thing he does with his hands, but that dissipated after a while.

The fourth time I went over, telling Dani I was off to "a quick house-sitting gig, just a one-night thing," I walked into the house without first knocking on the door. I kicked my shoes off and launched myself into Rob's arms, speaking, for the first time in your house, at a volume louder than a whisper.

I looked at everything. I saw everything. We use the same shampoo, the same moisturizer too, and you stock your pantry with all the same things I do. Those similarities charmed me, back then. I never pointed them out to Rob or asked him if he'd noticed them.

I never did any real snooping, though, save for the time I opened your underwear drawer, curious to see what you wore. I know I'm acting like that doesn't qualify as real snooping, but it's not like I went through your datebook or any of the many notebooks you kept by your side of the bed for when "inspiration struck in the middle of the night," as Rob would say.

I was curious, obviously, but I knew I'd find something that would solidify your place in Rob's world to me, and I didn't want that. Not that you and your place with him wasn't perfectly solid before; it's just that I could ignore it back then. Or pretend to ignore it, at least.

To me, you were his wife in name only, but if I knew the date of your anniversary, or the pieces of poems that had come from him, then you couldn't be so easily ignored. I didn't want that. I wanted to bask in my childlike rationalizations. I wanted to keep you vague and shadowy and villainous.

When I slept at your house, he always took your side of the bed and I'd pretend that this was our house, our bed, our world. With every minute spent there, I was claiming bits and pieces of your connection with Rob. I'd thought I wanted that, back then.

For two weeks I stole hours and nights of your husband's time in your house, and I was happy to do it. I'd return to my apartment, my face flushed and my heart still hammering, my lips itching to share my secrets with Dani, but instead I'd duck my head and futz with my hair and ask her about Craig, distracting her from the love that was surely shooting out of each and every one of my pores.

I was too happy to consider whether she was aware of my lying; it didn't matter, I thought. I was in love, and if I had to lie to keep it, I would.

28

On our last night together before you returned, we had dinner out in the world. This sounds small, but I know you'll understand how major that was for me, for us both.

We had built our relationship behind walls and doors and windows, keeping it away from the world outside and the people in it. Our love was something to be hidden but not that night, though.

Rob picked me up from the apartment (or, more accurately, a block away from the apartment so Dani wouldn't see him; I'd told her I was going out to have dinner with my agents) and he drove us up Laurel Canyon, navigating our tried-and-true route home (sometime during those two weeks, I'd started referring to your place as "home") with one hand on the wheel and the other on my knee, when, instead of turning up to our street, he kept going straight, eyes forward.

"You lost?" I asked, smiling, trying to grin the reality of your arrival away.

"I was thinking we'd do something different tonight, actually," he replied, smiling slightly.

"Like what? Fight club?"

"Like a date," he answered.

"Isn't that what we've been doing?" I asked, confused.

"Not properly. I want to take you out to a dinner that we don't have to cook or clean, where people will see us and we'll be just like any other couple, only much better looking, of course."

"Of course," I agreed, speaking softly because my smile was too big for any real volume.

"Is that okay? Are you all right with that?"

"Yeah. I am perfectly okay with that."

"Good," he said, bringing the hand on my knee over to my hand and squeezing it.

He took me to that place at the foot of the canyon. You know it. I'm sure you guys went there together, sharing a bottle of wine and a starter or two. I didn't think about that on that night, though.

He took my hand and we sat at a table with paper and crayons and a candle that illuminated his face the way my lighter had that night on the boat, and we didn't let go of each other's hands until our waitress brought us our drinks.

He sat facing the room, and he didn't ever say it, but I knew he was surveying the other restaurant-goers, checking to see if there was anyone he knew.

I don't remember what we talked about, that night. I don't remember what we ate or drank. I know it was good, though. All of it.

I felt like I'd swallowed the candle's flame. I was warm throughout my body and my smile felt limitless. I was glowing and he was glowing, and we were sitting at a table, glowing together.

I didn't see who was there until after dinner, when we sat at the table surrounded by empty and half-empty plates, our drinks sipped and swallowed, our hands linked.

Rob was drawing on the paper with the crayons, and I was watching him work, soaking up the way he'd stick the tip of his tongue out between his teeth, brow furrowed in concentration, shoulders hunched. He looked like a little kid when he did that, and I was so distracted by him and his him-ness that I didn't even look at the paper beneath his hands to see what he was drawing.

There was a couple seated at the table behind him, the man's back to me, and the woman facing me. I could only see her because of Rob's focused, slouching posture, but when I looked up, I realized who it was. Elsie. You know, Jackson's ex. The one whose coat I was wearing the night on the boat. The coat I was wearing that night too, at the restaurant, in front of her.

I'd never seen her in person before. When Jackson died, I thought she'd be at the memorial, but as it turned out she'd been in Montauk with Ray, meeting his parents.

She'd posted about it on Instagram. They made her carbonara because they knew it was her favorite, and she'd met the family dog, Dougie. Here she was, though. No longer a two-dimensional figure made up of pixels and Instagram filters; she was here and she was real and she was staring at me the way Jackson had that day in Skylight when we first met.

My breathing got shallow and my eyes watered. I glanced at Rob to see if he'd noticed, but he was still focused on his crayon masterpiece, swept up in artistic inspiration, and so I was alone in this. Just me and Elsie.

I frantically shrugged the coat off, then realized that it would only draw attention to the coat, which I wasn't sure she knew I had, so I put it back on.

I wanted to say something, but what was there to say? I didn't know, don't know. I couldn't stop staring. Neither could she, it seemed, but it didn't faze Ray, who sat back, scanning his splayed-out menu.

I almost got up and went over to their table, but to do what, I didn't know. Hug her, maybe? Laugh? Cry?

I thought about what Jackson would've said if he were there, but I wasn't sure. Somewhere along the line of my being with Rob, I'd lost sight of what Jackson would say or think about things. His voice was no longer in my head. I'd stopped looking at his Instagram, too.

So I didn't do anything. Neither did she. We just looked at each other, staring, until she smiled, a small, tiny sliver of a smile, and nodded slightly. I did the same. What she was trying to tell me in that nod, I'll never know, but it was enough for me, because I looked away, burrowing into the collar of my, *her*, coat and looking instead at Rob's drawing.

It was a portrait of me. A series, actually. Three tiny portraits, one after the other, of me in various moods and expressions.

The first was of me that night on the boat, sitting and smoking with big, sad eyes. The second was me at the beach that day, my lips big and kiss-swollen, my smile wide. The third was me asleep, curled up into a ball and my face open and clear.

They were beautiful. They were spectacular, really. Looking at them, I realized that all that time I'd been watching him, he'd been watching me right back. He'd seen more than I'd realized, and, even more, he'd liked it. He considered me to be beautiful, to be worth studying and memorizing.

He ripped an edge of the paper tablecloth and began tearing the trio out, which he then flipped over, signed, and dated. He looked up, straightening his posture and blocking Elsie from view, before he looked at me and handed me his crayon trio.

"These are . . . ," I said, before trailing off, trying to find the words.

"It's nothing, just a few sketches," he answered, but I knew those were just words. It wasn't nothing. It was a summation of our Ingrid-less time together. A celebration of an easiness that we both knew would vanish the next day.

"I love them," I said, slipping them into my coat pocket, one hand softly caressing the paper, the other hand holding his across the table.

"I love you," he replied, his voice full and crackly.

I looked at him, *really* looked at him, and, like I had with Elsie just moments before, I smiled, nodding slightly. He squeezed my hand, smiling too.

We didn't yet know that that night would be the last one we'd spend like that, with hope and wine and crayon portraits and sex in the car outside your house because we were in too much of a hurry to move ourselves inside, and then sex again inside, this time with me on your side of the bed (that was not intentional, I swear), and then he drove me back to the apartment, holding my hand the whole way.

When we reached my street, he squeezed my hand and looked at me as he put his car in park.

"I love you," he said.

"I love you, too," I replied, because it was true.

"I know things are going to be . . . different. They're going to be difficult, but it won't change anything between the two of us, I swear."

How wrong he was.

"Okay," I answered, staring out the window. I didn't want to look at him; it would make things too hard in what were already hard circumstances.

"I want to leave her," Rob said.

I froze, then turned slowly to face him.

"I do. I wanted to before you came into the picture and I want to now, but Ingrid's been my family for ten years, Maggie. I can't just . . . uproot her life the second she's home. I have to do this right. Just give me some time, okay?"

His eyes were wide as he said it, and he didn't break eye contact with me as he reached for my hand again and squeezed it. I opened and closed my mouth, wanting to say something, to say the *right* thing, but I didn't know what that would be, so I just squeezed his hand back and gave him a slight smile.

"Okay," I answered in a whisper, after a long beat of silence. He moved his hand to my neck and kissed me on the cheek.

"I'll call you, okay? I'll see you soon. Maybe not tomorrow or right away, just because—"

"Because Ingrid. I get it," I said, thinking that I did. "Don't worry, I won't call or anything. I won't go and boil any rabbits or confront her or anything." I was trying to make a joke, trying to be the kind of girl who could joke about these things and really mean it, but Rob didn't laugh, he just sighed and squeezed my hand again.

"I know," he said. "I'll just miss you is all."

"I'll miss you too. You have to go now, though, because I don't want to cry, and if we do the sweet, sappy goodbye thing, I will, so I'm gonna get out and you're gonna go, okay?"

"I love you," he said.

"That's exactly what we're not gonna do," I said, shaking my head and opening the car door.

"I know, I just had to say it one more time."

"Sap."

"Baby."

"Softie."

"Hon."

"Shut up," I said through my teary smile, shutting the door and taking a step backwards to the curb, still looking at him.

"I love you," he said once more through the open car window.

"I love you too," I repeated. "Now get out of here, please." And so he did. He drove off and I stood on the curb, watching as his taillights disappeared on their way to your house, on their way to you.

29

Dani was asleep when I walked into the apartment after standing on the curb for five more minutes, trying to remember the feeling of Rob's hand in mine.

I sat on the porch, staring straight ahead, trying to prepare myself for what your arrival would mean. I thought about Elsie, her stare, her coat, and then I thought of Jackson. I hadn't thought of him much, my mind too occupied by thoughts of Rob for anyone or anything else, but Rob was off to you, and so my thoughts drifted back to Jackson.

I guess I should get into how we ended—Jackson and I—shouldn't I? It's come up, obviously, in bits and pieces, but I've been putting off talking about it and I'm not sure I should anymore.

We'd been together for a while and were in what Dani used to call "the shit-or-get-off-the-pot stage."

He'd celebrated his sobriety birthday that day at the beach with the hat and the cake and the love, and two months later I got my tattoo. I should've realized something was up then. I should've been looking for it, taking in the warning signs and the blatant red flags, but, as these stories have made pretty clear, I am very good at making red flags look green.

I later learned that Jackson had started getting high again pretty much the week after his sober birthday. I don't know how or why, because by the time I figured it out, he had one foot out the door.

The tattoo day, he was slow, like his reactions were dipped in amber, suspended in something requiring effort to move through, but I thought it was excitement. *Love can make you slow down*, I thought. *This is just that. He's full of love and excitement and all things good and loving and sober.* I was, in other words, a total idiot.

I knew things were bad when he started spending less and less time at the apartment, saying he was "swamped with work," forgetting that, just days ago, he'd told me he'd scaled back on his hours at the bookstore. I tried not to worry, really, I did. Cool Girl, remember? They don't worry. They don't overthink minor details and fragments of truths and half-truths, but, as we've established over and over again, I'm not a Cool Girl.

When we would see each other, it would be at my apartment always. He said he "liked the vibe there better," but I knew that was bullshit. He'd hated the too-sheer curtains, the upstairs neighbors and their noise-carrying dinner parties, the lack of parking spots . . . I could go on, but I won't.

After a while, I started asking questions. Too late, I know. I confronted him more times than I can count, telling him I was worried about him and I wanted to help, I wanted to be there for him but I couldn't if he wouldn't let me in. I'd cry and plead and yell, and he'd scoff and laugh and throw things and cry too, accusing me of not loving him and making up excuses to leave.

He was the one to leave, though. We were having "the talk" again, though in this case talk really means a tear-filled argument about track marks between toes, cash missing from wallets, and sweating through the sheets. Jackson had started referring to these talks as "the victim hour with Maggie Hoyt." He thought it was funny, made funnier still by how much I hated it.

We were in our third hour of "the victim hour with Maggie Hoyt" when he did it. Ended things. I don't remember what I said, only that something about my tears made him stop yelling. His face froze in an expression of total disinterest, and he scoffed at me, a reaction I'd gotten all too used to.

"Yeah," he said to no one, "this isn't it."

"What do you mean?"

"Us. This isn't it. I'm done. I don't want this shit."

My stomach lurched. I felt like I was going to be sick.

"What?" was all I could think to ask, trying not to puke. Or cry.

"If I wanted to be nagged at, I would move back with my mom. This is fucked. This isn't worth it anymore. It's not fun anymore."

"But you said you loved me," I said, regretting it instantly as those words made two things happen at once: I began to cry, silent, hot tears streaming down my cheeks, and Jackson started to laugh maniacally, itching at his skin and breathing slowly, too slowly.

"I did, didn't I?" he asked, after he'd stopped laughing. "But I say a lot of shit I don't mean."

I sank down to the floor. He left. I stayed like that, sobbing, weeping, yelling, for hours until Dani and Craig got home, laughing as they came through the door about something that dared to be funny while I was in the midst of heartbreak, until they saw me. Dani sat next to me, rocking me back and forth, while Craig ran me a bath and grabbed me a glass of whiskey and a mug of tea.

So, that's it. That's how it ended. Was it as dramatic as you thought it would be? When I found out he died, I didn't speak for three days. And then I fixed the tattoo and forgot how to sleep and fucked DJs until Rob.

30

I spent the next few days sitting by the phone, waiting for Rob to call, and trying to convince myself that I wasn't *just* sitting by the phone, waiting for Rob to call. You know, like a pathetic, delusional liar would.

I wasn't completely pathetic, though. I had an audition to prep for, one that I would've been more excited about if I weren't so busy waiting for Rob to call.

He didn't call your first day back, or your second one, or your third, but I did get a text. He sent me a song. "Sweet Thing" by Van Morrison. (I know, it's *so* on the nose, but when was Rob ever all that subtle?) I listened to it nonstop, analyzing the lyrics, looking for signs and hidden meanings, too obsessed to think that maybe the song itself *was* the sign.

I didn't respond to the text right away, promising myself that if I did well in the audition, I'd reward myself by texting him. And maybe, by reminding him of my existence, I'd hopefully make him think of me.

The audition went well. Really well. I'd done a good job and I knew it, so as I walked out of the casting offices, I started typing my heavily crafted text to Rob.

With all of the overthinking and drafting and redrafting of texts, you'd think Rob and I hadn't had sex yet. Or said I love you.

It was as though the second you came back, I forgot that I didn't need to use my cleverness and quips to win him over. I'd already done that, even though it didn't feel like it. Evidently, I didn't need quips because right before I hit Send on my effortful text meant to appear effortless, Rob called me. I paused, waiting three rings before picking up.

"Hi," I said, trying to sound calm. The butterflies were back. You brought them back.

"I missed that," I heard him say, smiling.

"What?"

"The way you sound. Your voice."

"Well, it's still right here where you left it," I said, going for casual. I'm not sure I achieved it.

"I know. I know. Fuck, I miss you."

"I miss you too."

"I'm on a food run, so I thought I'd try you."

"Oh," I said, trying not to picture what the two of you eating dinner together would look like. "Nice."

"Maggie," he said, and I could *hear* him run his hand through his hair.

"What?"

"I don't like this either, you know." He said it as though someone had forced him into this predicament.

"I know," I replied, trying not to pout while pouting.

"She's only just got home. I can't do anything yet, that would be cruel. You know that, we've talked about it," he said, which was kind of true, but mostly bullshit.

We hadn't talked about what would happen, as much as I'd asked and he gave me an assortment of hazy, half-answers. He told me he'd leave you, and I'd frozen, unsure of what to say. He'd said it in the car on our last night together and once before that in the tub, *your* tub, where we were soaking in steaming water, my back against his chest. *When it's over and done with and I've left her, we'll do this all the time*, he'd whispered into the back of my head.

I'm only just now realizing how all of his confessions and declarations were delivered to the back of my head.

I didn't push him to say it again there on the phone, but I wanted to.

"I know," I said again.

"Can I see you soon?"

"When?"

"Monday? I won't be able to get away until then."

It was Friday. I tried to settle my disappointment, but it raged and roiled inside of me.

"Maggie?"

"Yeah," I said, attempting a chipper voice, "Monday works."

"Good. Did you get the song I sent?"

"Yeah. I loved it."

"I didn't hear back, so I wasn't sure," he continued.

"I didn't know if I could write back, so I didn't."

"You can write back," he said, sounding unsure.

"Okay."

"Okay. I have to go. I love you."

"Say it again, please," I said.

"I love you, Maggie." And I knew his grin matched mine.

"I love you too," I said before hanging up.

31

I spent the rest of my Friday night sulking. Saturday, too. I sat on the couch, drinking wine and watching movies where people fall in love and no one is addicted to heroin or married or a DJ.

On Sunday, Dani forced me off the couch and into a dress, saying that my choices were as follows: free brunch with her, Craig, Joey and Liv, or she'd call Pearl.

I relented, allowing her to brush my hair and drive me to Santa Monica for brunch. Anything was better than facing the interrogation I knew would come if my sister was informed of my sadness.

So, brunch. With two couples who were deeply, ridiculously in love. Joey smirked at me when I sat at the head of the table, like the matriarch of some boisterous, brunch-loving family, and Liv kissed him on the cheek before nibbling his earlobe.

I wanted to die, but Dani reached over and squeezed my hand, a knowing look in her eye. I smiled back, taking a sip of my Bloody Mary and pretending that I wasn't thinking about Rob, but it didn't last. He was so on my mind that I was convinced I'd seen his face out of the corner of my eye. I tried shaking it off when Craig launched into a story about something Dottie had done the other day, half listening as I worked to spot the Maybe Rob again.

I knew I must've imagined it. The Bloody Mary wasn't helping, either. I said all of this to myself and it worked, allowing me to tune into the last bit of Craig's Dottie story (she'd seen a possum and chased it) and order food.

"Holy shit," Craig exclaimed, cutting his story off. "Rob?!"

I looked up.

Everyone at our table looked in the direction of Craig's stare, and, sure enough, it was Rob. And . . . you. You with your white linen pants and blond hair and birdlike features. You with your ring and your smile and your laugh. You with your husband.

I stared at your hair for a while, remembering a night when Rob and I'd had too much to drink and wound up in bed, my head on his shoulder, as he wound his fingers through my hair. "I've always had a thing for brunettes," he said, and I smiled, humming as he pulled on my strands. I guess I'd just figured you'd be a brunette too.

When Rob saw me, his face froze. I started tearing up, trying frantically to appear unfazed.

I took a gulp of my Bloody Mary, and a bigger gulp of Dani's mimosa, and prayed to anyone listening that he wouldn't get up and come to our table.

"Dude, what are you doing over there? Come here," Craig called, ushering the two of you over.

Evidently, god wasn't on my side. Rob glanced at me for a moment, a fraction of a moment even, before smiling big and wide, getting up, and walking over to our table. You smiled at us, got up, and followed him, your husband.

"Hi," Rob said once he got over to us, giving Craig one of those ridiculous half-hugs that men give one another. He nodded at Joey and leaned over to kiss Liv on the cheek before hugging Dani, who'd stood up, and then it was my turn. I stood, gripping the table to keep myself upright, and plastered a smile on my face. He'd been staring at me the whole time he greeted the others.

"It's good to see you," he said, wrapping me in a hug. I was frozen. I didn't remember that hugging him back would be the normal thing to do until a few seconds in, when I quickly wrapped my arms around him before pulling away.

You just stood by him, smiling at all of us. At *me*.

"You too," I said, sitting down and downing the last of my Bloody Mary.

"How've you been, Rob?" Craig asked, all smiles.

"Good," he replied, eyes still locked on me as he continued. "Just here for some brunch with my wife. She just got back into town."

"Do you want to join us?" Craig asked. "We just ordered, but we can pull up two chairs."

He said more, I know, but I didn't hear it, because before I knew what was happening, I'd pushed my chair back and stumbled towards the bathroom, saying something about having to make a phone call.

I barely made it into the stall before I threw up. I stayed like that for a while, head over the toilet bowl, trying to calm my breathing, before Dani came in. I could pick her footsteps out any day.

"Mags? You here?"

I didn't say anything, using all of my focus to keep my breathing calm and even and stop the hot tears from streaming down my cheeks. It didn't matter, though. My breathing was all over the place, my tears kept coming, and Dani found me, opening the stall door I'd forgotten to lock.

She rushed to my side and sat on the floor of the bathroom, stroking my hair and wiping my cheeks. We were silent for a while, save for my shaky breathing.

"It's Rob, isn't it," she said, still stroking my hair. "Rob's the guy you've been sneaking around with."

It wasn't a question. I nodded and my tears quickened, making everything a blur.

"Fuck," she said, pulling me close and rocking me back and forth, just like she'd done after Jackson.

"I'm sorry," I cried between heaves.

"I know," she said, "I know. How long have you been carrying this around, Spoon?"

"Since the party," I confessed, still crying.

"You poor thing." She squeezed me, and I looked up at her.

"You're not mad at me?"

"No. I don't know what I am . . . hurt, maybe. And I'm worried about you."

"He's married," I said, feeling like I really understood what that meant for the first time since the party.

"Yeah, he is."

"I love him."

"I know."

"You do?" I asked, my head shooting up.

"Yeah. He loves you too. The way he was looking at you . . . it was pretty clear."

"Do they all know?" I asked, suddenly frantic all over again.

"God, no. You both played it off. If I didn't know you so well, I wouldn't have been able to tell."

I breathed a sigh of relief, but I shouldn't have. After all, you knew Rob very, *very* well. It should have been obvious to me that you could see through him, but I didn't put it together at the time.

"What do we do now?"

"We can stay in here as long as you want. Or we can go eat, or we can go home. Your choice."

"You won't call Pearl?"

"I won't call Pearl," she reassured me.

We stayed on the floor of the bathroom for a while longer before I decided to go back. I stood up and Dani helped clean me up, making me look something close to normal.

We returned to the table holding hands and let out twin sighs of relief when we saw that you and Rob had gone back to your table. I saw Rob visibly straighten and relax seemingly all at once, but Dani squeezed my hand and I looked away, sitting just in time to hear Joey talk about his and Liv's shroom trip.

32

Rob called me that night around seven. I was on the couch with Dani after having told her everything, and she tensed up, reaching across my lap to decline the call almost instantly.

I would've questioned her, fought her, slapped her, something, but as soon as the call ended, he called again, and I was quicker than she was, so I picked up the phone and left Dani for the porch, closing the door behind me.

"Hi."

"Are you all right?" he blurted out, his voice hoarse.

"Yeah."

"Maggie—"

"I'm okay," I said, trying to ease the tension. "I was just thrown."

"I didn't know you were going to be there. It's our standing place, we go there every Sunday and—"

I cut him off before he could use the words *we* or *our* again. "I know. It's fine. I'm fine."

"You're sure? I wanted to go to you, you know that I did, I just didn't want to . . . I didn't know what to do."

"Rob. I know. It's fine. Really." I thought that if I spoke in short, declarative sentences, he would ignore the way my voice was still hoarse from my tears. "Dani knows."

He sighed. "I figured."

"I'm sorry," I said, before he cut me off.

"Maggie, it's okay. I'm the one who should be apologizing to you. I am so sorry. More than I can say. Seeing you like that, so . . . *hurt*. It broke my heart."

"So," I said, clearing my throat, "Ingrid seems nice."

It was silent for a bit before Rob coughed. "You didn't speak to her."

"Yeah, that's why I said she *seemed* nice. Pretty, too."

"Maggie," he said before trailing off into another one of his patented sighs.

"What? It's true! It's a genuine compliment."

"Whatever you say," he said, not believing me. I did mean it, though. I swear.

"She's not there, is she?" I asked, knowing the answer, but needing some reassurance.

"No, god, no. I'm heading to work."

"Oh. Right. And tomorrow—"

"I'm off work in the day, so whenever's good for you."

"I've got a callback tomorrow at two, so after that, I can come to you, or—"

"You got a callback?" he asked, sounding genuinely excited. I'd forgotten all about the callback until I mentioned it, actually, but as soon as I did, I was excited for it. Thrilled, even.

"Uh-huh," I said through my smile.

"Maggie, that's phenomenal. I'm proud of you."

"Thanks," I responded, meaning it.

"I don't work until seven tomorrow. Do you want to meet at your apartment after the callback? Will Dani be there?"

"She'll be at Craig's," I said, which was a lie, but I figured that if I asked, given everything, she'd agree, however reluctantly.

"Okay. I'll be there."

"Okay."

"I'm sorry about today. Really, I am."

"I know," I repeated for what felt like the hundredth time.

We talked for a little while longer before I hung up, leaving the porch for the couch, where Dani sat, arms open. I sunk into them, pressing my face into her neck.

"He's coming here tomorrow," I said. "Can you go to Craig's? Please?"

Dani was quiet, so I looked up at her, pouting.

"Please," I repeated.

She sighed. "Okay. I'll go. But Mags—"

"I don't want to talk about it anymore," I said, which was true, for the most part.

"You'll let me know when you're ready?"

"Uh-huh."

She kissed the top of my head and we sat like that, pretzeled and quiet. I'd missed that. I'd missed the easy rhythm we shared, a rhythm I'd either forgotten about or ignored while I'd been up in the canyon, my focus solely on Rob. He was splitting his focus, though, so I would too.

33

The callback went well, but I was too focused on seeing Rob to care much. All the way home, I kept doing the silent math, running through yellow lights and going five, ten, twenty over the speed limit. If I got there faster, I'd have more time with him before he had to go.

What is typically a thirty-minute drive took fifteen, and as I pulled up, I saw Rob sitting on the stoop, eyes scanning the road ahead. He perked up when he saw my car, smiling his open, wide smile.

I barreled towards him. He opened his arms and hugged me tight, pressing me closer and closer to his chest. I could feel his heartbeat.

"You have no idea how much I've missed you," he said, hands moving from my shoulders to my waist.

"I think I do," I said, unlocking the door and pulling him in with me.

"How was the callback?" he asked, leaning down so our faces were inches apart. I saw his gaze dart from my eyes to my mouth and back again.

"I don't really want to talk about that right now," I replied.

"And what is it you want to do?" he asked. Less than a minute later, we were in my bedroom, the door closing as our world shrank.

We went on like this for a few months before shit hit the fan. I got the job, which we celebrated with champagne drunk out of teacups in the alley of the tattoo parlor in between shifts. The movie wouldn't shoot until the spring, so I had time to revel in my newly acquired job before I was set to dive back into the world of sets and lines and Rob-lessness.

I never asked him when he was going to leave you, but I wanted to. There was a lot I wanted to know, but I don't think I was ready for the answers.

Every once in a while, though, I'd ask him what the deal was, either when I was drunk or just tired enough not to care about how it might seem, and he'd respond the same way each and every time.

"The deal is," he'd say, "I'm going to tell her. Soon. In a month."

So we spent month after month stealing snippets of time, kissing and fucking in cars, seeing movies at two in the afternoon or three in the morning, living for the in-between hours of the day, when you'd be asleep or writing or otherwise occupied.

I used to get dressed up for these rendezvous, dressing to kill my time, turning what are normally fast, easy steps into events.

I'd spend twenty minutes applying lotion to every part of my body, reveling in how soft I could make my skin.

I got better at looking artfully disheveled, mastering the messy bun, picking tendrils of curls out so that no one, not even Rob, would know just how much time and effort went into my look of effortlessness.

He appreciated it, I know he did, but once you were home, he spent less time looking at me and more time checking his watch to see how much time was too much time away from you.

We spent some of our time at the movies. A little theater in North Hollywood I used to go to with Jackson, one I was sure you'd never been to.

We always sat in the back, away from everyone else, and spent less time watching the movie than we did looking at each other.

I settled for catching moments of action movies or movies with victim roles I had almost been cast to play (but wasn't) in between kisses and whispered exchanges, hearing cars explode and people being punched while Rob sucked on my neck. I couldn't mark *him,* but my skin was free territory. *His* territory.

He was never jumpy or anxious when we were out in the world, but I knew that he preferred it when it was just the two of us, either in my apartment or in the car, and so that was where we spent the most time.

He always said he wanted to be able to take me out, on "a proper date," and I always told him I didn't mind, but I'm not sure if that was true. I envied the couples we saw in the lobby of the theater, flaunting their coupledom, holding hands as they ordered popcorn and a soda to split between the two of them.

I tried not to want that, I'd make fun of them to Rob, whisper comments that would make him laugh, a loud, barking laugh he'd try to disguise as a cough, but my snide remarks felt hollow to me. I wonder if he knew what I was hiding in them.

I missed your house, the house I'd started considering my own, but I knew that I wouldn't be back there, not unless you left town again. Every time I left to go see him, Dani would watch me silently from the couch. I knew she was worried, but I didn't care. Not enough, anyway.

34

We saw *Beautiful Boy* by accident. We had meant to see *Bad Times at the El Royale*, but we missed the start, so instead of getting back in the car and aimlessly driving around for an hour or so, we decided to see whatever was playing soonest, which was . . . a movie about addiction.

Rob turned to me, brows furrowed. "We don't have to see anything, we can just drive, or—"

"No," I said, surprising myself, "let's watch it. I want to watch it."

"Maggie . . ."

He was studying my face, staring straight at me the way Jackson used to.

"I want to see it. I do. I want to see it with you."

Rob stared for a bit longer, biting his lip as he mulled his words over, but instead of saying anything else, he just pulled me into his side, kissed the top of my head, and squeezed my hand.

"We'll take two tickets for *Beautiful Boy*, please."

The second the lights of the movie theater dimmed, I felt my heart pound so hard I thought I was going to throw it up. My hands were sweaty, but Rob kept holding them, one of them anyway, squeezing it gently as the movie started.

"If it gets to be too much, just say the word and we'll go, okay?" he whispered to me, squeezing my hand again. I just nodded, giving his hand a light squeeze back. I didn't know how to express just how grateful I was for his sensitivity, and so instead I kept my eyes fixed on the screen and practiced box breathing: four seconds to breathe in, four to hold the breath, four to exhale, and another four of holding.

For the first time ever, we watched the entire movie. No kissing, no hickeys, no whispered play fights. We sat in the back like we always did, but other than that, it was unlike any of our other movie theater excursions.

The movie *did* get to be too much, but we didn't leave. I didn't want to leave. Instead, we sat there, in the back row of an almost-empty theater, and Rob held my hand as I sobbed, big, heaving sobs that rattled my body and blurred my vision.

For the first time in a long time, I thought about Jackson and his needles and his track marks and his laughter and his joy. I thought about how happy he had made me and how scared he had made me. I thought about the frustrating desperation I carried around our last few months of dating, the deep desire to fix him, to force him to get clean, to *stay* clean. I thought about the night I learned he'd died. I thought about the memorial and the vigil, and the time spent at Pearl's house.

I don't think I'd realized just how much of my grief I'd been pushing down until that night. I had been in a state of perpetual mourning up until the night of the boat party, but then I met Rob and he made me happy, and I hadn't wanted my newfound happiness to be marred by anything, so I just . . . ignored it. I thought my grief had gone away, but it was still there, I guess.

When the movie ended and the lights came up, we sat in silence. I tried to steady my breathing, to stop my tears, but Rob just squeezed my hand again and said, "Let it out, Maggie. Don't make yourself okay. Feel it."

And so I did. I sat and cried for what must have been another ten minutes as the staff came in to clean, sweeping up kernels of popcorn and disposing of cups of half-flat soda.

After the tears subsided and my breathing evened out, I stood and Rob followed, my hand still in his. We walked out of the movie theater and got into his car in total silence. We stayed that way as he turned the car on and put it in drive, and I knew that he was waiting for me to speak. He was following my lead.

I didn't say anything until he was driving, eyes fixed on the road ahead. He was giving me space and time and silence and privacy, but I didn't want to be private. I wanted to share this with him, so I spoke.

"Do you remember that thing you said on the phone? The thing about grieving being like going to the beach and getting sand everywhere?"

"Yeah," he said softly, "I do."

"I think I've still got some sand in some places."

He looked over at me and pulled the car over, putting it in park before turning to me, drinking me in just like he used to.

"That's okay," he said, "I've got plenty of sand myself."

"Yeah?"

"Yeah. I have these moments sometimes where I forget that she's gone. My mum. When I'm happy about something, or frustrated by something, or not knowing what to do, and I just want to call her, because she's the person I want to talk to, you know?"

I nodded.

"Sometimes I'll even pick up the phone and call home, and it's not until my dad answers that I remember, and it destroys me all over again. I'm back where I was three years ago and I'm grieving all over again. I did that a while ago, actually."

"You did?"

"I did."

"When?"

He smiled, then. A small, soft smile. His eyes were teary, for me or for himself, for his mum, I didn't know, but it made my heart swell.

"The night we met," he said, simply, "I was confused and scared, and I wanted to hear her voice, you know? I wanted her to tell me what to do."

"What do you think she'd have said?"

Rob laughed ruefully, scratching the back of his neck with his hand.

"She would've cursed me out, probably. Yelled at me for kissing you, for *wanting* to kiss you, and then she would've said you better be sure you know what you're doing."

"Do you?" I whispered, not sure if I wanted the answer.

"Yes," he said after a pregnant pause, "I think I do."

35

Dani finally opened her mouth on Halloween, when we'd returned home from a party we hated and were on the porch in our costumes, looking straight ahead.

"I'm worried," she said, and I knew what she was talking about. I made to say something, but she cut me off. "Just let me say this and then we'll drop it. I know you love him. I know he loves you. But what if love isn't enough?"

"What if it is?" I said, because that's all I could think to say.

"Then I'm wrong and I'll be the first to admit it. But Maggie, he's married. And you know, historically speaking, these kinds of stories don't often work out for people in your position."

"And what position would that be?" I asked, pushing for a fight. I wanted to be angry at someone, blow up at them, because if there was no one else to be angry at, that meant that I'd have to be angry at Rob, and I wasn't interested in that.

"Do I really have to say it?"

"Clearly you want to, so just say it."

"I don't! All I'm saying is that men don't often leave, no matter how much they love the other woman."

"Some do," I said, feeling like a child.

"Okay," she said, calmly, evenly, "who?"

"My dad. Over and over again, actually," I said, trying to make it sound light, a joke, but she knew better.

She looked at me with that wide-eyed fawn-like face of hers, all heart and warmth and love, and I just . . . I lost it. Again. She reached out and held my hand as I cried.

"I can't believe I'm in the position of hoping the guy I love takes a page from my dad's book," I cried, letting my tears turn to snot-filled laughter. Dani laughed too, softly at first, but then we were sitting there, laughing hysterically in our costumes under the moonlight.

For a while after that, things were good. Really good. Dani was spending more time at Craig's; she never said as much, but I knew it was so that Rob and I could spend less time in cars and movie theaters and more time in an actual bed, and we did. Lots of it.

I got used to falling asleep with him again, feeling warm and safe in his arms, and tried not to be hurt or sad when I'd wake up to an empty bed. He'd leave around three in the morning any time he came over at night, showering before he snuck out the door.

He only ever came over after I'd assured him Dani had left, and so the front door of my apartment felt like a revolving door of the people who mattered the most to me.

I never asked him why he was so insistent never to see Dani, but I thought about it a lot. I'd fantasize about the three of us spending time together at the apartment, cooking dinner and drinking wine as a joy-filled, easy trio. She'd tell him embarrassing stories about me and he'd laugh, grinning at me as I pretended to be more embarrassed than I was, but it didn't happen.

Instead, he'd come in, kick off his shoes, and we'd sit on the couch, making excuses to touch each other more than we needed to, if only to remind ourselves that what was happening was *real*; he was there and so was I, and we were in love.

We tried taking a bath together in the apartment, but it wasn't the same. It was too small, and so we sat in the hot water, cramped and pretending that we weren't thinking about how much easier everything had been when you were gone.

We spent months like this, trying to convince ourselves and each other that nothing had changed. For the most part, it worked.

When he kissed me, I could close my eyes and force myself into forgetting that he had a home and a wife just a few miles away, but that false security only lasted until I woke up in the morning alone, with nothing to assure me that the previous night had been real save for an ache between my legs and a note on the bedside table, scrawled in his messy handwriting, saying something like "I love you," or "I'll see you soon. Sleep well!!!"

You were still a threat, though. A looming figure who cast every moment with Rob in shadow, and I longed for the end of your marriage-filled reign.

I didn't know that it was coming sooner than I realized. I didn't know that it wouldn't make things easier. I know now that even your shadow was tinged by the rose-colored glasses I'd donned the moment Rob and I got together.

36

Before I get to that part, though, I should tell you about Pearl, because she found out before you did.

Maybe *found out* isn't the right term, though. It's not like she ran into us or something. I told her.

I was at her house, a few weeks before she was due, and we were out in the backyard while Jonah and Harper went to pick up dinner.

I was drinking wine and she was drinking a strawberry milkshake (her pregnancy craving item of choice), and it just came out.

We'd been talking about Harper, who had decided that she was in love with a classmate of hers, but it was "tricky," because he had just been married to another of her classmates the week before.

Pearl told me that Harper was heartbroken, not understanding why Beckett (the married four-year-old in question) wouldn't just "die-vorce" Willow, and I started to laugh.

"Tell her I can relate," I said, still laughing.

"What do you mean?" Pearl asked, setting her milkshake down.

I froze. I hadn't meant to say it.

"Nothing," I said quickly. "Has she said anything to this married man of hers?"

"Maggie," Pearl said, gentle but firm, "what do you mean?"

I looked at her and saw that she was fixing me with her patented Tell Me Your Secrets Now stare. I took another big sip of my wine and exhaled.

"Promise you won't freak out?"

"I can't promise that."

"You don't have to *mean it*, just . . . can you say it?"

"I won't freak out."

"Okay. So. You know Rob?" I asked, digging my nails into my palms.

"Rob as in the guy you're seeing?"

"Yeah. Him. So the thing is . . . he's married," I said it quickly, hoping that the faster I said it, the less she'd react.

"He's *what*?"

"Married. To a poet. But I didn't know it at the start. Like when I first kissed him, I didn't know, and then I knew, and then we were friends and then . . . and then we were more than friends."

Pearl sat there, staring at me, silently. I wanted to throw up. I wanted to take it all back, pretend it was a joke, but I knew I couldn't. I'd said it, and it couldn't be unsaid.

"Please don't hate me," I said, on the brink of tears. "It's awful, I know. *I'm* awful, but just . . . can you just not hate me right now because I don't think I could take that on top of everything else."

"Does Dani know?" was all she said.

"Yeah, she does."

"Does Mom?"

"God, no."

The air was too hot and too cold all at once, and I couldn't look at Pearl's face; instead I focused on how her maternity shirt was thin, thin enough that I could see the outline of her belly button, which I fixed my gaze on.

"Okay," she said, sipping her shake again. "Good."

"You hate me, don't you?"

"I don't hate you, Maggie," she said.

"Are you sure? Because *I* kind of hate me."

"I don't hate you. I'm just . . . processing."

"Right. Okay. It's a lot to take in, I know."

"He's married?" she asked.

I nodded and the tears spilled down my cheeks. I kept brushing them off, refusing to acknowledge them, refusing to stop looking at Pearl and her shake and her shock.

"Oh Mags," she said, opening her arms, "I was hoping you were going to make things easier for yourself this time."

I crawled into her arms, not fitting all that well thanks to her enormous bump. "I know," I said into her shoulder, "so was I."

We sat like that until Harper and Jonah returned, when we straightened ourselves up and plastered smiles on our faces until Harper went to bed and Pearl and I were alone again, this time on the couch. She turned to me, staring, and pushed my hair away from my face, picking lint off my sweater.

"I just wish I could make you understand that love doesn't always have to be this *hard*."

"So do I."

"Is he worth it?"

"Rob?"

She nodded. I didn't have to think about it.

"Yes," I said, so sure of it, "he is. I love him."

"You do?"

I nodded. "This isn't going to end well, is it?"

"I don't know," she said, stroking my hair some more. "You know who you should talk to about this?"

"Who?" I asked, knowing what she was going to say before she said it.

"Dad."

"No."

"Maggie . . ."

"*No,*" I said, forcefully, "this isn't like it was with him and Lily. Or Rose. Or Flora."

"Or Ana?"

"God, no. This is . . . it's real. It's *good.*"

Pearl laughed softly.

"What?" I asked, looking at her.

"Nothing. It's just . . . that's what Dad says every time."

That stopped me. It was true; that's what he said when he met Lily, and when he left Lily for Rose, or Rose for Flora, and then again Flora for Ana. They were all "real" and "good." Rob *was* both of those things, though. I was sure of it.

I was so, *so* sure.

PART IV

Love without You

37

Do you want me to tell this part, really? You know it better than I do; it's your story now too. I guess I'll just go through what happened step-by-step, what you did and what Rob and I did in response.

1. I woke up on the day after New Year's Eve to a text from Rob. He'd called seven times. I rubbed at my eyes, still sleep-filled and puffy from last night's drinks, and opened the text. It had two words, but those words sent chills down my spine and awakened the butterflies, who morphed quickly into yellow jackets, stinging at my insides. The text was, of course, this: Ingrid knows.

2. I listened to Rob's three voicemails, trying to pretend I wasn't even a little pleased that finally, *finally*, you knew.
   a. The first one was left when he was in tears. I know this because of his heavy, labored breathing and occasional sniffs. "Maggie," he said, "Ingrid knows about us. She confronted me just now. Please call me when you get this."

b. The second: "Maggie, wake up. Ingrid knows. She knows. She's suspected something since that brunch, and then last night she found that photo, the one we took at Lucy's, in my truck, and . . . fuck. Fuck! Please, babe, just call me."

c. The third one was left two hours after the first two. It was the hardest one to listen to, but, mercifully, it was the shortest one. He sounded exhausted, totally drained: "She's leaving. It's done."

4. I called Rob, who sounded just as drained as he had in the last message. He said, very slowly, that you'd made him tell you everything, this whole story in *his* words, and, when he was done, you'd told him you "weren't interested in pretending that this was just an affair." You said, "If it's just sex, that would be one thing, but you *love* this girl?" And he'd admitted it. I tried not to gloat when he told me that. I tried not to, but I wasn't successful. (Also, fuck you. I'm not a girl.) He said you packed some of your things and went to a friend's place in Big Sur.

5. I drove up to your house, now Rob's house, I guess, letting myself in and finding Rob on the couch, eyes red-rimmed, staring straight ahead. I held him silently as he sobbed, his shoulders shaking so violently I thought he'd fall off the couch.

6. We had sex in the kitchen. Quick and messy and he cried throughout, even after I asked if he wanted to stop.

7. He smoked an entire pack of cigarettes, and I sat watching him.

8. We had sex in the living room on that green velvet love seat he said you'd bought the day before your wedding.

9. We had sex in your office, and his tears covered my chest and tangled my hair.

10. He drank half a bottle of whiskey and told me all the reasons he loved me more than you. I'm not sharing them, so don't even ask.

11. We slept in ~~your~~ *his* bedroom and he held me so tight I lost sensation in my arms.

That was the first night after you left. It got easier after that. It took some time, but it really did get easier. He boxed up your things and shipped them to your Big Sur address, and I sat on the deck as he did it, not wanting to interfere with your things any more than I already had.

I kept thinking about my mom, how she was in the weeks after my dad left for London with Lily. She didn't speak for three days, spending her time staring out of windows and through space.

I remember one night she got drunk and rented one of his movies, *Button Nose*, I think, and made me watch it with her. I was six and it was late, but she made me sit down on the couch and watch all two hours of it. At the end she turned to me, her eyes glossy, and said, "At the end of the day, Maggie, he needed someone who thinks his name deserves to be in lights as much as he does. He needs someone to adore him. All men do."

I think about that a lot. I'm still not sure if she meant it, but I think she was on to something. It's not just men, though. We all need to be adored, don't we?

My mom used to talk about how my dad was needy. She called him a spoiled toddler, always reaching out to be seen, to be admired, and to a point, she was right, but I think we're all a little like that. That's what relationships are, aren't they? Two people reaching for one another, both needing something from the other.

38

A month and a half after you left, Rob came out to the deck, where I'd been reading *The Chronology of Water*, one of his favorite books. He'd given it to me after finishing *Love Is a Mixtape*, saying we were now a book club on top of everything else. He paced around the table, lighting a cigarette and stewing.

"What's wrong?" I asked, setting the book down.

"Nothing," he said, still pacing, "I'm good."

He pushed the sleeves of his sweater up and kicked at the ground with his socked feet.

"You sure?"

"Yeah. I was just on the phone with a friend, Patrick, and he invited me for dinner. And you. Us. Together."

I didn't know how to respond. He wasn't pacing anymore, but he wasn't looking at me either.

"Oh," I said, slowly, "and that's bad?"

Rob looked up at me, resuming his pacing.

"No, it's good. It's great, actually. You wanna come? You don't have to, but—"

"I'll come." I'd said it before I'd even realized it. "I want to come. He's your friend. I want to know your friends."

"Yeah?"

"Yeah."

He smiled, but it didn't quite reach his eyes.

"Okay," he said, clapping his hands together, "I'll call him back."

We got into the car that night in silence. Rob wore that shearling jacket he always wears, the one with the deep pockets, and his dark jeans. I started dressing as if I were going in for an audition, analyzing and reanalyzing my wardrobe choice until I decided it wasn't at all slutty or trashy. Blue jeans and a bagel-and-lox tee are not at all Mistress Clothes, I'd decided.

Rob's knees were bouncing the whole drive from Laurel Canyon to Los Feliz, and I watched him out of the corner of my eye, trying to emanate calm and positivity for him. It wasn't working.

"You sure you're okay with this? I can always just go back to my apartment, and you can go on your—"

"No," Rob said, his knees slowing, "I want you to come. I'm just in my head. It's fine. I'll be fine."

"You don't have to be," I said, thinking of how he'd said the same thing to me that night on the boat. Rob laughed softly.

"Remember when you thought I was cool and collected?" he asked. "Those were the days."

"Who said I *ever* thought you were cool and collected," I teased, hoping to bring him out of his head some more. It worked: he laughed and his knees stopped bouncing.

"Asshole."

"Yeah, but you love me anyway," I said, smiling.

"Yeah," he said, looking over at me and squeezing my hand, "I do."

"So who exactly is Patrick?"

"He's the first friend I made when I came out here. You'll love him."

I sat for a second, thinking. Patrick lived in Los Feliz. He was Rob's first friend in LA. Rob had met *you* in Los Feliz.

"You met Ingrid through Patrick, didn't you?" I asked.

"Yeah," he answered, "I did."

"Okay then," I said, my heart rate picking up.

We were quiet until Rob slowed to a stop in front of a green Craftsman-style house surrounded by orange trees. It was beautiful, but it felt haunted by something. By *you*, I guess. Your legacy.

Before we got out of the car, Rob grabbed my hand and looked at me, eyes wide.

"If you don't want to come, we can turn around now, okay? If this is too soon or too scary, or—"

I loved him so much in that moment that I almost couldn't look at him. Almost. His concern, his support, made me want to be brave. He deserved to be with someone who was brave.

"Let's do this," I said, squeezing his hand before hopping out of the car.

Patrick answered the door, lanky and full of whimsy in his mismatched socks and silk pajama shirt.

"Hey, brother," he said to Rob as he pulled him in for a hug, clapping Rob on the back. "How're you doing?"

"I'm good," Rob said, returning the hug, "really good."

Rob pulled out of the hug and Patrick's gaze shifted to me, his face tightened for a second, a fraction of a second maybe, before being replaced by a wide smile, but I'd seen it.

"You must be Maggie," Patrick said, smile still in place.

"Yeah," I said, trying to steady my breathing, "thanks for having me."

"Of course." Patrick pulled me in for a quick hug before leading us through the house and onto his deck, where a woman in a silk kimono was manning the grill.

"Katie," Patrick called out, "look who's here!"

Katherine, as I now know her, turned to face us. Her eyes glossed over Rob and landed on me. Her jaw tightened and Rob pulled me into his side. I wanted to hide in his jacket.

"Hiya, stranger," Katherine greeted Rob, shutting the grill before coming over and giving him a quick squeeze.

"This is," Rob started to say, but Katherine cut him off, addressing me. "Maggie, right?"

I froze. My tongue felt heavy and too big for my mouth. I nodded, unsure if I'd be able to speak.

"I've heard a lot about you," she continued, fixing me with a stare.

I wanted to disappear. Patrick coughed lightly, giving Katherine a pointed look, and she glared at Patrick for a moment before evening out her expression.

"So," Patrick said, shifting his weight, "drinks?"

After Patrick returned, drinks in hand, we sat at the table outside and I pretended to eat, looking anywhere but at Katherine, whose eyes were fixed on me.

"So, Maggie," she said, taking a sip of wine, "what do you do?"

I opened my mouth, but Rob was quick to jump in. "She's an actress."

"Impressive," Katherine said, not sounding impressed at all. "Anything I've seen?"

"She was in *Opening Up,*" Rob answered.

"Haven't seen it."

"It's an indie about two girls who decide to try having an open relationship," Rob explained. "It's really good. Great, actually. She's amazing in it."

I turned to Rob, forgetting for a second who was across from me. I didn't know he'd seen it. He'd never said anything.

"You saw it?" I murmured to Rob, shocked.

"Yeah, I did. Of course I did," he answered.

"When?"

"Sometime in August," he answered, smiling softly at me.

I was floored. The boat was in August. We had been friends in August. He'd looked me up when we were friends and he'd watched my movie. It's not a huge deal, I know that, but still, it made me grin and feel bashful. Rob grinned back at me, and for a moment it was easy and nice, until Katherine dropped her fork and its clattering brought me back to my reality.

"So when Ingrid was away," Katherine said, her tone even, her eyes icy.

"Yes, Katherine," Rob said, "when Ingrid was away."

"Hmm," Katherine said, eyes still fixed on me, "interesting."

"Kath," Patrick murmured, his hand coming to her back.

"I didn't say anything! Nothing at all," Katherine exclaimed. "Ignore me, I'm drunk."

That was a lie. She'd barely had anything to drink and she knew I knew it.

I wanted to melt in between the cracks of the wooden deck right then, just trickle down and be anywhere but there, on the deck with a woman who hated me on principle, her husband, and my formerly married boyfriend.

"So Rob," Patrick said, a false geniality to his voice, "have you met Kyle's new girlfriend?"

"No, I haven't. What's she like?"

Katherine rolled her eyes. "Not a clue."

"You haven't met her either?" Rob asked.

"God no," Katherine crowed, "she lives in fucking Sacramento, for crying out loud. I don't even know where he *finds* these girls, it's ridiculous."

"They're women," Patrick chimed in, but Katherine was on a roll.

"No," she said, "they're girls. They're girls and he's an overgrown child who gets excited the second a twenty-something barista smiles at him."

"You realize that you're saying this to someone dating—" Rob started, but Katherine cut him off.

"I didn't mean *her*," she said, gesturing to me, "or you. It's just . . . seriously? Is this a midlife crisis he's going through, or—"

"He's fine! He's happy, that's the important thing," Patrick stated, trying to backpedal.

"No, the important thing is the fact that he's incapable of being alone," Katherine stated. "*That's* the important thing."

Rob opened his mouth, but I stood, saying I needed to go to the bathroom. Patrick explained where I could find it, and I made my way across the deck and into the house, hoping for a momentary escape, but Katherine was loud, and the house was echoey, and so I could hear her.

"She's sweet, Rob, really. The whole doe-eyed thing is cute, but what the fuck are you doing? You threw away *ten years* to just . . . date some twenty-year-old actress? Really? You realize how clichéd that is, right?"

"Kath," Patrick warned.

"She's twenty-five," Rob said, and I could hear the anger in his voice. I should've gone to the bathroom, I shouldn't have listened, but I couldn't move.

"Right." Katherine scoffed. "Because *that* makes it so much better."

"What exactly *is* your problem with her, Katherine? Is it that she's young or that she's not Ingrid? Because if this is about Ingrid, and I'm sure it is, then your problem's with *me*, not with Maggie. My girlfriend. Who I love. Who makes me happy. She's kind and funny and smart and talented and—"

"And twenty-five," Katherine muttered.

"Katherine, enough," Patrick said, sounding, for the first time all night, angry.

"What? Are you seriously okay with this? Ingrid's coming here next month, Patrick, and here you are, playing host and pretending that this is fine? Really?"

"It's not fine," Patrick cried, "of course it's not fine, but Rob's our friend too. He's hurting too. It was his marriage too."

"Yeah," Katherine muttered, "he seems *really* torn up over it."

I could hear a chair scrape back and another fork clatter to the floor.

"That's enough." Rob was seething. "Katherine, you have every right to hate me for what I put Ingrid through. I hurt her. I know that. And I am sorry. Deeply sorry. You don't have to believe that, but it's true. Hate me all you want, but you have *no* right to blame this on Maggie. I didn't throw my marriage away for her, she didn't ask me to leave, I'd wanted to leave. For a while. I wasn't happy. I was miserable. And then I met Maggie, and I wasn't miserable anymore. You can think this is a midlife crisis, you can think I'm with her for her youth, but you're wrong. I'm with her because I love her. I am in love with her. My marriage didn't end because of Maggie. My marriage ended because it was already ending. It was over before Maggie was even in the picture. Patrick, I'll call you later. Thanks for dinner."

I heard his footsteps approaching the house, and he entered, face red and eyes teary. He looked at me, inhaling deeply.

"You heard that?" he asked.

I nodded.

"Let's get the fuck out of here," he said, grabbing my hand and leading me out of the house and into the car.

I was reeling. With what, I'm not sure; all I knew was that hearing Rob speak so definitively, so passionately, about us was terrifying and comforting all at once.

"I'm sorry." Rob blurted it out as soon as we got into the car. "I'm so sorry. I shouldn't have brought you. I should've known that Katherine would be . . . Katherine. That's why I was so . . . off today. I was dreading it. That was inexcusable and horrible and—"

"It's okay," I said, meaning it.

"No, it's not."

"Rob. I'm okay. I'm sorry for *you*. The way she was talking to you, the things she was saying, that was . . ."

"That's just Katherine," he said, half-heartedly.

"Patrick was sweet, though," I supplied, trying to find a silver lining.

"Patrick's always sweet. God, I'm such an idiot. I just wanted . . . I wanted you to like them, you know?"

"I *do* like them," I said.

"Liar."

"I like half of them!"

"You sure you want to stick around after that shit-show?"

"Unsure," I teased him, trying to ease the tension. "I'll tell you in the morning."

"What did I do to deserve you?" he asked, seriousness slipping back into the conversation. I looked at him and reached over to smooth his furrowed brow.

"You didn't do anything," I said, a lump forming in my throat, "you just do."

He let out a shaky exhale, closing his eyes. I pressed my forehead against his and we stayed like that, silent and linked, for a minute or so before he turned the car on and we made our way home.

39

We got home and went straight to the deck, where Rob drank whiskey like it was water and I sat next to him, trying to stay small and quiet. I didn't know what to say. I didn't know how to make things okay. I'd been feeling that more and more since you left.

Collectively, we were great; individually, he was a mess and I was—I only now realize—in over my head.

Rob liked having a wife. He'd liked having you. I knew it and I hated it and I did everything I could to ignore it, but the truth was, I liked Rob having a wife. I loved who he was when he was your husband and my . . . something. I may need some help with the terminology here.

After you left, I wasn't you and I wasn't a wife, and suddenly I found myself in a place where I was something new to him, and he was something new to me. I wasn't sure how to navigate our relationship any longer. Nothing was easy anymore.

I think that's when I really got a sense of how much I secretly liked having you in the background when I was with Rob. When you were in the picture, I told myself you were the reason we couldn't be together. I could blame it all on you, on the marriage, and that allowed me to float freely and easily through the relationship. Our love was Good and Strong and True and every issue was because of your marriage, not because of our affair. I didn't have to fear that he'd abandon me, like Jackson or my father, because he was never really mine. But now that he *was* mine, or wanted to be mine, it triggered a whole new set of issues for me. And now I just wanted to run away as fast as I could.

So Rob was ringless and dinner had been awful, and he was drunk, and he said that he "missed wearing something that showed the world he was loved and he loved someone."

I didn't remind him that when we first met he'd described his ring as merely a way of telling others that he was off the market.

I listened to him wax poetic (your influence) about wearing a "symbol of love" on his hand, and tried to find it beautiful, but the sky was spinning and I was just thinking about that night on the boat.

We were at the table on the deck, and he traced the lines of my tattoos as he slurred.

"I want one of these," he murmured as he kissed the strawberry on my shoulder, the wings, the JAM.

"A strawberry?"

"A tattoo."

"Oh," I said, unsure of where the conversation was going, a state of being I'd gotten used to the last month or so, "really?"

"Yeah. I want something permanent."

I wondered if his desire for permanence was more about your leaving or my guilt-induced distance, but I kept my mouth shut.

"Like what?"

"Dunno. Something to do with you."

This surprised me. It shouldn't have, I know, but the idea of someone walking around with a lasting mark of me, of their ties to me, on their body still shocked me. It's silly to say this after so many I love yous, hundreds of orgasms, and nights of linked limbs and hushed confessions, but I never thought about the fact that Rob considered our relationship to be something worth memorializing or, as I had begun to realize, something permanent.

"Me? Like a picture of me or something?" was all I could say, because I could hear my heart beating in my ears and I didn't know where the ground beneath me had gone to—somewhere far, far away, though, because everything was spinning and all I could think was *This happened before, a man loved you so much that he wanted you inked on his skin, and back then, you were happy. The last time this happened, you were smiling. So smile.*

And I did. I smiled, but my cheeks felt tight and I wanted to be back home, with Dani and Craig and Dottie.

"Not telling. It's a surprise."

40

He showed me the tattoo a few days later, after I'd come up to the canyon to see him when he'd gotten off work, when the day was new but the sky was still the vast, consuming blue-black of the night before.

"Hi," he said, smiling and pulling me into him for one kiss, then another.

"Hi," I said through a semistifled yawn.

"I have something to show you."

"Yeah?"

"Yeah."

With that, he pulled his sleeve up, revealing a tattoo. His first tattoo. A tattoo for me.

I want you to imagine the shock that coursed through my body when he pulled up his sleeve and revealed a tattoo of a winged strawberry, which is, to this day, the weirdest phrase I've ever said. It's small, tiny even, but that night, it felt like the biggest thing in the room.

"So?" he asked, smiling. "Do you like it?"

I was at a loss for words. I kept opening and closing my mouth, waiting for the words to come, but they didn't, not quickly enough, at least.

"You hate it," he said, his smile fading as his sleeve dropped down.

"No," I blurted out, "no, I love it. I do, I just . . . I wasn't expecting it! You were right, it's a total surprise."

"I was expecting a bigger reaction," he said, and I felt like laughing at him. For the first time since the boat, he felt like someone who deserved pity. This was not how I was supposed to feel. I was supposed to be in love.

"I'm sorry," I said, reaching out to touch him, but he pulled away. "Rob. I love it. I do. I'm sorry it didn't seem like I did. I was just surprised. Really. I'm bad at surprises, but I love it. It's beautiful."

I made an excuse to leave pretty soon after that, saying something about Dani needing my help with something, and I got in the car to drive nowhere in particular. The winged strawberry flew around my mind the whole time I drove.

It was both the most romantic thing anyone had ever done for me, and the scariest. I wasn't sure why; it was romantic. It was a grand gesture, one of those gestures I'd see in movies and wish was happening to me. But after you left, I kept feeling an urge to get away, to put some distance between us, and so that night, I ran. Not far, just to my apartment, where I got into bed and dreamt of strawberries flying away from me, to something better, prettier, more deserving.

41

Rob and I were stumbling through our time together, clinging to each other because what kind of people end a marriage and then break up? At least that was how I saw it. The thought of breaking up with him after he'd ended his marriage made me feel guilty all over again. And I didn't want our story to end that way.

I love him. But our love doesn't change the fact that he wants a wife, and I want a boyfriend, and his life had blown up, resulting in a broken home, lost friendships, and divorce papers, while mine had just . . . shifted. He never admitted it to me, but I think he resented me for it. I'd resent me, too.

So now to the part I'm sure you're dying to hear about. The bad bits.

He suggested that I move in with him, at your old house, and when I said no, he got angry, asking me, "What is the point of all this if not for us to build a life together?"

He had a point, I know. I'm still not sure why I didn't say yes. It sounded just like everything I'd been so sure I wanted, but the idea of living there with him, in the house he shared with you, made me feel like I was playing house.

He wanted us to skip ahead, go from whatever we were to a couple who lived together, almost as if by moving me into the house he once shared with you, he was erasing your presence from our story, from *his* story. I couldn't do that, though.

I had become what I'd hated so much: a woman who ended a marriage.

I wanted to talk about it, to talk about *you*, but whenever I brought you up, he bristled, saying that you didn't matter, you were gone and we were together and that was that.

One night, when we'd been fighting about you, he said, "You didn't know her. You have no right to say her name. She wasn't some *thing* we shared, she was *my wife*, and now she's not. She's not because of *you*."

I froze.

So did he.

He'd said it.

He'd said the thing I'd been thinking since you broke up, the thing I'd wanted him to say, hoping that saying it would make it better, would free up space, let us address it and move on. But it didn't work like that.

"Maggie, I—" he said, reaching for me with his ringless hand, but I backed away.

"I wasn't the one who ended your marriage," I said, willing myself to believe it. "She did. She did because of *you*, not because of me. She did because you loved me and she knew it. Don't blame me for the things you did to your marriage," I said, scrambling for my keys and walking to the door. "I'm sleeping at my place tonight."

He called me seven times that night, but I didn't pick up.

Instead, I called my dad. He picked up on the fifth ring.

"Maggie," he boomed, sounding happier than I thought anyone had the right to sound.

"Hi," I said, my voice cracking.

"Are you okay? What's wrong?" he asked. "Hold on, let me get some-where quiet."

"No, it's fine. I'm fine. You have people over, we can talk later," I said, hoping he'd allow me my exit.

"They're Ana's friends, they won't miss me," he said, and I heard a loneliness in his voice I hadn't heard before as he closed a door, shutting out the sounds of laughter.

"Okay," I said.

"What's wrong, darling?"

And so I told him. It was the most I'd said to him in months, in *years*, maybe, and, for once, he listened. No interruptions, just the sound of his breathing as I told him about Rob and the boat and you and the fight. When I finished, I took a drag of my cigarette and let out a shaky exhale, letting go of a breath I didn't realize I'd been holding, as I felt my anger, the anger of my six-year-old self, rise up at him.

"This is your fault, you know that?"

He was quiet for a moment before letting out a sigh. "I can see how you would feel that way, I suppose."

"You broke Mom. You *broke* her and I had to sit there and watch, and then you just kept on doing it! You ended *four* marriages and you were *fine,* but Mom wasn't, and I watched that and now I'm doing the same thing to people and it's your fault."

"I—" He started to speak, but I cut him off.

"I don't want to be this person. I don't want to be a person who breaks someone else, and I don't want to be a person who ruins a marriage, but I am, and I keep wanting it to be okay, because I love him, I do, but you said you loved Mom and then you met Lily and you said you loved Lily and then you met Flora and I don't want that. I don't want to be like you, but what if I am?"

"I did love your mother. I love her still," he said, pained.

I scoffed. "You loved her so much you left."

"I did," he said simply.

"I don't want Rob to be like you either," I said, my voice thick with anger and sadness and love and fear and everything else.

"He might not be."

"But he might be."

"That's for you to decide for yourself."

I took a shaky breath, clenching my fists and closing my eyes. "He's not. I don't think he is, anyway. I don't want him to be."

"Lily wasn't the reason I left, Maggie. I should've explained that to you, I should've explained it all to you, but you were so young and I wanted you to stay young. I didn't want to drag you into my chaos."

"I didn't feel young."

"No, I suppose you didn't. I hadn't been happy, darlin', not for a while. I loved your mom, but I hadn't been *in* love with her for quite some time. I was going to leave before I met Lily. I'd been leaving for a while, bit by bit, before Lily was even in the picture."

This was news. I felt the blood rush to my ears and I tried to remember something, anything, that would confirm this, but my memories of our Lily-less time were hazy and I couldn't picture anything except my mom on the couch, teary and silent.

"You didn't ruin a marriage," he continued, "he left one. People don't leave unless they've wanted to for a while. I would've left your mom even if I didn't meet Lily. She was just . . . she was a light at the end of the tunnel. She was hope. And I needed hope. Maybe you needed some hope yourself after Jackson passed."

For the first time in a long time, I could hear the sadness in my dad's voice, and I remembered him when I was six, on the couch day after day, quiet and distant and wounded. I remembered listening to my mom scoff at his napping form, hearing their silences that were worse than their fights, watching them go out of their way *not* to touch one another. I don't think I let myself remember how bad it had been before Lily. It was easier to pretend that things were fine until they weren't, I suppose.

"He didn't leave," I said, teary. "She left him. She found out and she left, and when he told me, when I found out, I wanted to run away. I wanted to call things off and leave, because—"

"Because you were afraid," my dad supplied, "because once he was free to really be with you, that meant he was able to leave you. You've been burned before. Badly. Of course you're scared. After everything that happened, after that pain, that grief, fear is natural."

Everything got quiet once he said that. He was right; he knew it and so did I. I think maybe I'd known that all along, I just hadn't let myself think about it until then. Guilt was easier than fear, but the fear was always there.

"Mags," he said, a warmth in his voice that made me wish I could see him, could hug him. I hadn't realized how much I'd missed him until I heard him call me that.

"I don't know what to do," I said. "I'm scared."

"I know you are," he said, "and I wish I could say that it will get easier, but I don't know if it will. That fear, I don't know if it goes away. It hasn't for me. And, in my experience, love doesn't make it easier. For people like us, love is rarely easy. Fear gets in the way."

"But I don't want it to," I cried, rubbing my face. "I just want to love him. I want to let him love *me*."

"I know. I want that for you, too. I wish it was different. I wish . . . god, there's so much of me in you, you know that?"

"I'm figuring that out," I confessed, "and I don't really like it."

He laughed ruefully. "I'm sorry for that. It doesn't make for an easy life."

"No," I answered, "it doesn't."

"An exciting one, though."

"It doesn't feel that exciting right now. Just . . . sad. And scary."

"I know."

"I love him," I said.

"I know you do."

"So why does it feel so shitty?"

"Because love makes you vulnerable, and the more vulnerable you are, the more it hurts if it ends."

"What if he leaves?"

"He might. He might not. You've just got to trust him. You've got to lean into the love, not the fear."

"I want to trust him."

"So trust him."

"I don't think I know how."

"That's okay. You'll get there. One day."

"Maybe."

"Are you sure you're okay? I can get on a plane and be there in the morning."

"No, I'm okay."

"Have you told your mom?"

"No."

"Okay. How is she?"

"Mom?"

"Yeah."

"I don't know. Good, I think. I don't know."

"You should call her. You don't have to tell her, but you should give her a call. It'll mean a lot to her. This meant a lot to me, you calling."

"Me too. Thanks, Dad."

"I love you, kiddo."

I was quiet for a moment. I could tell he was waiting for me to say it back. I think I was too.

"I love you too, Dad," I said, knowing that I meant it but also knowing it wasn't that simple. Love doesn't fix everything.

"I know you do," he said, voice soft, "you just . . . don't like me very much."

I laughed a bit at that, the simplicity of it. Such a complicated thing said so simply . . . it was funny.

"I'm getting there," I assured him. "It's just gonna take time." What I'd really wanted to say was *It's going to take more than one phone call,* but he knew that.

"I'm here," he promised, and I knew he meant it.

I hung up and felt like I had a clearer sense of why my father married and remarried so much. But I still didn't know what to do about my relationship with Rob. When something is born from lies and secrets, how does it survive?

42

The next morning, I called Rob, who apologized a million times, saying all the right stuff, and I forgave him. We didn't talk much about the fight. Or about you. Rob just said that he was trying and that it would take time. I understood. I hadn't been able to talk about Jackson until recently.

So I tried to make it okay. I tried to forget about you, but I couldn't. He'd taken his ring off so long ago, yet it felt more permanent than his tattoo. Your marriage was more real than anything I'd shared with him, and despite the commitment, it had ended. Just as my father's marriages had ended.

I told my mom about Rob a few days after I talked to my dad. We had been on the phone catching up when she asked me about my love life.

"So," she said, "Harper told me you have a boyfriend."

I froze. Harper hadn't met Rob yet, and I hadn't planned on telling my mom about him yet, not until she was here and could meet him, could see him for herself and understand why I'd gotten myself in this situation, but apparently it wasn't going to happen that way. I took a deep breath before answering.

"Yeah," I said, "I do."

"Well? What's he like?"

"He's great," I said, really meaning it. "He's smart and funny and talented and he's really wonderful. I'm happy. He makes me happy."

"Angel, that's amazing! I'm happy for you! Truly! Why haven't you told me about him before?"

I took another deep breath. A long one this time.

"Mags?" my mom asked, "you there?"

"Uh-huh," I said, "I'm here."

"Well?"

"Well what?"

"Well why has it taken you this long to tell me about him? He's not married, is he?" She laughed as she said it, joking, but my blood ran cold and I squeezed my eyes shut, digging my nails into my palm.

"Maggie," she repeated, sounding serious now, "is he—"

"No," I said quickly, "he's not."

"Oh, thank *god*," she cried, "I was about to get—"

"He's not married *anymore*," I said, speaking quickly, hoping that if I said it fast enough, she wouldn't register it.

"What are you saying?" my mom said, her voice low. "Are you saying that he, that he was—"

"He was married when we met. And now he's not. He's not married anymore," I said, feeling hot tears slide down my face.

My mom was silent; years passed in the quiet.

"I'm sorry," I said, still crying, still speaking quickly. "I'm sorry I didn't tell you and I'm sorry that I . . . that he . . . I'm sorry. I didn't want this to happen, I didn't want to be like . . . Lily, but we met, and I didn't know he was married and then I kissed him and then—"

"Stop," my mom said, voice firm. "I need you to stop talking right now."

I stopped. I wished that Rob was with me, that I was back on his deck with him, or else that Dani was home so she could hold my hand and pat my cheek and rub my back and tell me it would be okay, but I was alone. It was just me and my mom and the silence that sat between us, heavy and charged with something that felt like poison.

"How long has this been going on?" she asked, her voice breaking through the silence, but doing nothing to relieve the tension.

"Since August," I answered.

"I see."

"Mom, I—"

"No. Don't say anything. Maggie, I love you, I do, but I cannot believe that this is who you are now. Ending a marriage? Ending a *partnership*? You *saw* what your father's leaving did to me. How could you willingly put another woman through that?"

I couldn't breathe.

"Mom—"

"If I don't hang up right now, I'm going to say some things I know I'll regret, so I'm going to hang up. I love you. But I . . . I need time."

And so, she hung up. She hung up and I sat on my couch for three hours, staring at nothing, rocking myself back and forth as wave after wave of tears hit me.

43

Rob took a few days off work after I told him about what happened with my mom. I hadn't wanted to tell him, but he could sense that something was wrong, and so, in that gentle, persistent way of his, he got it out of me.

When I told him, he didn't say anything for a while. He just pulled me onto his lap and held me.

I don't know why that's as important to me as it is, but there's something about the fact that he knows how to sit beside me in all my moods that feels profound to me. I'd never had that before.

Rob looked after me, treating me with love and warmth and all the things I'd wanted to be treated with, but I kept thinking about my mom, my memories of her on our couch, drunk at ten a.m. and crying, and the way her voice sounded on the phone, and it made me think of you. Somewhere down the line, I'd linked the two of you in my mind. You and my mom were members of the same club.

I didn't want to be left. And I didn't know how to put that fear aside.

Rob wanted to take my guilt away from me, I knew that. My fear, too. He'd said as much to me a few times, but I didn't want him to carry any more of my psychological baggage than he already had, and besides, I wasn't sure how to put it down.

It's hard to be in love and be drowning in fear at the same time. It's hard to build something that lasts in the wreckage of something that didn't. I think that's why my dad's always getting married. It's easier to start something new than to face the grief of what's ended. Beginnings are easier. Cleaner.

44

I'd tried getting advice from people, anyone who I felt could help me figure out how to build something made to last, and they were helpful, but only a little. My situation was compounded by grief and was a little too complicated for all their advice to apply, I suppose.

I found myself spending more time with couples whose relationships I deemed to be solid, healthy, good. Pearl and Jonah, Dani and Craig. I watched the way they interacted with one another, hoping that in spending enough time with them, their stability would rub off on me, erasing my guilt and everything else that seemed to be tainting my relationship with Rob.

Craig and Dani are always touching each other. It's never full-on make-out sessions in public, just little things: Craig will drum his fingers on Dani's knuckles as she's talking; Dani traces invisible circles on Craig's knee when she's thinking about him, little things like that. I spent a long time being hard on Craig because, to me at least, he was the guy who stole my best friend from me. I don't feel that way anymore, though.

Dani's happy when she's with him. The two of them are good together. No guilt, no shame, just . . . love.

Dani tried to give me a healing the other day, just to "ease my guilt and grief and shed my generationally inherited trauma," but the ritual just left me smelling like cloves and feeling the same as I had before the ritual began.

"You guys are building fresh," Dani told me as she rubbed essential oils into my temples, "and that takes time. It's the way of the world, Spoon. One thing ends so another thing can begin."

I tried to explain to her that what had begun began before the previous ending had ended, but she wasn't listening, not really. I think she was just so happy to see me with someone, someone who ran lines with me and folded my laundry without me even asking and made me laugh harder than I had in years, that she'd do anything to gloss over the mess of it.

Pearl was different, though. She called me a few times a week, just to check in. She was the one I could talk to about all this. I told her once that I felt like I had to remind myself to smile, to do the things that happy, in-love people do, but it was all hollow. I was in love, I knew that, I *know* that, but I wasn't being filled by the love I once thought I could survive on.

Pearl said that it was because I was too scared to let someone in, all the way in. She also said I was still grieving and still felt too guilty to allow myself happiness, and maybe she was right. That didn't stop me from feeling shitty, though.

She, more than anyone else, was sympathetic. Not just to me, but to Rob. That surprised me. I figured that she would paint him with the same brush I'd painted Dad with so many years ago, but when I asked her about it, she looked at me, still rocking her baby, and said, "I never hated Dad, Mags. Or maybe I did hate him once, a long time ago, but I understand it. I understand why you'd stray, what it takes to stay, I get it. When you build your life with someone, you have to choose that person every day. And there are some days when you absolutely do *not* want to choose them. You'd choose anyone *but* them, really, except you choose them anyway. I choose Jonah every day, but I understand why some people can't do that. They're not bad people, Dad and Rob. They just . . . made different choices."

"So, what am I supposed to do now?" I asked, eyes wide.

"You've just got to decide if Rob's the guy you want to choose every day."

She said that like it was simple, like it was the easiest question on a multiple-choice quiz. *Is Rob the person you want to choose every day? Yes or no.* The question I knew I was asking myself, the question I didn't know how to answer, though, was *Am I the person Rob wants to choose every day?*

45

I didn't know how to answer that question, and my hesitancy, my confusion, pushed me further and further from Rob. I started to get a sense of how he must have felt with you when you were home before you left, or the way my father must've felt before leaving for Lily, or the way Jackson felt in the weeks before he left me: I couldn't look at Rob without hearing the questions echoed over and over: *Am I the person Rob wants to choose every day? Is Rob the person I want to choose every day?*

I didn't know how to make that decision. All I knew was that I felt like it should be an easy one, and the fact that it wasn't meant that he *could* leave, he might leave, and so it was easier for me to act as though he already had. So I avoided him. I spent more time at the apartment, telling him that I was working on auditions and needed some time to prep, and he gave me the space. For a while, at least.

Two weeks after my conversation with Pearl, Rob called me. I was at the apartment, just like I'd been for the last nine nights, and I froze, staring at the phone as it rung once, twice, three times. I picked up, butterflies in my stomach still there, just like they had been at the start.

"Hey," I answered, my finger poking through the hole in his T-shirt, the one he'd worn when we first got breakfast, the same one I was wearing now. I'd forgotten how badly I'd wanted to do that, to poke my finger through and touch his skin. I'd done it so many times by this time, though, that I'd forgotten how much I'd thought about it.

"Hi," Rob answered, clearing his throat, so I knew he was nervous, "are you at your place?"

"Yeah, what's up?"

"Could I come by?"

He didn't answer my question. I poked another finger through the hole, then another one.

"Uh-huh," I said, feeling the butterflies multiply. "Is everything okay?"

"Yup," he said, sounding very not okay. "I'll see you in five."

He hung up and I got up from my seat on the porch and walked into the kitchen, where I made myself a drink. Actually, "made" makes it seem like I mixed a cocktail or something vaguely impressive. I was too worried, too in my head to do anything like that, so I just poured myself a whiskey and paced around my living room, not even bothering to drink the whiskey. I just held it, my grip so tight I'm surprised I didn't shatter the glass.

Rob knocked on the door five minutes later, and after taking my first gulp of whiskey, I opened it, seeing my formerly married boyfriend's face for the first time in over a week.

I'd forgotten how I reacted to being around him. The second I saw his face, I felt myself let go of a breath I didn't know I'd been holding on to. The nerves didn't vanish, neither did the doubt, but I could feel my pulse calm down and the butterflies faded.

"Hi," I said, my voice a whisper.

Rob smiled at me, but it didn't quite meet his eyes.

"Wanna come in?" I asked.

He nodded, stepping inside and removing his sweater, that camel-colored one that he loves so much, revealing that striped T-shirt he'd worn the day we ran errands together, the one that makes him look like a sailor.

I handed my drink to him, and he took a long sip, closing his eyes as he did so. I stared at him, trying to soak it all in. *This might be the last time I see him like this*, I remember thinking. *It may be the last time I see him at all.*

We walked out to the porch and sat across from one another. Rob handed the whiskey back to me and stayed quiet as I took a sip and lit a cigarette. As nervous as I was, I knew that whatever this conversation would turn into, it was one that Rob needed to start.

We were quiet for a while, with Rob looking down at his hands, his brow furrowed, his mouth opening and closing as though he was trying to figure out exactly how to start the conversation he wanted us to have, and I let him be quiet as I studied his face, thinking all the while of what my dad had said to me: *The more vulnerable you are, the more it hurts if it ends.*

"You've been avoiding me," Rob said, shattering the quiet.

He looked up at me as he said it, meeting my eyes in an unwavering stare. He didn't sound accusatory or angry, he sounded . . . hurt. Confused.

I took a deep breath, preparing myself for the inevitable: he'd decided that I wasn't the person he wanted to choose, that this had been a mistake, and he was going to leave. He was done and it was over.

"Yeah," I said, "I have been."

"Why?"

It was my turn to open and close my mouth this time. I didn't know how to answer that question, really, but I knew that he deserved an answer. I poked my finger through the T-shirt's hole once more and tied my hair up in a bun that fell out seconds later as Rob sat, watching me.

"Maggie," Rob continued, taking my hand in his, "I'm in this. I know things have been hard, I know I've been making it hard, but I love you and I am in this with you. I don't think I ever really took a second to think about what this might be bringing up for you, things about your dad, about . . . Jackson, but I've been thinking about it this past week, and I get it. I get it and I want you to know that whatever's making you distant, it won't change how I feel about you. I want this. I want a life with you. But you have to tell me if that's something you want too, because I'm scared too. And I want to be scared with you, if that's something you want, but if you want out, you have to tell me, because if staying with me isn't what will make you happy, then you have to leave. If me letting you go is the best way that I can show you I love you, I will."

He stopped talking and I felt tears build up in my eyes. I opened and closed my mouth again; my palms got clammy, and I knew he could tell because he squeezed my hand and stood up.

"Take your time," he said. "Take as much time as you need, just—"

I cut him off then, pulling him into me and hugging him tight, so tight I could feel his heartbeat against mine. I'd missed that feeling.

"Thank you," I whispered, my lips on the shell of his ear.

We both stood like that for a while, teary-eyed and wrapped up in each other's arms, before he pulled back a little, fixed me with his gaze, and gave me a quick peck on the lips, leaving without another word.

I sat back on the porch once he was gone, my head spinning with love and grief and fear.

I still didn't know what to do. I didn't know how to make a decision as big as that one: how to be scared *with* Rob, and not *of* him.

46

And then your letter came.

Rob was out at work, and I was in the kitchen of your house, debating what I should make for lunch, when the mail arrived. I grabbed the pile, mostly bills and spam, and went to set it on the table for Rob, when I saw my name. I'd never had mail come for me at the house; it felt serious. Adult. The sort of thing that is symptomatic of being in a Serious, Committed, Adult Relationship.

There was no return address on the envelope, so I had no real way of knowing who it was from until I opened it. But even before I saw your address on the top corner of the letter, before I saw your name signed at the end, I knew it was from you. I'd seen your handwriting enough in the margins of books and on the scraps of paper you and Rob used to use for grocery lists to recognize the way you write your Rs, all loopy and large. You're the only person I know whose handwriting looks like art.

I stood by the door, frozen as I stared at the envelope for a while. I'm not sure how long, really, I just remember my eyes blurring and refocusing and blurring again several times.

I wanted to open it.

I didn't want to open it.

I wanted to have someone else open it for me.

I didn't want anyone else to see it.

I put the rest of the mail down, not bothering to look where, and walked back to the kitchen, where I grabbed a glass of mescal before heading onto the deck. It was the afternoon, two, I think, too early to be drinking, but I needed something to ground me in my body. I needed something to burn my throat and warm my stomach and render everything a little fuzzy around the edges.

I opened the envelope after I downed the first glass and smoked two cigarettes back-to-back. I considered burning the letter at one point; I looked at the embers of the cigarette and thought about how easy it would be to erase any trace of whatever you had written, but even while I considered it, I knew that I couldn't do it, not really.

Maggie,

Before you panic too much, I'll start by saying that I'm not going to attack you here. Or curse you. Even though I'm sure you think I am; I'm sure seeing this letter filled you with panic. I hesitated to write this but, while I'm not sure why, I thought it was important for you to know: you didn't end my marriage.

I'm sure you think you did. I'm sure you've been feeling guilty as you and Rob sleep in my old bed in my old house. Guilt is natural in this situation, but it's not warranted.

The truth is our marriage ended long before you came into the picture.

That doesn't mean I'm happy about the way things ended. And that doesn't mean that I haven't ever blamed you, because I did. At the start, I did. It was easier to make you the villain, to pretend that you were the one and only reason Rob and I didn't work out, but that's not fair. To you or to Rob.

Rob and I married early, too early, maybe. We were both young and scared and lonely, living in a new city, so we did what lonely people do: we clung to each other, thinking that would be enough. It wasn't. We'd been drifting apart for years, long before you were even in the picture.

I don't hate you, Maggie. I hate what happened. I hate the _way_ it happened, but I don't hate you. You're the reason I found myself loving Rob more in those last months than I had in the last few years. You brought him back to life. You opened him up and you made him someone I remembered loving. That's no small thing. Looking back, I should've realized he was having an affair sooner than I did—he was kinder, more attentive to me when I came back than he had been in months. Maybe years. I assumed he had just missed me, but I know it was more than that now: your love turned Rob back into the man he used to be, and I hope that you will be happy with him. This too will surprise you, I'm sure.

I left because I decided it was time to end my own suffering. When I was away, I spent a lot of time thinking about my marriage. Things hadn't been good for a while, and I found myself dreaming about freedom, other people, other cities, independence. I haven't been alone for a long time. I didn't know who I was on my own. That thought sobered me. It scared me. I came back knowing that it was time to end our marriage, but I didn't have the courage to do it. And then came you. I will admit, despite the hurt and the anger, I was somehow relieved when I found out about the affair. You gave me an out. A much-needed excuse for my escape. And so, I took it.

In leaving, I set myself free. I hoped that I was setting him free too, and, by extension, you. So you can pursue your own relationship free of the constraints of our worn-out marriage. I still love Rob in many ways, though the love I have for him is different now, and I hope that we will one day be friends. Before we were anything, we were friends.

If I could ask you one thing, it would be this: I want to know how you found yourself here. You know about my marriage; I would like to know about your relationship. I want to know how you fell in love with Rob. He's told me his side of things, but I'm more interested in yours. We share some-

thing, after all. We both know what it's like to fall for the same wonderful, infuriatingly decent man.

I'm not entitled to it, I know. It's a lot to ask. I don't expect you to respond, but if you do, I would like to hear your love story. I want to hear all of it. I've spent hours imagining it, every detail. Maybe it's masochistic, but let's call it benign curiosity.

Warmly,

Ingrid

I read the letter seven times in one sitting. After that, I stood up, paced around the deck, and sat back down to read it another four times. I wanted more. I wanted less. I wished I had never read it and I wanted to read it again.

When I first opened the letter, I had done so in the hope that someone would finally, *finally,* look at my guilt and fear and tell me that it was what I deserved, that I deserved *more* of it, that I was no longer entitled to happiness or joy or Rob. I'd hoped that you would be that person for me, but you were even better than that.

You were a kinder, more gracious person than I know I deserved.

What your letter brought me was a sense of release, I think. In writing to me, you cut the ties of this affair that had bound us, the ties that I felt were still strangling me, and that kept me (and us) from moving forward.

I traced the lines of your words the way Rob traced the lines of my tattoos, hoping to feel the ghost of you once more, but I didn't. Not anymore. It was like you had exorcised yourself from my relationship with Rob.

You removed yourself from the equation, leaving me without the guilt, but still with the weight of a choice: to stay or to leave.

I hated you in that moment. And loved you. In equal measure.

47

turned my phone off after I got over the initial shock of your letter. I sent Rob a text telling him I was feeling sick and I'd see him later. I couldn't face him yet. I knew I wouldn't tell him about the letter or this response; I haven't told anyone about it, actually, and I don't think I will. More secrets I'm harboring from the people I love most.

But at least now you're caught up. I didn't see Rob that night; I chose instead to spend the night at the apartment, where I knew Dani wouldn't be. I need some time alone. There's a lot to think about.

I've been thinking, not for the first time, about my dad, Jackson, and Rob. I used to think of them as entirely separate figures in my life, each totally different from one another, sharing nothing but a connection to me. I don't think that anymore, especially when it comes to my dad and Jackson.

My dad left me, my mom, my sister, for other women. He took off, started new lives and bought new houses, always running towards something, someone, who was just around the corner, never wanting to face the grief and guilt left in his wake, his own or anyone else's.

I don't blame him for that. Not anymore. I know what it is to try to build a home in the ruins of a wrecked one. Just because I don't blame him anymore doesn't mean there aren't still scars. My dad left me, again and again, and I was taught to believe that was normal.

Jackson left, too. I'm not talking about his dying. Before that, back when he thought he was immortal and I thought I could fix him, he left me. This was different than it'd been with my dad, but not much. Jackson didn't leave me for a person; he left me for something more dangerous. He left me for drugs and, in the end, for his own death, and I thought that was normal, too.

I think I grew up feeling like I was only worth being loved until something better came along. Love and leaving were always linked for me. That's why I turned to the training-wheel rebounds after Jackson, including Rob. I knew they wouldn't leave me, and if they did, it didn't matter, because I knew love wasn't a part of it.

When we first met, I think I saw Rob as a life vest of sorts. I thought he'd be the thing to lift me up out of my grief. I didn't think about the possibility of him leaving me, not at the start. And then I thought about it too much.

But now I know Rob is different. He wants to stay. I think. I hope.

I don't know if he means it. I don't know if he'll turn around and find someone else and I'll be left again, but love is about trust, right? It's about faith. I want to have faith in him, but faith is hard for me. Your letter helped, though. It made things a little clearer.

Now that I'm almost finished writing, I realize I don't think this letter is *for* you, Ingrid. I think it's for me. I needed to figure out what happened so I could move forward, improve.

Maybe one day we'll sit down and I'll tell you everything you want to know. I'll answer all of your questions, but not yet. It'll hurt more than it will help, I think. Besides, this is a still a story without an ending. So I won't send this letter just yet.

You deserve an ending, and so do I, a happy one even, once I've figured it all out.

ACKNOWLEDGMENTS

Henry Carr, you're in everything I do. This is the last of my writing that you read. Everything that comes next is with and because of you. I hope I make you proud. You made me proud every day.

Sabrina Padwa, you are family. Thank you for welcoming me into Club 44 and for providing me with comfort, support, saunas, and loungewear.

Antonio Stefan, thank you for being my first and favorite reader. You are a truly singular person and someone I am honored to know.

Louise Salter, you gave me my first notebook and told me to get to writing. This book (and everything that will come next) is because of you.

Glen Hirshberg, you taught me everything I know and a bunch of things I haven't yet learned. Thank you for telling me to keep writing this and for helping me turn this into what it is.

Emma Thompson, you've filled my life with support, encouragement, love, and dungarees. You are glorious (and exactly the same age I am!).

Janice Zawerbny, thank you for shaping this book into what it is and for sharing a birthday with Bill Hader, two things that I deem equally important.

Catherine Dorton, Noelle Zitzer, and Lisa Rundle, thank you for your guidance, your edits, and your support of this book.

Gaby Edwards, we met on a log and I am oh so glad that we did. You see me more clearly than almost anyone, and for some unknown reason, you stick around. Thank you.

Brian Buckley, thank you for all of it, even though you seem to think I'm "always smiling," an observation that is as charming as it is wrong.

Natalia Cordova, you are a true friend and I am lucky to know you.

Gaite Jansen, thank you for your encouragement and for holding my face between your hands while shouting kind and loving words at me.

Alice McMillan, thank you for making me laugh and for refusing to let me be unkind to myself. You light me up, you make me brave, and in my darkest days, you held me from thousands of miles away.

Gaia Wise, thank you for your strength. Your name lives on my wrist and your voice echoes around my head.

Sydney Botko, thank you for famously sticking with me through my flop era. You are a Diamond Dog and I love you tons.

Payson Whitwell, you and your constant support mean more to me than I can ever say.

Lily Jackson, your fire and wit are electric.

Molly Kirschenbaum, thank you for your grace, your kindness, and for listening to me read the first twenty pages of this novel before I even knew what it would turn out to be.

Lillian Fox Peckos, you have nurtured me with tough love, long hugs, and lots of cuddles.

Nick Friedlich, your unwavering kindness and support are unbelievable to me, as are you.

Gabrielle Baba-Conn, you, my Best One, are spectacular. Thank you for holding me. I'm holding you right back.

Daphne, Garry, and Sabrina Carr, I love you. Just float.

Dadoo, thank you for your wisdom and for your absurdity.

Mom, thank you for your strength and thank you for your frills.

Susan Williams and Steven Poster, thank you for being my family.

Martha Frankel and Stevie Heller, I love you more.

Elana Rabinovitch, thank you for getting this book into the hands of the people who released it to the world.

Carla Gugino, you have never not supported me. You have also never not been glamorous. Thank you for both of those things.

Sebastian Gutierrez, you exposed me to music, books, and movies that lit me up and set me on fire. Thank you.

Gio, I know you hate books but thank you for reading this one. (Yes, you *do* have to read this one.) I'm proud of you.

Alix Legrand Wittich, you are the big brother I always wanted. Thank you for your guidance, your support, and for reading this book even though you "don't normally read books like this." I love you very much.

James Paxton, thank you for your rambling voice memos, your kindness, and for inflating my ego more than anyone should.

Harper Zuma and Hayes Blue Koellner, neither of you is old enough to read this book but you're *definitely* both old enough to read this bit. I love you both more than I can say.

Emma Hoyt, I don't have the language to express just how much I love you. But you know. You must know.

Abi Hardingham, my sister, I love you with all the oranges and strawberries in the world. Thank you for your insight, your joy, and your infectious smile.

Mariasha Altynbaeva and Katherine Gage, you two creatures entered my life when it was small and closed and dark and you lit it up and blew it open.

Sarah Lutzky, you and me. Always.

Alison Segel, you walked into my life when I most needed help and you changed my life. Thank you for helping me rewrite my negative patterns and for filling my world with good tears, Dolly Parton pictures, and so, so much support.

Molly Baz, you don't know me, but thank you for your recipes, many of which sustained me while I was writing and later proved to be handy distractions when I was looking for delicious and salty ways to avoid editing this book.

To all the artists and musicians named in this book: thank you for your art.

And finally, to my friends and chosen family who lift me up and fill my life with joy: thank you to Lothaire Bluteau, Ruby Bond, Shannon Connolly, Ruth Dickinson, Jasmine Djavahery, Allyson Fanger, Maxine Fanger, Erin Fite, Gracie García, Eve Harlow, Lauren Katz, Danny Mailey, Cele Pasternak, Lorry Pasternak, Aislinn Paul, Minnie and Sophie Perry, Tracy Pion, Milo Reed, Desi Reed, Jillian Sanders, Isabel Stern, Jack Wareham, and Greg Wise.